LEGION
BOOK
FIVE

Hallowed Ground

A.D. STARRLING

COPYRIGHT

Hallowed Ground (Legion Book Five)
Copyright © AD Starrling 2020. All rights reserved. Registered with the US Copyright Service.
Paperback edition: 2020

Edited by Right Ink On The Wall
Cover design by 17 Studio Book Design

Want to know about AD Starrling's upcoming releases? Sign up to her newsletter for new release alerts, sneak peeks, giveaways, and more.

The right of AD Starrling to be identified as the author of this work has been asserted in accordance with the Copyright, Designs and Patents Act 1988.
All rights reserved. No parts of this book may be reproduced in any form or by any electronic or mechanical means, including information storage and retrieval systems, without the prior written consent of the author, excepting for brief quotes used in reviews. Your respect of the author's rights and hard work is appreciated.
Request to publish extracts from this book should be sent to the author at ads@adstarrling.com
This book is a work of fiction. References to real people (living or dead), events, establishments, organizations, or locations are intended only to provide a sense of authenticity, and are used factitiously. All other characters, and all other incidents and dialogue, are drawn from the author's imagination and are not to be construed as real.

www.ADStarrling.com

CHAPTER ONE

Jeremiah Chase did not believe in monsters.

As he lay sprawled in a dirty alleyway in Chicago's North Side, the metal dumpster he sat against leaching the warmth from his back and the savaged body of his partner and fellow Chicago PD detective Tony Goodman lying limply in his arms, Jeremiah repeated those words over and over inside his head, as if they were a prayer that would dispel the horror of what he was witnessing with his own eyes.

Monsters don't exist!

The shrill howl of police sirens rose in the distance to the west, the sounds muted by the blood thundering inside his head. Though he knew his unconscious partner would not register the words, Jeremiah felt compelled to comfort him nonetheless.

"It's okay, Tony," he mumbled. "Help is coming!"

He pressed a hand against the gaping wound on the detective's chest. The coppery smell of blood filled his nostrils and hot wetness soaked his fingers; Tony was bleeding profusely, his body growing colder and heavier with every passing second.

Jeremiah had already stripped his and Tony's belts from their waists and tied them above the jagged lacerations in the detective's leg and arm. Though he could feel Tony's heart racing beneath his touch, his frozen gaze remained locked on the creature crouching over the remains of a dead man some twenty feet away.

Jeremiah could not have taken his eyes off their attacker even if he'd wanted to. Every instinct he possessed told him that to look away was to invite instant death.

Gore and human remains coated the vile beast's jowls and fell thickly from his wicked talons. He buried his maw in the corpse's gut, his strong jaws working hungrily while he crunched and chewed and swallowed.

Bile rose in Jeremiah's throat at the wet sounds the creature made as he feasted on the dead man's entrails. His knuckles whitened on the empty gun in his right hand.

He had already fired every round he had at the beast, to no avail. Though the monster had oozed black blood from his wounds, the gunshots had not impeded his ferocious assault on Tony, nor the men who had once been his allies.

The mangled bodies of the four drug dealers Jeremiah and his dying partner had hoped to question lay scattered across the alley behind the creature, the ground beneath them dark with blood. One of them was still breathing, albeit shallowly, his chest rising and falling raggedly with his labored gasps.

Even if Jeremiah managed to recover Tony's handgun from where it had skittered under the dumpster behind them, he knew there would be no point using it on the beast to try and save his partner and the criminal. The creature was insanely fast and had avoided half the shots Jeremiah had aimed at him.

Jeremiah didn't know if it was dumb luck or some stupid twist of fate that had kept him alive and unharmed so far. What he didn't doubt though, was that he would not leave this alleyway alive. Not if the creature who had just manifested its evil presence inside the body of the fifth drug dealer had anything to do with it.

A low moan left Tony's lips.

The beast's head snapped around. Ochre pupils dilated in a sea of obsidian as he stared at Tony, his expression ravenous despite the gruesome meal he was gorging upon. Jeremiah could barely make out the features of the man he had once been, so grotesque was his ungodly transformation.

The creature looked up and met Jeremiah's petrified stare. A diabolical smile split his mouth wide, much wider than should have been humanly possible. The beast raised his hideous face to the sky and roared.

He moved in the next instant, his actions so fast he was already halfway to Jeremiah before the detective was even aware that he was closing in on them.

A knife! Jeremiah looked frantically around the alleyway, despair a living entity throbbing through his veins. *I need a knife, dammit!*

Coldness filled him as the monster's shadow engulfed them. Jeremiah instinctively covered Tony with his body to shield him from the attack and raised a hand defensively toward the claws descending upon them, conscious of how futile his actions were.

Something flickered in the air above the creature, drawing Jeremiah's gaze through a gap between his fingers.

An object sailed the length of the shadowy alley and crashed into the back of the monster's head. The creature jerked to an abrupt halt a few feet from Jeremiah, his claws raising sparks on the asphalt as he dropped on all fours.

The item peeled away slowly from the monster's misshapen skull and thudded to the ground. The beast stared at it, its ugly features growing perplexed.

It was a backpack. A red one, with bright, colorful stickers all over it.

Jeremiah blinked.

He recognized the bag.

Terror clutched icy fingers around his heart at the same time an achingly familiar voice bellowed out a warning that echoed against the grimy walls of the alley.

"*Get away from them!*"

The words resonated starkly in Jeremiah's ears. His stricken gaze found the figure standing braced at the opposite end of the gloomy passage. His stomach twisted.

No!

CHAPTER TWO

Five Days Ago, Chicago.

"Leah, dinner is ready!"

Silence fell in the wake of Jeremiah's call. He sighed, placed the salad bowl on the kitchen table, and undid the apron from around his waist. He wandered out into the hallway and stopped at the base of the stairs.

"Leah! Dinner!"

This got no reply. He started up the steps and was on the second-floor landing when a door flew open at the end of the corridor. Leah rushed out, her auburn hair trailing wildly around her face before she grabbed the stubborn strands and tucked them firmly behind her ears and under her *Chicago Cubs* cap.

"Sorry, Dad. I can't make dinner tonight." She pressed a quick kiss on his cheek as she stormed past him. "There's an advanced watercolor class starting in an hour and I just heard about it!"

Jeremiah frowned. "That's the third time this month. It was the same last month and the month before that. Can't your art professors manage their schedules better?"

Leah shrugged her arms through the straps of her backpack and started rapidly down the stairs. "Yeah, well, you know what those creative types are like. Plus, I need the extra credit if I want to ace this course, so I can't exactly complain."

Jeremiah followed slowly in her wake. "Take your bike."

Leah slipped her sneakers on before grabbing the front door handle. "I will."

"And be careful of bad guys," Jeremiah warned.

Leah cast an exasperated look at him over her shoulder. "I'm nineteen, Dad. I'm not exactly going to take candy from a stranger and climb inside their car for a ride. Besides, I have a black belt in Taekwondo. Most bad guys wouldn't stand a chance against me."

The door slammed shut after her.

Jeremiah ran a hand through his hair, blew out another sigh, and went downstairs. He paused next to a shelf in the hallway.

A collection of framed photographs crowded the surface and the wall above it. A melancholic smile stretched his lips as he gazed at the figures in the pictures.

Even as a child, Leah had been the spitting image of her mother.

Pain twisted his heart as he gazed at the woman who stood with her arms looped around the little girl with red hair and hazel eyes in most of their family photos.

Four years had passed since Joanna Chase's death. And Jeremiah still missed her just as badly as the day she'd left him. The last time he'd seen her alive, she'd been in the hospital bed where end-stage ovarian cancer had finally claimed her life.

"I could really do with your help," Jeremiah mumbled

to his dead wife. "I think our daughter is finally going through her rebellious phase."

He blinked. It had to be a trick of the light that had just made it seem as if his dead wife's smile had grown wider. Heat warmed his ears. As a senior Chicago PD detective, he hated showing any sign of weakness. Joanna had often teased him for it. After all, she'd known him better than anyone in the world.

Jeremiah took his dinner into the TV room and settled down in front of an old soap rerun. Lines wrinkled his brow as he thought back to the conversation he'd just had with his daughter. He took a small diary from his pocket and made an entry to remind himself to have a word with Leah's supervising professor next week.

It's absurd. They can't expect their students to just drop everything every time they make a last-minute change to their schedule.

I'm going to burn in Hell.

The wind cooled Leah's hot cheeks and stung her eyes as she cycled furiously through the city. The School of the Art Institute of Chicago was five miles north of her home in Bridgeport. Instead of heading there like she'd told her father she would, she was riding south.

He'll kill me if he finds out where I've been going these past few months. Leah grimaced. *Well, maybe not kill. But he'll ground me for sure.*

Guilt wormed through her at the thought; it pained Leah to no end that she was having to lie to her father about her recent activities. Her self-reproach gradually turned into irritation. She pursed her lips.

He has no one to blame but himself, really. If he wasn't such a stubborn old coot, I wouldn't have to hide this from him.

A town car pulled up beside her a moment later. The driver's window wound down with a soft, electronic whir.

Leah braked to a stop and smiled at the man inside. "Thanks for picking me up, William."

"It's a pleasure, mistress," the butler murmured solemnly. "Here, some pastries to tide you over until we get to the house."

He passed her a paper bag.

Leah accepted the offering and sighed. "I've told you a dozen times, William. Just call me Leah."

"That would be most inappropriate, mistress."

Leah rolled her eyes, folded her bike, and popped it in the trunk. She climbed into the back of the town car and munched on a selection of tasty mini eclairs and macaroons while she gazed at the landscape rolling past the window, the vehicle's tires swishing hypnotically as it whisked her away to her final destination.

She still recalled her mother's funeral as if it were yesterday. Joanna Chase had passed away exactly one day before Leah's fifteenth birthday. They'd buried her a week later, in a cemetery near Jackson Park. It had been the only time Leah's father had openly broken down in front of her. He had shed tears many times before and since, but never when he'd thought she was looking. Her father was a headstrong, proud man.

He'd also lied to her, as had her mother.

Because, contrary to what they'd told her when she was a child, her maternal grandmother was very much alive. And the woman had made contact with Leah six months ago, on the anniversary of Joanna Chase's death.

Leah had been shocked to discover not only that her

mother was the daughter of Barbara Nolan, one of the wealthiest people in Chicago, but that the Nolans were among the oldest families in the country.

She had been wary of the older woman's claims at first. But it hadn't taken long for her to research the origins of the Nolans and to find a birth record for her mother that stated plainly that Barbara Nolan was indeed whom she said she was.

As to the reason why her parents had cut all ties with Barbara Nolan, that remained a mystery. Despite Leah's repeated questioning over the past few months and the sad expression her grandmother often wore, the old woman had never revealed the motive behind the separation.

Leah had only ever brought up the thorny subject with her father once, a short time after her first meeting with her grandmother. Wracked with guilt over the secret she'd been keeping from him, she had finally confessed the truth. Jeremiah Chase had become angry and agitated, and had banned Leah from ever seeing the old woman again. When Leah had challenged him about the lies he and her mother had told her, he'd shut down completely, his aloof expression telling her that no answers would be forthcoming.

This had only served to intrigue her more. Since she had a stubborn streak a mile long, Leah had carried on seeing her grandmother behind her father's back, not just in the hope of solving the mystery of why Jeremiah and Joanna Chase had ceased all contact with Joanna's mother, but also because she found Barbara Nolan genuinely fascinating.

It only took twelve minutes for the town car to reach the private, wooded estate atop a hill in one of the most exclusive neighborhoods in Beverly. Leah's heartbeat quickened as she observed the rose-vine-and-ivy-covered frontage of the three-story brick mansion that appeared at the end of a long, serpentine driveway winding through thick trees and undergrowth. Soft light glowed behind dozens of leaded glass panels and balcony doors, dispelling some of the darkness that shrouded the stately home.

Though she had been to the place dozens of times before, Leah couldn't shake the spooky feeling that sometimes came over her when she entered the Nolan estate. There was nothing in the least bit Gothic about the manor house, yet it still projected an eldritch aura that made her think of things that went bump in the night. She recalled her impression of the residence the night she had first visited her grandmother.

This is a place where witches live.

Leah had chided herself in the next instant, surprised by the fanciful direction her mind had taken. Things like witches and magic didn't exist.

A single bay window stood illuminated on the second floor of the west wing. It was where her grandmother would be waiting for her, in the mansion's library and study.

Leah disembarked from the town car, flashed a smile at the maid who stood waiting to take her backpack in the foyer, and rushed up the stairs.

Barbara Nolan turned from where she stood looking out of the window when Leah entered the library. She was dressed in a severe black dress that reached her ankles and wore a large ruby pendant on a silver chain around her neck.

Leah crossed the floor, kissed her grandmother on the cheeks, and closed her arms around the old woman. "Hi,

Grandma." She glanced at the gray-haired terrier snoozing on the floor next to a desk. "Hey, Thorn."

The dog opened a lazy, cataract-filled eye and blinked a silent welcome.

Barbara stiffened slightly before relaxing and returning her embrace. "Good evening, Leah."

Leah grinned and stepped back. "You're getting better at that."

Barbara arched an elegant eyebrow. "And you are getting cheekier by the day, child."

Leah chuckled. Her grandmother was not the most physically affectionate person in the world. It had taken Leah several weeks to get her to crack a genuine smile and many more to receive a hug in return.

"So, what are we talking about today?"

Barbara smiled faintly at her question. Leah blinked. Her grandmother was still arresting, despite her age. Leah could see a lot of her mother's features in the older woman's face.

I hope I look as good as she does when I'm her age.

"I thought I'd tell you more about our ancestors."

Barbara guided Leah to a couch and sat her down. Thorn yawned, lifted his arthritic body off the floor, and joined them.

Leah stared curiously at the thick tome on the coffee table while she picked up the terrier and settled him on a cushion next to her. She could tell the book was old.

"I haven't seen this before."

She picked up the volume and carefully thumbed through its well-preserved, yellowed pages.

Barbara had shared her love of Irish history and folktales with Leah ever since they first started meeting at the estate. They talked about life, politics, and philosophy too, but Leah very much preferred listening to the fables of old and the rich tapestry her grandmother weaved about the days of yore, before the Nolans migrated from Ireland to the Americas in the seventeenth century. Despite the fact that her true love lay in the classical arts, Leah found the stories captivating.

"I normally keep it in the family safe," Barbara murmured.

Surprise shot through Leah. She hadn't realized there was a safe in the house.

She rebuked herself silently. *Of course there's a safe. She must have a lot of expensive items in the house.*

Something else on the coffee table drew Leah's attention. "What's that?"

Barbara followed her gaze to the black jewelry box next to the book. "It's a gift. For you."

Leah's eyes widened. "What's the occasion?"

Barbara carefully lifted the box and opened it. A beautiful, silver pendant on a chain glittered against the dark, velvet interior.

"No occasion. I just thought it was time I gave this to you. It's a family heirloom." She hesitated. "And your mother's inheritance."

Leah's heart clenched as she stared at the intricate jewelry inside the box. The medallion was shaped like a compass. Instead of the traditional cardinal points and directions, strange letters occupied the eight tips.

"Take it," Barbara said quietly. "It's yours."

Leah faltered before extending a hand and lifting the pendant from the box. Something hot throbbed through her body when she touched the metal.

She blinked, startled at the sensation.

A sudden gust of wind rattled the window. Leah turned

and looked through the thick glass panes. Dark clouds raced across the section of sky visible above the trees surrounding the estate, obliterating the stars and the moon. Lightning flared and thunder boomed in the night.

Thorn raised his head off the couch and let out a low bark.

Leah stared at the storm, mesmerized. She rose and crossed the floor to the window. "Oh wow. That came out of nowhere."

Barbara joined her. The older woman's face was pale and her eyes full of apprehension.

"Grandma?" Leah asked hesitantly. "Are you alright?"

"Yes."

Barbara's expression softened slightly. She faltered before raising a hand and touching Leah's cheek gently.

Leah stiffened, more than a little stunned. She was normally the one who initiated any kind of physical contact between them.

"I'm so sorry, child," Barbara whispered. "I hoped and prayed that I was wrong. That it wouldn't be you."

Leah stared. "What do you mean?"

Barbara's gaze found the tempest once more. Her face turned grim.

"It has begun."

CHAPTER THREE

An unholy shriek roused Artemus from a deep sleep. He bolted upright, fumbled around for his knife, lost his balance, and tumbled backward out of his bed. A curse left him as his head struck the floor.

"What the—!"

Gray light filtered through a gap in the curtains covering the leaded windows of his bedroom. Though he couldn't see the antique clock on his nightstand from where he lay, he could tell it was barely dawn.

Silence filled the mansion. Artemus frowned in the gloom. From the lack of activity, none of the other residents had heard the noise that had woken him.

He sat up and rubbed the back of his head gingerly. *Did I dream it?*

Artemus climbed awkwardly to his feet. He checked the bottom of the bed.

Smokey was missing from his usual spot. Which meant he was probably still in the TV room with Haruki, where Artemus had last seen them.

The Yakuza heir had received his monthly consignment of sake from the Kuroda Group the day before. As per tradition, he and Smokey had opened the first bottle and were more than likely currently passed out on the couch downstairs after getting thoroughly inebriated and spending the night watching some mindless drivel on TV. The fact that they would have to suffer through Sebastian's usual tirade that morning had evidently not deterred them.

Even Daniel had rebuked the hellhound and the Dragon when he'd first witnessed the aftermath of one of their drinking sessions.

Artemus had initially feared the priest would struggle to fit in with them following his forced relocation from Rome to Chicago five weeks ago. Daniel had soon proven him wrong, and in spades. It turned out he was as much of an ornery bastard as the rest of Artemus's tenants. And, as they all rapidly discovered, the guy could be brutally cutting.

Artemus was about to get back in bed when he heard a rustling noise.

He stiffened, his gaze gravitating to the east-facing windows once more. His eyes having adapted to the shadows, he found his knife where it lay under his pillow and silently approached the curtains.

The rustling came again.

Artemus swallowed, his pulse now racing. It didn't matter that he was the son of an archangel and a goddess, and likely one of the strongest beings on the planet. Strange noises in the night were just plain creepy. He gripped the edges of the curtains, took a shallow breath, and opened them with a brisk move.

A large, black shape outside squawked at him loudly before rising from the windowsill and fluttering noisily against the glass. Artemus stumbled backward.

"Oh," someone murmured behind him. "It's a raven."

Artemus looked over his shoulder.

Daniel was standing on the threshold of the bedroom in the new pajamas Callie had bought him. The heiress had declared the priest's wardrobe an unmitigated disaster when he'd first arrived at the mansion and had taken it upon herself to give him a makeover. Much to Daniel's ire, this had included contacts and a snazzy new haircut. He yawned and rubbed his eyes sleepily as he came inside the room.

Artemus's gaze shifted to the window. "You heard it too?"

The bird examined them with a beady eye, flapped its wings, and rose toward the pale sky.

"Yeah. I'm a light sleeper."

A figure loomed into view behind Daniel.

"Is something wrong?" Sebastian said gruffly.

"Not really." Artemus crossed the room and put his knife back under his pillow. "There was a raven outside my window."

Sebastian stiffened. "A raven, you say?"

"Yeah."

"Those are birds of omen."

"You don't say." Artemus stared. "Is that a new dressing gown?"

Sebastian looked down at his dark blue, silk robe. It was decorated with splashes of color in the shapes of flowers and birds. "Yes. It is my new made-to-order peignoir. It arrived from London two days ago."

"You look like a peacock," Artemus said bluntly.

Daniel's lips twitched.

Sebastian's expression grew frosty. He drew himself to his full height. "I will have you know that this was the height of fashion in my day."

"You mean the nineteenth century? Well, I hate to break it to you, but this is the twenty-first century and you still look like a peacock. Now, if you two will excuse me, I'm going back to bed."

Sebastian perused the shadows while Artemus climbed under the covers. "Where is my brother?"

"The wino hellhound?" Artemus rolled his eyes. "Presumably passed out with Haruki downstairs." He fluffed his pillow and snuggled down into the bed. "Close the door on the way out, will you?"

Daniel mumbled something under his breath, turned, and headed back to his bedroom.

Outrage clouded Sebastian's face. "Why, that little—! I shall whip his furry hide into shape!"

He twisted on his heels and stormed noisily down the corridor.

A faint shout reached Artemus from somewhere inside the mansion.

"*Will you guys shut the hell up?!*" Serena yelled in the distance.

"Yeah, keep it down!" Callie bellowed dimly from the floor above. "I need my beauty sleep and Nate is reading."

"Unlike someone who shall remained unnamed, some people have to go to work in the goddamn morning," Drake grumbled lustily from his bedroom in the west wing.

"I heard that!" Sebastian snapped.

Artemus scowled at the ceiling.

"Why the hell did I ever let you guys move in?" he muttered darkly.

The atmosphere in the kitchen was fraught with tension when he entered it two hours later. Artemus opened the refrigerator, poured himself some orange juice, and observed the glum faces around him.

"Did someone die?"

Haruki eyed him sullenly where he sat nursing a glass of water at the kitchen table. "The only thing dead is my dignity. Smokey and I have a hangover. I think Ogawa sent a dud consignment of sake. I have never puked so hard in my life." The Dragon glared at the man at the cast-iron range. "Of course, our headaches were made infinitely worse by all the unnecessary shouting this morning." He grimaced at the sound of his own voice and dropped his head into his hands with a low moan. "Shit, that hurts."

Artemus indicated Smokey. "Is that why he's munching on lettuce leaves instead of bacon?"

The rabbit was perched on the window seat, his butt to the room and his hackles raised. His eyes flashed red as he glanced at Artemus over his shoulder, his jaws busy chomping on a mouthful of greenery.

"Don't give me that look," Artemus said mildly as he sipped his juice. "It's your own damn fault your head is sore."

The rabbit growled.

Sebastian sniffed where he stood making himself coffee.

"You are both divine beasts," he told Haruki and Smokey in a remorseless voice. "You should demonstrate the gravitas appropriate to your station."

Artemus glanced at the black enamel pot Sebastian was using to prepare his drink. The Englishman still hadn't come to grips with Nate's newfangled coffee machine and preferred to brew his the old-fashioned way.

A wave of nostalgia washed over Artemus.

The pot had belonged to Karl LeBlanc, the man whom he'd considered his adoptive father and who had bequeathed him his antique shop in Old Town and his estate upon his death several years ago.

"Yeah, well, there is one divine beast who isn't displaying any kind of gravitas whatsoever," Haruki said grimly. "Especially at night. I thought they'd calm down after a couple of months, but *noooo*. Those two are still at it like a pair of rabbits." He glanced at Smokey. "No offense."

Smokey huffed. Sebastian frowned.

Their sister Callie was now in a firmly established romance with one of the super soldiers residing at the mansion. From Haruki's disgruntled reports, they were evidently still hot and heavy when it came to the physical aspect of their relationship.

The back door opened. The super soldier making up the other half of the ardent liaison appeared, a wicker basket full of eggs in hand.

"Now, now, Henrietta, go back to the yard."

Nate gazed fondly at the stout, orange-feathered chicken who'd followed him inside the house. The hen clucked and looked curiously around the kitchen, head bobbing to and fro. She froze and straightened when she spotted the rabbit.

"I thought that one was Charlene," Artemus muttered as the chicken squawked and defecated in alarm.

"Charlene has a distinctive patch of pale feathers on her breast." Nate gently removed the bird from the mansion and cleaned up the poop. "You might be thinking of Gertrude. They look alike, but they have completely different personalities. Henrietta is more sociable." He paused. "Why are you guys looking at me like that?"

Artemus sighed.

It was with some reluctance that he'd agreed to let Nate keep a brood of chickens in the grounds of the estate. It wasn't that he was against having an open-air aviary roaming in his back garden per se. He'd just been worried about the birds' chances of survival with a carnivorous hellhound on the loose.

Strangely enough, apart from the occasional threatening growls in their direction, Smokey had mostly left the flock alone. Artemus wondered whether it was out of respect for Nate, who was inordinately devoted to the birds.

Callie walked inside the kitchen and pressed a kiss to Nate's lips while he stood making breakfast at the range. Serena and Drake appeared a moment later.

Drake cocked a thumb at Haruki and Smokey. "What's wrong with them?"

"They have hangovers," Artemus said.

"That time of the month again, huh?" Serena placed a cup under the gleaming piece of shiny, sophisticated machinery on the counter and raised an eyebrow. "How many bottles of sake did you guys have?"

The monstrous device whirred to life and started making a latte.

Haruki winced at the buzzing noise. "Two."

Smokey huffed.

"Okay, four," the Yakuza heir confessed. "Each."

"I'm surprised you can still walk," Serena drawled.

"I'm surprised they can still see," Drake muttered.

"Where's Daniel?" Artemus asked as they sat down to eat.

"He departed for the church an hour ago," Sebastian replied.

Artemus frowned.

They always made it a point to have their meals together when they were home. It was a habit Karl had instituted when Artemus had moved in with him and one he'd carried on when he'd suddenly found himself the unwitting landlord to a group of supernatural tenants.

"I made sure he ate something before he left," Nate said.

"That's not the point," Artemus grumbled. "We have house rules for a reason."

"If it is any consolation, the religious studies class he usually gives at the orphanage starts at seven this week," Sebastian explained.

This went some way toward mollifying Artemus.

The local church Daniel had been assigned to upon his transfer from Rome to Chicago had a children's home attached to it. The priest had spent half of his own childhood in a series of such residential institutions in the Ukraine. It was at his last orphanage that he'd met Persephone DaSilva, the Pope currently heading the Catholic Church and the woman who had become his adoptive mother over the following century.

Artemus had just cut into his eggs when a strange cry echoed from the direction of the garden. They all froze. Nate paled.

"Uh-oh," Callie murmured.

"What was that?" Artemus said stiffly.

The cry came again.

"I thought you were keeping her in the woods," Serena hissed at Nate out the corner of her mouth. "You know, until you broke the news to him."

She cast a surreptitious glance at Artemus.

Suspicion filled him. "Keeping what in the woods? And break the news about what?"

"She must have chewed through her rope," Nate mumbled.

"That's one tough broad," Drake said.

Something white bobbed past one of the kitchen windows. The clippity-clop of hooves rose from the back porch.

"Is that a goat?" Artemus said leadenly.

A pair of golden eyes set in a wizened face sporting a pair of short horns was gazing at them benevolently through the glass. The goat let out a genteel bleat.

"Her name is Daisy," Sebastian said.

"She makes good cheese," Haruki added.

"You all knew?" Artemus glared at a sheepish-looking Smokey. "Even you?!" He jumped to his feet, stormed to the back door, and yanked it open. "What the hell is this, bloody Animal Farm?!"

The goat and the chickens came to greet him with excited bleats and clucks.

"*Shoo!* Go away!" Artemus waved a hand wildly at the creatures before scowling at Nate. "I swear, I'm going to have a cow if you have any more farmyard creatures lurking around the estate!"

"Daisy is the last one, I promise," the super soldier said remorsefully.

"Though it would be a shame to have just the one

goat." Sebastian shrugged nonchalantly at Artemus's expression. "She might get lonely."

Artemus was about to voice a cutting remark when motion in the grounds drew his gaze. A raven descended from the skies and settled on one of the many tombstones dotting the estate. A second one followed.

CHAPTER FOUR

Leah glanced at her cellphone as she rushed inside the large building on South Columbus Drive.

Dammit!

A text message came through just as she was about to shove the phone in the rear pocket of her jeans.

Where are you?

Leah slowed and tapped out a reply. ***Sorry! On my way!***

Her phone pinged again.

You have thirty seconds to get here.

Leah swallowed a curse and took the stairs two steps at a time. *She'll have my hide for this!*

The irate face of Professor Naomi Wagner greeted Leah when she barged inside her airy office on the second floor of the campus building exactly twenty seconds later.

"You're late," the professor said accusingly.

"I know," Leah panted. She shrugged her backpack off her shoulders and plopped down on the chair across from the frowning woman. "There was an accident on Roosevelt."

"If you weren't the top student in my class, I'd be tearing strips off you right now," the professor muttered.

Leah masked a smile as she leaned down and took her laptop out of her bag.

Despite her strict manner and often aloof appearance, Naomi Wagner was a considerate and fair person at heart. Known as the dragon of the Department of Fine Arts, her presence struck fear in the hearts of most of the undergraduate and graduate students, and justifiably so. At the age of thirty, she was one of the youngest Fine Arts tenured professors in the country, with a host of solo exhibitions and projects that had seen her work displayed all over the world. That she had left such a promising career as an artist to return to her alma mater to teach still puzzled many of her peers.

Leah turned her computer on and took out a notepad. "I heard you gave Professor Vaudeman a tongue-lashing in the canteen the other day."

Naomi narrowed her eyes. "You did, did you?"

"Yup," Leah replied, unfazed. "Our online chat room was buzzing with comments."

Naomi put on a disinterested air. "Really?"

Leah wasn't fooled. "At this rate, you're gonna be single forever." She grinned at Naomi's scowl. "Vaudeman is pretty hot for an old guy. Why not just go on a date with him?"

Naomi's expression grew frosty. "The man is only forty-five. Not exactly over the hill. Not that my love life is any of your or the other students' business, but he does nothing for me."

"Oh yeah?" Leah said curiously. "So, what's your type?"

Naomi ignored her question. "Let's review your progress, shall we?"

They spent the next hour going over Leah's course work and art projects. As usual, Leah was surprised by the unusual insights Naomi brought to the table. She studied the older woman admiringly out the corner of her eye while she commented shrewdly on one of her assignments.

The only reason I'm top of her class is because of her.

They'd just finished when a knock came at the door. It opened before Naomi had a chance to respond. Leah looked over her shoulder and paused in the act of packing her backpack, her eyes widening slightly.

Naomi rose to her feet. "Director Patel." She dipped her chin at the plump, Asian man with the graying sideburns standing on the threshold of the office. "To what do I owe the pleasure of this…impromptu visit?"

If the head of the Art Institute detected the professor's dry tone, he turned a deaf ear to it. His lips curved in a beaming smile.

"Naomi." Patel glanced at Leah. "And I see your star student Miss Chase is here too."

Leah stared. She hadn't realized the director knew of her personally.

"The benefactor I told you about the other day is here and would like to make your acquaintance," Patel gushed.

Two figures appeared behind the director.

The first was an elegantly coiffed blonde with gray eyes. She was dressed in an expensive, cream pantsuit that showed off her lithe figure and held a pale clutch purse under her left arm. Diamonds glinted in her earlobes and at the base of her throat. The second figure was a man with dark hair and eyes. He stood slightly behind the woman, as if in deference to her.

The pendant tucked against Leah's breastbone vibrated slightly against her skin. She blinked, startled.

"Jane McMillan," the blonde said with a disarming smile. She stepped past Patel and crossed the office to shake Naomi's hand, her stilettos clattering leisurely on the floor. "I have long been an admirer of your work, Professor Wagner. It's a pleasure to finally meet you."

"Please, call me Naomi," the professor murmured.

"Um, I best be going. I'll be late for my shift," Leah mumbled. She grabbed her backpack and made for the door. "See you later, Professor." She inclined her head politely at Patel. "Director."

The blonde and her companion barely looked at her as she darted past them.

Leah was frowning by the time she reached the bike rack outside the building. Her pendant felt hot where it kissed her flesh. She lifted it from inside her T-shirt and stared at it. Sunlight glinted innocently on the metal.

It looked no different than usual.

It had been four days since her grandmother had given her the jewelry. Leah had lied to her father when he'd asked her about its origins the following morning and told him she'd bought it from a shop in town. To her relief, he didn't appear to recognize it and hadn't questioned her further.

Which means mom probably never wore it.

Leah recalled the mysterious words Barbara Nolan had said the last time she'd seen her and the peculiar weather that had sprung out of nowhere that night. It was as if her grandmother had perceived some dark omen in the windstorm that had swept through Chicago. She'd refused to elaborate on her puzzling statement and had told Leah she would call her next week. But that wasn't the strangest thing. No, the really freaky stuff had started happening the next day.

Leah had begun seeing faint tendrils of darkness above some people's heads when she was out and about. At times, she even sensed something ominous coming from them. And then there were the nightmares she'd started having the night she returned from the Nolan estate. Dark dreams of monsters and beasts, of death and destruction. She'd been experiencing weird flashes during the day as well, when she'd suddenly glimpse fleeting images of places and people she didn't know.

Maybe I should see a doctor. It could be epilepsy.

By the time she parked her bike in the storeroom of the coffee shop where she worked part time in River North, Leah had almost forgotten about Naomi's visitors and the pendant's strange reaction. She removed her helmet, hooked it on the handlebar, and headed into the staff room to change into her uniform. She was walking toward the exit when she spotted her reflection in the floor-length mirror next to the door. She stopped and grimaced.

It was an unusually muggy day and her hair had gone frizzy with the humidity. She combed her unruly locks with her fingers. This only made things worse.

Great. I look like a giant poodle.

She sighed and went out into the shop.

"Afternoon, Leah."

"Hey, boss," Leah replied distractedly to the Korean man who stood manning one of the sleek coffee machines behind the counter.

She shoved her cap firmly on her head and tucked her stubborn curls beneath it. Her gaze roamed the open seating area of the shop as she tied an apron around her waist.

"He's not here yet," Ken Noh drawled, his eyes wrinkling with amusement.

Heat warmed Leah's cheeks. "I don't know what you mean."

"Liar."

Leah pinched her lips and started cleaning the work surfaces. "Like I said, I have no idea what you're talking about."

Ken finished preparing a drink for the customer waiting at the serving station and joined her.

"I'm talking about the Japanese hottie you've been ogling lately. You know, the one who started coming to our shop two weeks ago." The shop manager pressed a hand to his heart, his expression dramatic. "If I wasn't in a happy and insanely hot relationship with my man, I would lick that guy like a lollipop."

Leah's mouth fell open.

"I can't believe you just said that!" she hissed, her ears burning. "And I have *not* been ogling him." She paused. "What makes you think he's Japanese?"

"His bracelet is pretty unique." Ken shrugged. "And I can tell these things."

A young man with blond hair, piercings, and a tattoo covering the left side of his neck appeared from the back of the shop.

Ken's expression cooled slightly. "Your shift started thirty minutes ago, Patrick."

The blond shrugged laconically. "I had something to do for my mom."

"You've had an excuse every single shift you've been late for this week," Ken retorted.

Patrick's face darkened. "Like I said, I had something to do for my mother."

Several of the customers looked around at his raised voice.

Ken flushed. "Just...get to work! And don't let it happen again."

Leah kept her expression neutral as she stepped out from behind the counter and started clearing tables. Patrick was the coffee shop's newest employee. Though he'd only been working there for a few weeks, it was clear he wasn't a good fit for the place. She suspected Ken was waiting until the end of the month to give him his notice.

She felt Patrick's stare as she worked the floor and suppressed a shiver. Although she was confident she could take him on if he tried anything funny, Leah didn't like the way he looked at her. And there was something...odd about him.

Leah's hand automatically went to the pendant beneath her uniform.

Though she hadn't perceived anything spooky above Patrick's head, she had sensed a menacing undercurrent at times when he'd been in her proximity. The only way she could describe it was that something appeared to be lurking behind his eyes.

Something sinister.

The doorbell jingled. Leah straightened when she saw the figure who entered the coffee shop. It was the guy who'd been coming to their place lately. The one Ken thought was Japanese.

Instinct had Leah cutting her eyes to Ken. The Korean man was grinning at her from behind the counter. He mouthed the word 'lollipop' slowly and winked. She scowled.

"Is this table free?"

Leah startled. The guy was standing next to her.

Shoot. I didn't even hear him move.

Leah swallowed and nodded, suddenly tongue-tied. Up close, the stranger's eyes glittered like dark gemstones. He moved past her and sat at the table she'd just cleared.

She sniffed the air furtively. *And he smells as gorgeous as ever.*

Leah realized the guy was looking at her questioningly.

"Would you like your usual?" she blurted out before wincing internally.

Sweet Jesus, Leah, calm down. You sound like a moron.

The guy smiled faintly before dipping his chin, oblivious to her private rant. "Sure."

Leah blinked. She could have sworn the air had just sparkled around him.

Her gaze dropped to the bracelet on his right wrist. It was made of onyx beads and featured a central, metal dragon head with ruby red eyes.

"That's beautiful."

Warmth flooded Leah's face when she realized she'd said the words out loud.

The guy looked surprised for a moment. His expression softened as he studied the jewelry. "Thank you. It was a gift from my late brother."

Leah swallowed. She felt like she'd intruded on something she shouldn't have.

She started moving away from the table. "I'll be back with your drink shortly."

"Wait."

Leah stopped in her tracks.

The guy's gaze shifted to the counter. "Do you have a cake recommendation for today?"

The last of Leah's nervousness vanished as she recalled his sweet tooth. She bit the inside of her cheek to stop from smiling. "The walnut and coffee cake would be my personal choice."

"I'd like a slice of that, please," the guy said solemnly.

Leah found herself humming under her breath as she headed behind the counter to prepare his mochaccino.

"Make sure to put a lot of cream in there," Ken said. "Lollipops are best enjoyed with extra sweetness."

Leah stabbed a spoon in his direction. "Keep that up and I'll sue you for sexual harassment."

Ken chuckled.

Goosebumps broke out across Leah's nape. She looked over her shoulder and met Patrick's stare. His gaze gleamed with a faint, yellow light for an instant where he stood working the till.

Leah's breath froze on her lips.

Patrick broke eye contact and turned to take the next customer's order.

Leah stared, unable to shake the eerie feeling that had just swept over her. She frowned, told herself she was being silly, and turned to put the mochaccino on the counter. She grew still once more.

The guy she had a crush on was studying Patrick with a guarded expression.

CHAPTER FIVE

HARUKI TUCKED HIS HANDS IN THE POCKETS OF HIS jeans where he lounged in the alleyway. It was past eight o'clock and the sun was sinking steadily in the skyline to the west.

The coffee shop's back door stood twenty feet to his right. Judging from what he'd observed over the past couple of weeks, most of the employees used it to enter and exit the building.

He'd found the place quite accidentally, when he'd been wandering through River North one day. After the startling revelation Otis and Sebastian had found in Catherine Boone's journals upon their return from Rome, they'd all been spending their spare time searching the city for traces of divine energy that might indicate the location of the Guardian they now knew to be there.

Their quest had proven unsuccessful thus far. When Artemus had raised the question of whether Otis and Sebastian could have misinterpreted Catherine Boone's writings, the pair had been adamant that this was not the case.

"My mother's visions have not been wrong to date," Otis had stated firmly.

"Well then, unless this Guardian is masking her divine powers for some reason, she's proving to be pretty elusive," Artemus had muttered with a frown.

"It could be because she hasn't yet awakened?" Callie had suggested.

Sebastian had shaken his head at that. "All Guardians exhibit some vestige of divine energy, even in their unawakened state. From what we have all observed, this was the case with Callie, Haruki, and myself. And even Daniel." He'd hesitated before turning to Artemus. "Your theory may be correct," the Sphinx had said reluctantly. "This new Guardian may possess the ability to conceal her aura. We have visited every corner of this city and still not found any clues as to where she might be."

Haruki had pondered those words with a degree of unease. If Artemus and Sebastian's conjectures were on the mark, then this Guardian had different skills from theirs. The only beings they'd encountered to date who could mask their true nature were demon commanders.

Ordinary people could not detect the power of heavenly beasts or the evil presence of demonic souls inside the bodies of humans. Only those with divine gifts could. And one thing had become inherently clear to them in the past week.

Although Ba'al hadn't made a move to attack them since their return from Rome, Haruki and the others had detected a steady increase in demonic activity in Chicago in the last few days. Which meant this unknown Guardian could likely sense it too.

And there was more.

It was Drake who'd finally put words to the weird feeling they'd all been having lately.

"Seriously, it's like someone's walking non-stop over my grave," Artemus's brother had said one night at dinner.

Haruki shivered as the sun dipped behind a skyrise and shadows filled the alley.

He's not wrong. The city feels…different. Like there's some kind of cloud hanging over it.

His trips to River North had ended up becoming a regular occurrence, and not just because of the coffee shop. He'd been browsing the art galleries in the neighborhood for a gift for his father's birthday.

Now that he and Akihito Kuroda had started opening up to one another, he'd come to discover his father's varied tastes and hobbies. To Haruki's surprise, his old man had turned out to be a keen collector of fine art, with a selection of expensive sculptures and paintings in his suite of rooms at the Kuroda estate in Malibu.

A wry smile curved Haruki's lips. *And here I thought he'd be into traditional Japanese ceramics and calligraphy. I wonder if Yashiro knew.*

A bout of sadness danced through him as he thought of his dead brother. Haruki pondered what Yashiro would have made of his little brother being the host to the Colchian Dragon and the wielder of Camael's divine sword.

The back door of the coffee shop opened, distracting him from his despondent thoughts. Haruki straightened where he leaned against the bare brick wall.

The girl who'd served him that afternoon, the one he suspected was a college student, stepped out with her bike. She'd swapped her brown work cap for a helmet and had a red bag on her back. She checked her phone, replied to a message, and was just climbing onto the bicycle when a figure materialized behind her.

He tensed.

It was the blond kid with the piercings and the neck tattoo. The one Haruki knew was harboring a demonic soul.

~

Leah stiffened when she sensed a presence at her back. She looked over her shoulder, her fingers tightening slightly on the handlebar of her bike.

"Hi," Patrick said from a few feet behind her.

"Hey," Leah murmured in a neutral voice. "Do you need something?"

Patrick's eyes were strangely intense as he watched her. "Do you want to go out sometime?" he said brusquely.

Leah blinked, surprised. *Wait. He's asking me out?!*

She hesitated before shaking her head and giving him a small, remorseful smile. "I'm really flattered, but I don't think that's such a great idea. Besides, I'm pretty busy with work and college."

Something fluttered across Patrick's face, distorting his skin in strange shapes for a fleeting moment. "How about right now?"

Apprehension formed a pit in Leah's stomach. *Did I just imagine that?*

"I'm having dinner with my dad," she replied, her voice firm despite her misgivings.

This wasn't exactly a lie, although her father had just texted to say he'd be late getting home.

"Is that so?"

Leah stared. Patrick's voice sounded different. Deeper. More guttural.

"I think you're lying," he continued in a low growl. "In fact, I bet you think you're better than me."

Fear twisted Leah's gut as a dark cloud exploded above him. She leapt off her bike and staggered back a few steps, her eyes rounding.

A black aura crowned the blond's head.

What the heck is that?!

It was her first time seeing the strange phenomenon she'd observed in the last few days up close. Leah could no longer deny the truth before her eyes.

What she was looking at was real. As real as the warm, humid air filling the alleyway and the distant drone of traffic from the main avenue. Only one word came to her mind as she gazed unblinkingly at the inky wisps twisting and coiling agitatedly above Patrick's hair.

Evil.

The yellow light she'd glimpsed in his eyes flashed into existence once more.

Leah swallowed and let go of her bike. It clattered noisily to the ground and was followed by the thump of her bag, the noises muted by the roar of her racing heart.

Her every instinct told her that her life was now in mortal danger.

She could have tried to get away. She could have jumped back on her bicycle and ridden the hell out of that alleyway and away from whatever it was Patrick was changing into. But Leah knew, deep in the marrow of her bones, that she could not afford to turn her back on him right now.

Patrick's face quivered as he glared at her. "Is that it, bitch? You think I'm not good enough for you?!"

Leah gasped and leaned back sharply. His left fist whooshed past her face, missing her by a mere inch. His knuckles caught the rim of her helmet and sent it crashing onto the asphalt. Her hair tumbled down around her face and shoulders in a riot of copper curls.

Christ, he's fast! I didn't even see him move!

The air shifted next to Leah.

Someone appeared beside her and grabbed Patrick's arm in a white-knuckled grip. "Hey, kid. Take a hint, will you? The girl said no."

Shock reverberated through Leah. It was her crush from the coffee shop.

What's he doing here?!

Patrick scowled at the Japanese man. Leah's pulse jumped.

The whites of the blond's eyes had started to turn black.

He closed his right hand on the man's wrist and bared his teeth. "Get off me, asshole!"

Leah sucked in air. Patrick's incisors and canines were changing into wicked fangs. And his fingers and nails were darkening and lengthening to deadly talons.

He sank his newly formed claws into the Japanese guy's skin.

Which was now glittering with tiny, silver scales.

Leah's jaw sagged open. Her gaze moved up the man's arm to his face. Her heart lurched in her chest.

No way!

"You're about to transform into a demon," the stranger told Patrick calmly. "And I'm afraid you won't be leaving this alleyway alive if you do. So, fight it, kid. I don't want to kill you unless I have to."

The scales covering the man's skin framed his cheeks

and jawline. His pupils had changed to vertical slits that shimmered with an orange light. The same light Leah could see pulsing faintly under his T-shirt and beneath the flesh of his throat.

It was as if some kind of fire were boiling up inside his body.

Smoke curled faintly from his nostrils and mouth, confirming Leah's suspicions. She fisted her hands, her blood pounding wildly in her veins.

I'm dreaming. This has got to be a nightmare. Stuff like this doesn't happen!

"You'd better run." The stranger glanced at her. "This is gonna get ugly." He paused. "And it would be best if you never talked about what you just saw."

Leah stilled. *Wait. Is he—threatening me?!*

A grunt reached their ears. They looked at Patrick.

Convulsions shook the blond. He groaned and clenched his teeth, his body twitching uncontrollably and his every move accompanied by gruesome cracks. His eyes rolled into the back of his head. A thin trail of dark blood dribbled down his chin as he bit his lip. He gasped and bowed his spine.

Leah stumbled backward as Patrick transformed into a monster.

CHAPTER SIX

HARUKI CURSED UNDER HIS BREATH AS THE BOY achieved full demonic transformation. The girl stared open-mouthed, her face pale and her feet rooted to the ground.

It wasn't just fear he was reading in her hazel eyes. She seemed fascinated by what she was witnessing, as if this were some kind of freak show at a circus.

Haruki yanked on her arm and pulled her behind him. "Stay back!"

He felt her flinch at his curt tone.

The demon who had awakened inside the blond glared at them from obsidian eyes.

His fist flashed toward Haruki's face.

Haruki blocked the blow with his left forearm. Sparks erupted as the creature's claws scraped the silver plates protecting his skin. The dragon bead on Haruki's bracelet flared with crimson light before transforming into the flaming sword of Camael. He swung the holy blade at the demon's neck.

The creature somersaulted backward, the weapon's

edge missing him by a hairbreadth. His talons raked grooves into the ground as he dropped on all fours and skidded several feet across the blacktop.

Haruki narrowed his eyes. *He's fast.*

The demon rose in a low crouch and charged.

Surprise widened Haruki's eyes a second before the monster's shoulder struck his chest and carried him all the way across the alleyway and into the opposite wall. The back of his skull struck bare bricks. Black spots exploded across his vision.

Shit! And seriously strong!

The Colchian Dragon growled inside him as he deflected the monster's lightning-quick attacks. Haruki gritted his teeth, his beast's energy filling his veins and augmenting his strength and speed.

Is he a demon commander?!

His beast answered him. *He may very well be. Or he is a general, like Tian Gao Lee. He would be dead by now if he were a low-level demon.*

Anger danced through Haruki at the name of his brother's killer. He took a deep breath and prepared to unleash the holy flames simmering inside his stomach.

The monster looked to the left. He was gone in the next second.

"Shit!" Haruki's gaze found the girl frozen in the middle of the alleyway. *"Run, dammit!"*

The girl glanced at him a heartbeat before the demon reached her.

She twisted to the side, hooked her right arm under the monster's shoulder as he rushed her, and flipped him over and onto the ground.

The demon slammed onto his back with a startled grunt.

Haruki blinked. *Wait. Was that a Taekwondo move?!*

∼

Leah scowled at the creature rising to his feet before her. The demon bared his fangs, his distorted face radiating pure rage.

There was no time for her to process the insane events currently unfolding in front of her eyes or, strangely enough, to feel much fear. Only three things were clear to her.

This wasn't a dream.

The monster who had taken over Patrick's body was not of this world.

And he most definitely intended to kill her.

Talons darted toward her face. Leah grabbed the demon's wrist a heartbeat before his claws could tear her eyes out of her skull.

They both stared at where she clutched his flesh in an iron grip.

Leah blinked, unsure who was the more surprised of the two of them. Something that felt like a sledgehammer smashed into her belly an instant later. Pain choked her breath as she was lifted off the ground and sent flying.

A noise sounded somewhere behind her. Strong arms wrapped themselves around her body in mid-air.

The man who had come to her rescue cursed as they landed heavily on the asphalt, his body cushioning her fall when they tumbled and rolled.

A dull ringing echoed in Leah's ears as they finally came to a stop. Her pendant quivered where it had fallen out of her T-shirt and rested against her chest.

The man laid her on the ground, his embrace gentle

despite the fierce expression darkening his handsome features.

"Are you okay?!" he asked roughly.

Heat flared through Leah as she gazed up at him.

Thump.

She shivered as an alien heartbeat exploded into existence inside her.

Time slowed. The man's pupils dilated above hers. Something that looked very much like recognition flared in the orange depths.

Leah gasped. A creature was staring at her from behind his eyes.

Thump-thump.

Blood thrummed in her veins, the beat matching the strange pulsation throbbing within her. She could feel him. Not just where they touched physically. She could sense the powerful life force swirling through the soul of the man who was holding her.

An indistinct form swam before her mind's eye. Leah stiffened as it slowly took shape.

It was a beast. A dragon. One with blazing eyes and ivory horns, and a fearsome, spiked tail.

Thump-thump. Thump-thump.

An angry roar shook the air.

The Dragon broke eye contact and looked over his shoulder at the demon who stood glaring at them.

He clenched his jaw. "When the hell did he get a sword?"

Leah saw the dark blade the monster now clutched in his right hand. It was as different from the weapon the Dragon was wielding as night was from day.

"Here he comes."

Leah blinked. The Dragon was on his feet and moving, his fiery sword in hand.

She sat up and clutched the pendant now vibrating violently against her flesh, her fingers trembling almost as badly.

Up ahead, the Dragon crashed into the demon with a violent sound. He ducked beneath a mortal blow and aimed his blade at the monster, the weapon singing and trailing pale flames where it carved the air with a silken hiss.

A flash of gold and dark exploded when their swords met.

Leah watched the surreal fight taking place some dozen feet away with a strange sense of detachment. She shouldn't have been able to follow their moves. Yet, her eyes were keeping up with their blisteringly fast attacks, so much so she could almost foresee their next actions.

She realized that something was happening to her. Something unnatural. The terror she should have felt since the moment Patrick transformed into a monster finally erupted inside her when she discerned the otherworldly presence within her soul. She swallowed convulsively.

Who—who are you?!

As if in response to her silent question, a pair of golden pupils blinked lazily open in her mind's eye.

A whimper tumbled out of Leah's lips.

The apparition yawned and licked his chops with a large, pink tongue that scraped across two rows of formidable teeth.

Oh. That was a nice sleep.

The creature's voice was low and gravelly. He stretched his powerful limbs and peered out at the alley from behind her eyes. A rumble of excitement worked its way up his throat as he observed the violent battle taking place a short distance away.

Good. It seems it is finally time.

Leah started moving, her palms scraping across the asphalt as she backpedaled toward the other end of the alley. Since she couldn't exactly escape the creature given that he was very much inside her, her actions made no sense to her logical mind. But she wasn't thinking rationally right now.

I must have knocked my head! There's no way this is happening! Any of it! I'm going to wake up any minute now in my—

The beast spoke. *Rise, child.*

Leah found herself on her feet in the blink of an eye. Shock overcame panic. *What the—?! Did he just move my body?*

The beast's smug voice followed. *Indeed, I did. Now, take your key. We must finish this demon before that blasted Dragon takes all the glory.*

"Key? What key?!" Leah squealed. "And you can see the Dragon?!"

The Dragon's head whipped around. Orange pupils flared with surprise; he'd evidently heard her. Leah winced as the demon used the distraction to punch him in the gut.

Of course I can see the Dragon. He looks as smug as the last time we met. The beast sounded offended by her words. *And by key, I mean the pendant around your neck.*

Leah's fingers found the necklace resting against her breastbone. It felt hot where it touched her skin.

Although it is incomplete, it is your weapon. Just as the sword of fire the Dragon is wielding is his.

"I think you've got the wrong person," Leah mumbled. "I'm leaving!"

She tried to turn. Her legs refused to move.

I am afraid I find that proposition entirely unacceptable. The beast's tone had turned cool. *You are a Guardian. As my host, I expect you to stand and fight.*

Irritation rushed through Leah, dampening some of her trepidation. "Oh yeah? Well, find another host to be your Guardian, whatever the heck that is!"

A growl echoed inside Leah's skull.

You and I are bound by a blood pact. Only someone of your lineage can become my host. The beast's impatience resonated inside Leah's soul. *You will just have to come to terms with your Fate, Guardian.*

Surprise jolted Leah. "What do you mean?"

A garbled shout reached her ears. *"Look out!"*

Leah's eyes rounded.

The demon had breached the Dragon's defensive guard and was barreling toward her.

Ah, finally. A chance to show our skills.

The beast sounded pleased with himself. Leah scowled, forgetting her fear once more.

I'm gonna kill him!

The demon was thirty feet from her and closing fast, the Dragon on his heels.

Instinct had Leah snatching the pendant from her neck. "What the hell do I do with this?!"

The answer came to her from both within and without. A cool wind blasted through the alleyway. Dark clouds burst into life in the sky above. The rumble of thunder followed.

Shadows engulfed the passage.

Heat bloomed inside Leah and rushed through every corner of her body, filling her with the incredible power of the beast. Her hair thickened around her face. Her vision grew more focused. Her skin itched and took on a faint, golden glow.

Static filled the air and sparked across the pendant.

It shifted, lengthening and broadening until it took the form of a short, double-ended, silver spear. Electricity danced across the prongs just as the demon leapt toward her, his face a vicious mask and his eyes aglow with the light of Hell.

Leah widened her stance, dug her heels into the blacktop, and stabbed him in the heart with the spear, the force of her attack so powerful it drove the weapon all the way through his body and out of his back.

The demon gasped and froze. A puzzled expression dawned on his hideous features. He sagged slowly on the spear, his body going limp.

Leah stared.

The monster was changing back into Patrick, his towering form shrinking and his face morphing into a human appearance once more. He blinked at her, the yellow light that had lit his pupils and the obsidian color darkening his eyes fading. Awareness returned to his gaze.

He stared at the spear embedded inside his body. Incomprehension flooded his ashen face. Blood bubbled past his lips as he looked up at her.

"Leah?!" Patrick mumbled hoarsely.

It was the last thing he said.

He sank to his knees, the spear leaving his flesh with a wet sound. Leah stared where she still gripped one end of the weapon, bile rising at the back of her throat.

Patrick thudded lifelessly to the ground, the wound she had inflicted a crimson line carving his chest. Blood pooled beneath his body, staining the blacktop a rich crimson.

Oh God! I killed him. I killed a man!

Tears blurred Leah's vision. The spear shifted back into the pendant, unbidden.

This time, her body obeyed her will. She twisted on her heels and ran up the alley, fear and self-loathing twisting her belly into knots.

"Wait!" the Dragon shouted. "We need to talk!"

Leah grabbed her backpack, jumped on her bike, and bolted out of the back lane, her face hot with her falling tears and her heart heavy with guilt.

The beast remained silent where he lurked inside her.

CHAPTER SEVEN

Naomi winced and stretched out the kinks in her neck. She glanced at the antique clock on her desk before staring at the pile of reports sitting under the soft glow of her desk lamp.

"I'm getting too old for this," she muttered to the dark room.

A sigh left her lips. There were days when she sorely regretted abandoning her wildly successful artistic career for her current position as a college professor. This was one of them.

End-of-term exams suck.

Lines wrinkled her brow as she lifted the next student's file off the towering stack. Although she often begrudged her change in profession, there were very good reasons why she'd returned to Chicago.

Something moved in the shadows to her right. A pale, sinuous shape took form in the gloom and approached the desk, soft pads striking the floor silently.

"And where have you been?" Naomi asked in a mild tone.

Bright eyes blinked in the gloom, one blue, one yellow. The white cat's pupils constricted as she leapt on Naomi's lap. She meowed softly.

Naomi stroked the feline's back, her tension easing. "At least you didn't bring a live mouse as a gift this time."

The cat purred and headbutted her hand affectionately in response. She stilled a moment later, her head swinging to stare fixedly at the door.

The tightness in Naomi's muscles returned ten-fold as she followed the cat's gaze. Someone was headed for her office.

Though the hour was late and she was the only staff member left in the building besides the security guards manning the place, it wasn't fear that had Naomi on edge again.

She recognized the energy of the person drawing close. She'd felt it once before, many years ago.

A shadow appeared in the thin gap beneath the door. The knock came a second later. Naomi unclenched her jaw and put on a neutral expression.

"Come in," she called out lightly.

The cat jumped from her lap and curled up on the desk, her unblinking eyes focused on the office door.

It opened to reveal the silhouette of a man.

His voice came out somewhat uncertain as he peered inside the unlit room, his face shrouded in darkness. "Professor Wagner?"

"The light switch is on your left," Naomi said.

The cat did not flinch when the man flicked the button. Brightness flooded the office. The stranger blinked, his eyes adjusting to the radiance.

They were as dark and as serious as Naomi remembered.

And he's still as attractive as the last time I saw him.

The man's brown hair was graying slightly at his temples and curled over the collar of his shirt. Though cheap, his work suit fitted his tall, strong body perfectly. She noted the bulge of the gun and holster under his left armpit with mild interest.

"Good evening. My name is Jeremiah Chase. I am Leah Chase's father." The detective glanced at the cat on the desk before meeting her eyes once more, his face inscrutable. "May I have a word?"

Naomi hesitated before nodding. "Sure. Please, take a seat."

Jeremiah came inside the room and closed the door. Both she and the cat appraised the strands of color dancing above his head while he crossed the floor to the chair his daughter had occupied several hours ago.

He's upset about something.

Her instincts warned her that, whatever the reason he was here, this situation would not end in her favor.

The seat creaked under the weight of the detective as he perched on the edge.

"What can I do for you, detective?" Naomi asked in a polite tone.

"I didn't think I'd catch you when I came here tonight." Jeremiah looked around the room curiously. "Do you always work this late?"

Naomi cocked her head to the side. *He's stalling.*

"Yes, I do, actually."

Jeremiah blinked. "Oh."

Naomi swallowed a smile. The detective could be enchantingly disarming when he was flustered. She wondered if that was what had attracted Joanna to him. She, for one, wasn't fooled. The man was as sharp as a knife. She couldn't afford to be careless, however beguiling his manner.

Jeremiah cleared his throat and frowned. "I've come to see you about the impromptu evening classes Leah has been attending these past few months."

Naomi stared. "Pardon?"

The detective's gaze shifted to the jade bracelet on her right wrist. Surprise danced in his eyes for a moment.

He focused on her once more, his expression disapproving. "I know you and your colleagues have busy schedules, but it's a little much to expect your grad students to drop everything and rush over here just because you feel like teaching an advanced class in the middle of the night."

"I literally have no idea what you're talking about," Naomi blurted out.

Jeremiah's frown deepened.

That was when Naomi realized her mistake. *Shit.*

"Oh. *Those* classes." She flashed a contrite smile at the man opposite her. "I'm truly sorry. I shall have a word with the professors involved and—"

"You're lying."

Anger brought a rush of color to Jeremiah's cheeks. The wisps of energy above his head darkened.

Goddammit! Why didn't she tell me about this?!

"I'm afraid I don't know what you mean, detective—"

"You weren't lying before, when you said you had no idea what this was about." Jeremiah rose to his feet and planted his hands firmly on her desk, his tone stiff. "But you are most definitely lying now. I'm somewhat of an expert when it comes to deceit."

Naomi narrowed her eyes. Although she knew Jeremiah was just worried about Leah, she was not one to take blatant intimidation well.

She stood up, braced her hands on the table, and leaned toward him. "I have to say, I don't appreciate being called a liar to my face, Detective Chase."

Jeremiah did not back down at her icy tone.

"If you aren't lying, then show me the attendance records for the classes you claim Leah took part in," he demanded.

Naomi cursed internally. *I could, if I had five minutes. Of course, they'd be totally fake.*

The cat meowed out a warning, as if she'd read Naomi's thoughts and did not approve. Jeremiah arched an eyebrow at Naomi's silence. He straightened and crossed his arms.

"I have no idea why you would want to protect my daughter, Professor Wagner. She's in enough trouble as it is now that I've found out she's been lying to me all these months." Suspicion clouded his face. "Unless you know where she's been going all those evenings, when she claimed she was coming here?"

I don't, but I have a pretty good hunch.

Jeremiah froze. His eyes flared, as if he'd just guessed what his daughter had been up to. "Dammit!"

He turned and stormed out of the office.

Naomi's shoulders sagged as the door slammed shut in his wake. She closed her eyes briefly, lifted her cell phone from the desk, and calling a number on her VIP list. Someone answered after the sixth ring.

"Hey, it's Naomi here. Can I speak to her?"

She sat down and drummed her fingers impatiently on her desk while she waited. A woman came on the line a short while later.

"Why didn't you tell me?" Naomi snapped.

The woman at the other end sighed. "I know we have

abilities, Naomi, but remote mind reading isn't one of them."

Naomi bit back a curse. "Why didn't you tell me Leah has been visiting you, Barbara? It would have helped avoid the mess I just landed her in!"

Barbara Nolan remained silent for a moment. "What do you mean?"

"Jeremiah Chase just rocked up at my office wanting to know why Leah has been coming to all these last-minute evening classes that never happened. He knows she's been lying to him and he's pretty pissed about it!"

"It doesn't matter."

Naomi scowled at the older woman's lackluster tone. "What?! Of course it—"

She went deathly still in the next instant. A shiver raced down her spine. Goosebumps exploded across her skin.

Naomi twisted in her chair, her gaze gravitating to the window overlooking Butler Field and Lake Michigan. She rose on legs that suddenly felt weak. The cat jumped down beside her as she stepped over to the window.

Naomi laid a hand against the glass. Static danced across her fingertips. A low warning rumbled out of the cat's throat. The feline scaled the wall and perched on the windowsill.

They stared at the dark clouds spinning menacingly over the lake.

Naomi swallowed. She knew this was more than just a late summer storm. "It's happening, isn't it?"

"Yes," Barbara said in a tired voice. "I gave her the pendant the last time she came to the estate, four nights ago. It reacted to her immediately."

Trepidation coiled inside Naomi as she studied the

ominous phenomenon in the sky. "Weren't you meant to give the relic to Leah on her nineteenth birthday?"

"I...couldn't."

Surprise jolted Naomi. It wasn't every day that *the* Barbara Nolan admitted to a weakness.

"She looks so much like her mother." The older woman's words were full of sorrow and regret. "I wanted to get to know her a little bit first. I know she will likely come to hate us and curse our bloodline, but I pray that the memories she and I have made these past few months will endure somewhere inside her."

Naomi clenched her fists. The white cat headbutted her arm, the gentle move meant to reassure her. The jade beads on her bracelet glowed faintly in response to the creature's warm energy.

She knew why Jeremiah had examined the jewelry with a perplexed look a short while back. His wife Joanna had owned an almost identical item.

"Leah won't hate you, Barbara." Naomi's tone hardened. "This is bigger than her. Bigger than all of us. And you forget. Though she may choose to abandon us as a family when she discovers the truth of her fate, she will gain an even more formidable one in Artemus Steele and his companions."

CHAPTER EIGHT

Leah unlocked the front door of her house and stumbled inside the foyer. She pushed her bike against the wall, dropped her bag on the floor, and went to remove her helmet. She startled when she touched her bare hair.

Her heart thundered inside her chest as she turned and stared at her reflection in the mirror in the hallway. She'd forgotten to put the helmet on in her wild dash to escape the alleyway behind the coffee shop.

The silence inside the house weighed heavily on her.

Her father wasn't home yet.

Leah gazed blindly at her pallid face. Her eyes were swollen and puffy, the fresh shadows beneath them rendering her a haggard expression. She looked like she'd aged ten years in the last half hour.

The memory of what had happened stormed through her once more, just as it had done time and time again during her desperate ride home. She could barely remember the blurry trip, so overwhelmed was she by all that she had witnessed and done. A sob escaped her throat. She twisted and raced up the stairs to her bedroom, her vision swimming with fresh tears.

I killed him! I killed Patrick!

It didn't matter that it had been in self-defense and under the most extraordinary of circumstances. No one would believe her account of events. Not even if she dragged the man possessed by the soul of the Dragon to court to be her witness.

Her father's face flitted before her eyes as she flopped down on her bed. *Oh God! He could get fired over this. And we'll probably lose the house too!*

Leah pressed a hand to her mouth, her sobs choking her. She looked over at the photograph on her nightstand. Her father and mother smiled at her dazzlingly from inside the frame.

She'd taken the picture on her mother's birthday, five years ago. They'd dressed to the nines and gone to a fancy restaurant in the city to honor the happy event. It had been the first and only time Leah had ever seen her father get drunk; the special evening had been a double celebration to commemorate his recent promotion to senior homicide detective.

Five weeks later, Joanna Chase had received her terminal cancer diagnosis.

Despite the bittersweet feelings the memory of that evening evoked in Leah, the photograph remained her all-time favorite family picture.

What should I do, Mom? Should I just turn myself in?!

Her mother's eyes twinkled happily at her from the photo.

Leah sat up and lifted her pendant out of her T-shirt. A scowl scrunched her face as she stared at it.

This is all the fault of this medallion! This wouldn't have happened if I didn't have—

She froze, her eyes rounding.

Wait. Grandma gave it to me. Does this mean she was aware something—something weird might happen?!

The events that had transpired the last time she'd been at the Nolan estate raced through Leah's mind. She gasped.

She knew!

Leah's heart sank. It all made sense now. The storm that had sprung up out of nowhere. Her grandmother's strange words. The odd things she had started witnessing the day after she received the medallion.

The words the beast that had made its presence felt inside her had uttered back in the alleyway resonated through her skull.

"Hey, you," Leah mumbled to thin air. "You said something about a blood pact and my lineage. Did you mean the Nolans?"

There was no reply forthcoming.

Anger surged through Leah. She could tell the creature had heard her where he skulked inside her soul.

A distant thud made her jump.

"Leah?"

Leah gulped at her father's loud call. Footsteps sounded on the staircase. Sweat broke out on her brow. Her hands turned cold and clammy.

Oh God. I think I'm gonna throw up.

The door to her bedroom opened with a violent motion. Jeremiah Chase stormed inside.

He rocked to a stop when he saw her. Concern flashed in his heated gaze briefly as he registered her tears. It was replaced by the fury she'd sensed in his voice and could feel radiating from him.

"Did she call you?" he snarled. "Is that why you're crying?"

Leah blinked, startled.

"What?" she mumbled numbly.

He slammed a hand on the dresser next to him. "Did Naomi Wagner call you to tell you that I've discovered the truth about your lies?!"

Leah's stomach contracted painfully. She'd never seen her father so angry before. "I—I don't know what you're talking about!"

"I mean your advanced drawing classes, Leah," Jeremiah grated out. "The ones you claim you've been attending for the last few months. The ones you deliberately lied to me about."

Deafening silence fell between them.

Leah looked blindly at her father. She couldn't deny his words. Not after everything that had happened tonight.

"Dad," she started tremulously, "there's something I have to tell—"

"*I don't want to know, Leah!*" Jeremiah barked, his fingers fisting at his sides. "Actually, strike that." He scowled at her, his tone turning cold. "There is only one thing I want you to tell me. Were you seeing Barbara Nolan all those times you lied to me?"

Leah swallowed convulsively. There was no point hiding the truth anymore. "Yes."

Jeremiah swore at her whispered confession. His face darkened. "You're grounded. Indefinitely."

Leah gaped at him, too shocked to speak for a moment. "What?!"

"You're not to leave this house for anything except to

go to your classes," Jeremiah elaborated between gritted teeth. "And I will drive you there and back myself!"

The torrent of emotions that had been bubbling inside Leah since she had stepped out of the back door of the coffee shop in River North and been confronted by Patrick exploded in a flood of anger.

"I will do no such thing!"

She jumped off the bed and faced her father, her nails digging into her palms.

Jeremiah did a double take. He recovered his composure and glared at her. "You're still a minor, Leah. And you broke the promise you made to me when you said you would stop seeing Barbara."

"*And you are still lying to me!*" Leah yelled. "About everything! About Mom! About why you guys stopped seeing Barbara! I mean, did Mom even have can—"

She stopped and pressed her hands to her lips, appalled at the words that had almost tumbled out of her mouth.

The color drained from Jeremiah's face. He looked as shocked as she felt.

"Did your mother really have cancer?" he said hoarsely. "Is that what you were going to say?"

Pain twisted Leah's heart. She found herself on the verge of tears once more.

"I'm—I'm sorry!" she stammered. "I didn't mean—"

"We would never lie to you about something like that, Leah."

Jeremiah's leaden words hung heavily in the air between them.

A suffocating feeling filled Leah's chest. She stared wretchedly at her father, wishing things could go back to the way they had been. Wishing that she had never accepted the damn pendant.

For the first time in six months, Leah regretted ever having agreed to meet Barbara Nolan.

None of this would have happened if I'd said no to her request.

Sorrow filled her, so much so she feared she would drown in it. Though she knew her grandmother was to blame for much of what had happened in the last hour, she could not dismiss one truth; she and Barbara Nolan had a special connection. One that felt deeper than the affection between a grandmother and a granddaughter. Which made the older woman's betrayal all the worse for it.

I need to get out of here.

Leah took a shaky breath, walked past her father, and headed down the corridor to the stairs.

"Where are you going?"

Leah ignored her father's stilted question as she descended the steps, her legs heavy. She snatched her backpack from the foyer floor, took her bike, and paused in the hallway.

"I love you, Dad." Her voice broke as she gazed at the pale-faced man standing frozen at the top of the stairs. "I'm so sorry about what I did. Not just the lies I told you, but what—what happened today." Leah swallowed. "I want you to know that I will always love you, no matter what. And I hope you will forgive me, one day."

"Leah?" Jeremiah mumbled in a stunned voice. "Leah! *Come back!*"

His shout rang in her ears as she bolted from the house and vanished into the night.

CHAPTER NINE

THE MAN SQUATTED AND TRACED THE BLACKTOP WITH his fingertips. He didn't have to sniff his hand to know that a demon had perished there. He could feel the dark essence that had filled the alleyway, as well as faint trails of the divine power that had clashed with the newly awakened fiend.

"What a pity," his commander murmured behind him. "That boy would have made a splendid general."

"Indeed he would have, my liege," the man said respectfully. "It's a shame he lost his life so soon."

"Do we know who fought him? I was looking forward to grooming someone to take over the vacant seat of power in New York." A weary sigh left the commander. "The Supreme Leader does exaggerate at times," the demon grumbled. "I grow tired of running two cities."

Unease darted through the man.

He looked anxiously around the shadowy alley.

Though he was aware that Ba'al's Supreme Leader had something of a soft spot for his commander, the high demon was also renowned for not tolerating insolence or the slightest hint of defiance against his ultimate power. His loyalty to Satanael was legendary among the Grigori and he had been known to eradicate entire legions of demons if their commanders dared mention a single word against the one whom they called their God.

"What's the matter?" His commander sounded mildly amused. "You look worried all of a sudden."

The man sighed. His commander had a nasty habit of teasing him.

"I am, a little bit, my liege. And, to answer your question, I believe the Dragon was the one who confronted our newly revived brethren."

"Oh." His commander's interest was clearly piqued. "The Yakuza boy did this?"

"I believe so, yes."

A hand grabbed the man's chin. He stilled, unmindful of the forceful grip. His commander leaned in and sniffed his face.

"There is more, isn't there?" Excitement made the demon's voice deepen with a guttural undertone. "I can tell from your scent."

The man masked a grimace. He disliked it when his master smelled him so.

"There was someone else here," he admitted. "A human. Female."

The commander's eyes widened. "And she walked out of here alive?"

The man hesitated before nodding.

"Hmm." A thoughtful moue clouded his commander's face. "And you can't detect anything else about her?"

"No, my liege."

Traffic hummed and roared in the distance as the demon gazed at the inky firmament above their heads. The strange phenomenon that had attracted them to this location had started to dissipate, the turbulent clouds breaking at the edges as they dispersed. Stars started to appear in the night sky.

It wasn't the only storm cloud that had sprouted above the city that evening. There were several more, including a large one over Lake Michigan.

"Could this be the work of our elusive Guardian?" his commander mused.

The man stayed silent. It wasn't his place to make conjectures.

His commander's expression turned serious.

"The fact that a human girl witnessed the fight between a demon and a divine beast and survived to live another day tells me there is likely more to her than meets the eye. We know this Guardian has abilities Artemus Steele and his friends do not possess. Such as the power to conceal their presence from the one who boasts the most refined animal instinct in this world."

The man shivered as the demon caressed his face with a gentle hand. He could feel his commander's excitement once more.

Except this feeling was different than the previous thrill the demon had displayed.

His leader was aroused.

"Do you mean me, my liege?"

The demon smiled at the man's softly mumbled words. "I do."

The man trembled at the naked lust in the demon's gaze. He knew what was in store for him tonight. His commander would not let him sleep a wink. And he would relish every single minute of the savagely sweet torment the demon would put him through.

"And you are *my* beast," the fiend purred.

"What is that?" Serena muttered.

Static raised the hairs on Drake's arms. He frowned. "I don't know."

They were standing on the rear porch of the mansion. A ring of clouds spun menacingly above the estate, the mantle billowing and contracting in eerie shapes.

The back door squeaked open. Artemus appeared, the others in his wake.

"Can you feel that?" his twin said with a faint frown.

"Yeah. It's what brought us out here." Drake indicated the strange mass in the night sky. "It's coming from whatever the heck that is."

"What in God's name?" Sebastian stared. "I have never seen a cloud formation like that."

"The atmospheric pressure has dropped," Nate observed.

"And there is no wind," Serena added thoughtfully.

"So, what's making that thing rotate?" Artemus said.

"Is it a twister?" Daniel asked anxiously.

Tornadoes weren't a natural phenomenon in Europe, so the priest had likely never seen one.

Callie shook her head. "Twisters don't look like that. We used to have them where I grew up."

"Well, whatever it is, it's making my skin crawl," Daniel mumbled.

Artemus shared a guarded glance with Drake. "Like someone walking over our graves, huh?"

Drake shrugged.

Smokey's eyes flashed crimson where he sat by Artemus's feet. He jumped onto the railing and rose on his hind legs, his nose twitching as he sniffed the air.

They followed his gaze.

"What are you sensing, brother?" Sebastian asked, puzzled.

That is not the only one. There are others.

As if on a cue, a giant bolt of lightning cracked the sky above Chicago, sending dazzling brilliance arcing through the darkness.

"Holy shit," Callie blurted out. "Pardon the language," she added hastily, looking over at Daniel.

"I believe that expletive is entirely warranted, given the circumstances," the priest said, ashen faced.

They gazed uneasily at the multiple vortexes spiraling ominously over other parts of the city, the largest one above Lake Michigan. A few of them started to disperse even as they watched.

"Still no news from Elton?" Drake asked Artemus stiffly.

He could sense the strange activity rousing the demon inside him. It appeared Samyaza was as intrigued by what he could feel as the rest of them were. Which meant the uncanny phenomenon, whatever it was, was not demonic in origin.

"No." Artemus looked at Daniel. "Have you heard anything from Persephone?"

The priest shook his head. "I spoke to her this morning. If she knew something, she would have told me by now."

The sound of a car engine rose from the direction of the driveway.

"Is that Haruki?" Serena asked.

"Yeah." Callie grinned at the super soldier. "You're getting better at detecting our energies. We'll make a divine beast out of you yet."

"No, thanks," Serena muttered. "Nanorobots and Immortal genes are more than enough. Besides, having some mythical creature creeping around inside my soul would give me the heebie jeebies."

Drake swallowed a wry smile. He doubted anything could scare the super soldier. And, despite her disinterested air, he could tell she was pleased by the compliment.

The divine powers she and Nate had manifested in Rome were still evolving. Even he and Artemus could feel the difference in the energy the two super soldiers now emitted. It was warmer and richer than that which they had first sensed from them upon their first meeting.

A door slammed somewhere in the mansion. Haruki stormed out of the back door a moment later.

Drake tensed. So did the others.

The Yakuza heir was agitated and so was his beast.

Haruki rocked to a standstill in the midst of them, his irate gaze on the whirling mantle above the mansion. "Damn!"

"What's wrong?" Callie asked anxiously.

Smokey leapt to the ground and coiled himself around the Dragon's legs.

"Thanks, pooch."

Haruki lifted the rabbit in his arms and studied the revolving clouds with a heavy frown.

Intuition blasted through Drake.

"You know what that is, don't you?" Artemus said before Drake could voice the question.

Haruki nodded. "Yeah. I was there when the first one formed. It's the new Guardian."

Shock reverberated across the bonds that linked them.

"You met the Guardian?!" Callie squeaked.

"I did." Haruki's expression darkened. "But she got away."

CHAPTER TEN

Artemus stepped out of the shadows of the trees and slowed to a stop. He studied the mausoleum occupying a small clearing in the woodland to the west of his estate with a faint frown.

Six ravens perched atop the pale walls of the building. Their heads swung in unison when they detected his presence, their gimlet eyes focusing unerringly on him.

Artemus felt a trace of nervousness snake through Smokey where the beast stood beside him in his dark hellhound form.

"You find them spooky too, huh?"

The hellhound let out a low growl in response.

I am not scared of them. Smokey paused. *I have met them many times in my long life. They have unfailingly been portents of things to come.*

Artemus grimaced. "Why do I get the feeling you're not talking about winning the lottery here?"

He recalled Sebastian's words from a few mornings ago, as well as Haruki's account of his chance meeting last night with the girl he suspected was the Guardian prophesied to be living in Chicago. Much to Serena's ire, she and Nate had been unable to find any information on her when they'd hacked into the computer of the coffee shop's owner and the databases of the colleges in Chicago.

The only thing Haruki knew of the girl was her first name, from the tag she'd worn on her work uniform.

Artemus's frown deepened as he headed across the glade to the mausoleum. Haruki's description of what the new Guardian had done in the alleyway in River North has surprised all of them. Not just because it was apparent her powers were likely elemental in origin, but because she had defeated a newly awakened demon of the caliber of a general.

I wonder what kind of creature her beast is.

He unlocked the door and entered the crypt, the hellhound following in his steps. The musty smell of ancient dust and dying flowers filled the air inside the burial chamber.

Artemus squatted in front of the sarcophagus sitting on a pedestal in the center of the floor and exchanged the wilting bouquet in the crystal vase at its base for the bunch of fresh flowers he'd gathered from the gardens. He topped up the container with the water bottle he'd brought with him before rising to his feet.

A mournful feeling filled him as he gazed at the words inscribed on the gold-plated plaque on the tomb.

Karl LeBlanc, 1970-2033.

Artemus hesitated before placing a hand on the cool marble. "Time sure flies, huh? It feels like yesterday that you were teaching me how to manipulate metal in your workshop."

His quiet words echoed around the vault.

Artemus swallowed the lump in his throat and exited

the mausoleum, Smokey padding silently at his side. They'd just entered the woods when the hellhound stopped in his tracks and looked around at the crypt.

Artemus followed his gaze.

The ravens had disappeared from the rooftop of the building.

"What is it?" Artemus asked, puzzled.

Smokey hesitated. *Nothing. I thought I...heard something.*

∽

Elton LeBlanc stared at his smartband. "Are you sure?"

The woman on the screen scratched the back of her head and nodded, her expression puzzled. "It's the damnedest thing. And this isn't the only place it's happening. I've heard rumors on the grapevine of other morgues and funeral homes experiencing the same incident in the last couple of days."

A niggling feeling bloomed at the back of Elton's mind as he studied the medical examiner.

Ruth Bradshaw was a forensic pathologist working for the Chicago PD. She was also an expert in demon killings, having had personal experience with the occult on the night her sister had turned into a fiend and killed their mother.

She had come to learn of Elton and the Vatican organization he secretly worked for the same way most civilians who eventually pledged their allegiance to the group did. By sticking her nose in places it didn't belong. It was Shamus who'd found her one night, when she'd been ambushed by a fiend in a seedy alleyway close to where there had been a recent demonic attack. Had it not been for Shamus returning to examine the scene of the brutal killing, she would have become yet another victim of Hell's forces.

She had helped investigate many a suspect death in Chicago in the years since her mother's gruesome murder and her sister's eventual capture and execution at the hands of Vatican agents, her expertise allowing Elton and his team to rapidly identify murders committed by newly awakened demons.

"Thanks, Ruth," Elton murmured. "Let me know if you hear anything else."

"Will do. And Elton?"

"Yeah?"

"You be careful now. You and your friends tend to be in the thick of it when things go south in the supernatural world. There's a bad vibe in the air at the moment." Ruth faltered. "I can't put my finger on what it is, but, like my grandma used to say, these are the kinds of days when you should gather your children inside your home before dark and lock your doors."

She ended the call.

Elton stayed still for a moment before twisting in his chair and gazing out of the window of his study.

Could this be related to Ba'al?

It was a bright, sunny day. Branches swayed and leaves rustled gently in the trees lining the cul-de-sac where his auction house was located. The faint rumble of traffic from the avenue beyond mingled with the bird song filling the street outside.

Lines wrinkled Elton's brow. He knew what Ruth meant.

Despite the great weather they'd been experiencing lately, there was something strange afoot in the city.

Elton rose and went in search of Shamus. He found the head of his security team eating a steak sandwich in the canteen. His stomach grumbled as the delicious smell of freshly cooked prime meat filled his nostrils.

The chef turned from the stainless-steel cooking range where he was searing a second steak fillet. "Hi, boss. Want me to make you one?"

"No, thanks," Elton murmured. "I'm on a diet."

Shamus and the chef stared.

"I'm trying to lose weight." Elton hesitated. "Helen said my love handles were cute."

"Women like their men chunky," Shamus stated in an authoritative tone. "Especially in the bedroom."

The chef nodded sagely.

"Besides, you can't help it." Shamus shrugged. "Things tend to sag after you hit a certain age."

"I'm fifty-six," Elton declared haughtily.

The chef blinked. "Oh wow. I would have put you at sixty-three at the least."

Shamus's shoulders trembled as he bit into his sandwich, his gaze focused intently on the paper he'd been reading.

Elton scowled. "You two know I sign your paychecks, right?"

The chef grinned and went back to cooking his steak.

Elton waited until Shamus had finished his lunch before getting the former boxing champion to drive him to Artemus's estate. A goat was sitting on the front porch when they pulled up outside the Gothic mansion.

Elton stared at the creature as he climbed the steps and rang the doorbell. Artemus opened the door.

"What's with the goat?" Elton said.

"Don't ask," Artemus said darkly. "And why don't you use your key? This place is as much yours as it is mine."

"It wouldn't feel right," Elton muttered. "Besides, there are ladies in the house. They could be in a state of undress."

Artemus sighed. "There are times when I forget what an old fogey you are. I wouldn't put it past Callie to wander around *en déshabillé*, but the only circumstances in which I could envisage Serena doing the same would be if Hell froze over."

Clucking rose from the east side of the mansion. A chicken poked her head around the corner and eyed them suspiciously.

"Get inside," Artemus told Elton and Shamus hastily. "That's Gertrude."

"Who the heck is Gertrude?"

"Nate assures us she's a normal chicken, but the rest of us are pretty sure she's an agent of Hell."

Gertrude let out a piercing squawk and flapped her wings threateningly.

CHAPTER ELEVEN

Sunlight filtered through the blinds and struck Leah's eyelids. She winced and raised a hand sluggishly to her face. Pain throbbed through her skull. She turned over and squinted at her cell phone where it lay on the nightstand of the guest room.

It was almost noon.

Her heart grew heavy when she saw the number of missed calls and messages she'd received from her father. Leah slumped back on the bed and stared at the ceiling.

I should call him and tell him I'm safe, at least.

A soft knock came at the bedroom door.

"Are you okay in there?" someone said in a mildly anxious voice.

Leah swallowed. *Not really. I killed a man last night. And I'm pretty sure there's a monster living inside me.*

The voice came again, its tone now adamant.

"I'm coming in."

Leah sat up and swung her legs over the edge of the mattress just as the door opened. A tall, beefy figure with a shaved head and tattoos covering his forearms stepped inside the room.

Randall Lynch was wearing an apron proclaiming that bacon was mankind's best invention over his colorful T-shirt and shorts. He was holding a ladle in one hand.

"I made spicy beef soup for lunch." Ken Noh's boyfriend frowned slightly. "You look like you hardly slept. Was the bed too hard?"

Leah managed a weak smile. "It was fine, thank you. I just have a lot on my mind."

"Well, come eat when you're ready." He arched an eyebrow. "That looks cute on you. You should keep it."

Leah glanced at the loose-fitting, dark blue *Kermit The Frog* T-shirt Randall had lent her when she'd turned up at their place last night.

It came down almost to her knees.

"Are you sure? This looks like one of your favorites."

"It isn't," Randall said bluntly. "Ken got me that when we went to Disney World last year. Trust me, you'll be doing me a favor if you take it."

This time, a genuine grin curved Leah's lips. She waited until the game designer left the bedroom before trudging into the adjoining bathroom. She avoided looking at her reflection in the mirror while she brushed her teeth, took a quick shower, and changed into yesterday's clothes. She walked out into Randall and Ken's airy, open-plan loft apartment ten minutes later.

Located on the top floor of a converted warehouse overlooking Chicago River, the place was a short walk from Ken's coffee shop and Randall's company offices.

The pair had met at a Hawaiian hula party six years ago and had been an item since. Ken declared it had been love at first sight. Randall was more pragmatic and claimed Ken had become smitten with his cooking first.

There were any number of girlfriends Leah could have stayed with last night when she'd fled her home in Bridgeport. She'd decided to come to Ken's place since her father was unlikely to look for her there and her boss wouldn't ask too many questions.

"Where's Ken?" Leah murmured as Randall got up from the breakfast bar and served her a bowl of soup.

Her gaze gravitated to the TV in the kitchen. It was muted and showing the national news.

"Out getting groceries. He has to go to the shop later. One of his part-time employees didn't show up again."

Leah's stomach started churning.

"Oh," she said lightly. "Did he say who it was?"

"Some guy named Patrick."

The churning turned into a sickening feeling. The local news came on. She stiffened and watched the headlines streaming across the bottom of the screen.

Randall pursed his lips. "Are you sure you're feeling alright? You've gone as pale as a ghost."

Leah nodded wordlessly. She couldn't see any mention of a gruesome murder in River North.

"You can stay here for as long as you need," Randall told her once she finished lunch. "Ken's pretty worried about you. You're not the kind of girl who runs away from home."

"Thank you," Leah mumbled.

I bet they'll change their tune when they find out I murdered Patrick.

The guilt gnawing at her conscience suddenly made it hard for her to breathe. "I'm gonna get some fresh air."

"Okay."

She grabbed her backpack and left the apartment hastily.

～

Artemus stared. "Come again?"

"There are bodies going missing in Chicago," Elton said. "A medical examiner friend of mine called me an hour ago. A number of morgues and funeral homes in the city have reported corpses disappearing in the last few days."

Drake raised an eyebrow. "How come this hasn't made headline news?"

Elton shrugged. "Probably because the authorities are trying to keep it under wraps until they figure out what the heck is going on."

Artemus rubbed his chin where he leaned against a kitchen worktop. "What could Ba'al possibly want with dead bodies?"

Elton frowned. "You think this is Ba'al too?"

Artemus and Drake exchanged a glance.

"Considering the weird mood in the air lately, I can't think who else could be behind this," Artemus muttered.

Serena strolled inside the kitchen. "I still can't find anything about that girl." An irate expression clouded her face. "I examined every piece of security camera footage from the area for the last month. Her face and body are obscured in all of them. It's as if someone's tampered with the recordings."

Elton's brow furrowed. "What girl?"

"Haruki met the new Guardian last night," Drake replied.

Elton's eyes widened. "He did?"

"She works at a coffee shop he's been visiting lately, in

River North," Artemus said. "She killed a demon yesterday. Someone Haruki struggled to take down. That's when those strange cloud formations started appearing across the city."

Elton startled. "That was her?!"

"Yeah." Artemus studied Serena with a pensive frown. "So, nothing at all? Not even a general sense of where she was headed?"

"The only thing I know for sure is that she rode south and crossed the river." The super soldier gnawed at her lower lip. "I don't like this. Everyone leaves a digital footprint in this day and age." She faltered, her tone troubled. "It's like she doesn't exist."

Shrill squawks rose from the backyard. Shadows flitted past the kitchen. Artemus moved to a window. A heavy sense of disquiet filled him as he stared outside.

"What is it?" Drake said.

His twin joined him, Serena and Elton in his wake. They gazed at the LeBlanc family cemetery.

There was a raven perched on practically every tombstone.

"What on earth?" Elton muttered.

CHAPTER TWELVE

"Thanks for letting me know, Ken."

Jeremiah ended the call and stared at his cell.

"You okay?" Tony Goodman said opposite him.

"Yeah." Jeremiah sighed and raked a hand through his hair. "It's just—" He paused and grimaced. "Well, Leah and I had a fight last night."

Tony arched an eyebrow. "Teenage hormones?"

"That's the thing. She's never been a difficult kid."

"I hate to break it to you, boss, but your kid is a young woman. And a pretty one at that."

Jeremiah made a face.

Tony's lips quirked in a smile. "So, she brought any boys to the house yet?"

Jeremiah shuddered. "No, thank God."

"Wow. I feel sorry for Leah. Her old man is a total grouch."

"Thanks. FYI, I'm doing your performance evaluation next month, so you'd better be nice to me."

Tony grinned. They both knew he'd pass with flying colors, like he had each of the three years they'd been working together. His desk phone rang. He picked up the receiver and grabbed a writing pad.

Jeremiah glanced at his cell again.

Now that he knew Leah had spent the night safe and sound at Ken's apartment, the fear that had been weighing him down all of yesterday and this morning started to abate.

He'd gone back over their argument again and again while he'd been driving around town looking for her. Though he was aware his anger had been warranted, he realized Leah hadn't been upset about him finding out she'd secretly been visiting her grandmother for all those months she'd been lying to him. It was clear something else had been on his daughter's mind last night.

And all I did was bite her head off, instead of listening to what she was trying to tell me.

Sorrow swamped Jeremiah. He and Leah had never had a serious fight before. He hated that he couldn't talk to her.

Lines creased his brow a moment later. He'd called Barbara Nolan last night to ask her if Leah had come to her place in Beverly. She'd told him her granddaughter hadn't been in touch with her in almost a week.

It wasn't the fact that Leah had failed to seek her grandmother's help that had struck him as odd. Though it had been years since he'd last heard her voice, it was his mother-in-law's tone that had made a lasting impression on him. She hadn't sounded in the least bit concerned that Leah had gone missing. In fact, it almost seemed as if she'd been expecting it. Her final words to Jeremiah resonated in his mind once more.

Be careful.

Tony's excited voice distracted him from his troubled thoughts.

"Good news." The detective put the phone down and flashed a grin at him. "I know where our suspects are."

Jeremiah straightened in his chair.

They'd been investigating the murder of a drug dealer whose body had been found floating close to a pier a month ago. So far, the men they'd wanted to question in relation to the murder had proven elusive.

They grabbed their jackets and headed out of the precinct.

"By the way, I heard the strangest thing when I went to get us lunch," Tom mused as they crossed the parking lot to their car.

"Oh yeah?"

"A couple of detectives were talking about the case they'd just been assigned. Apparently, someone's been stealing bodies from the mortuaries around the city."

Jeremiah stared. "Really?"

"Yup. It's almost as creepy as those weird storm clouds we had last night."

It took less than ten minutes to drive to the dive bar in North Side where Tony's informant had told him their suspects were. They parked in an adjacent street, checked the building's exits, and entered the tavern.

The place was busier than Jeremiah had expected. He allowed his eyes to adjust to the gloom, looked around, and spotted their suspects.

The five men were seated around a booth next to the jukebox at the rear of the establishment. From the empty beer bottles crowding their table, they'd been drinking a while.

Jeremiah and Tony negotiated the crowd and stopped

in front of them. Four of the men stiffened. The fifth guy leaned back in his chair and eyed them leisurely.

Jeremiah studied Shane Maddox with an inscrutable expression while Tony grabbed a seat from an adjacent table and dragged it over. The younger detective straddled the chair and gave the men a friendly smile.

"Hey there. I'm Detective Goodman. This is Detective Chase." He indicated Jeremiah where the latter stood leaning against the booth's partition. "We'd like to talk to you about your deceased associate, Felix Hernandez."

Maddox stuck a toothpick in the corner of his mouth and started rolling it around his tongue, his expression mildly amused. The other four exchanged troubled glances.

"Come now, detectives," Maddox drawled. "You're kinda ruining what was turning out to be a nice Saturday afternoon. Can we do this another day?"

"I'm afraid that's out of the question." Though Tony's smile remained amiable, his tone was anything but. "It's taken us a while to track you guys down. Now, how about we all take a ride back to the precinct for that chat I just mentioned? The coffee's nice and the rooms are better ventilated."

Chairs scraped hurriedly around them. Some of the bar's occupants had overheard their conversation. They cast uneasy stares their way and beat a hasty retreat toward the other side of the room. Jeremiah saw the bartender frown at them out the corner of his eye.

He kept his gaze locked unblinkingly on Maddox. The drug dealer's mouth curved in a lopsided grin. Jeremiah blinked.

The man's eyes had just flashed with a strange, yellow light.

Maddox spat out the toothpick, leaned his hands on the table, and rose to his feet.

"Come on, guys," he told his associates. "The faster we get this over with, the faster we can come back here and continue our drinking session."

The other four stared at him as if he'd grown a second head.

Maddox's voice turned stone cold. "I said, let's go."

The men hesitated before nodding and getting up.

Tony rose and turned to Jeremiah. "I'll radio for a second car."

Maddox indicated a door to their left while Tony walked over to a quieter spot to make the call.

"How about we go out the back?" the drug dealer suggested to Jeremiah good-naturedly. "The owner of this place is a friend of mine. It wouldn't be good for business if some of his regulars were seen being escorted out of the premises by cops."

Jeremiah hesitated.

Tony returned. "A patrol car's on its way." He clipped his radio back in his belt and frowned slightly when he saw Jeremiah's face. "Everything okay?"

A strange foreboding crawled across the back of Jeremiah's neck. He couldn't stop thinking about the weird glow he'd just glimpsed in Maddox's pupils.

The drug dealer smiled at him mildly.

"Let's take the back door," Jeremiah said brusquely.

We've already checked out the alley behind the bar. There's more space there to maneuver if they try anything. And it's less likely innocent bystanders will be caught in the crossfire if things go south.

Tony's gaze told Jeremiah he'd gotten the gist of his thoughts. They weren't making an official arrest and had not checked the drug dealers for weapons yet. The younger detective took the lead, the suspects following in his steps. Jeremiah brought up the rear, conscious of the weight of his gun in the holster under his left arm.

They headed out of the bar and stepped into a grimy alleyway dotted with dumpsters. A high rise flanked the back lane, casting it in shadow.

Tony's pace quickened as he turned north, toward where their car was parked.

They were thirty feet from the opening of the alley when it happened.

One of the drug dealers stumbled into two of his associates with a choking sound before dropping to his knees.

Jeremiah slowed, fingers rising automatically toward his weapon. Up ahead, Tony stopped and turned, his hand reaching around his back to where his gun was strapped.

The man who had fallen to the ground was clutching desperately at his throat. Something splattered thickly onto the blacktop in front of him. One of the other drug dealers moved back hastily, a startled cry on his lips.

That was when Jeremiah saw the blood pulsing through the fingers of the ashen-faced man kneeling on the asphalt.

What the—?!

A crimson spray arced through the air and struck the wall of the alley to Jeremiah's left. Something wet peppered his face. He touched his check and stared dazedly at the red streaks on his fingertips.

It was still hot.

Another drug dealer fell to the ground, a gaping wound in his chest. A third one followed, a scarlet line blooming on his abdomen.

Tony's panicked voice reached Jeremiah's dully through the blood roaring in his ears. The younger detective was calling for backup. He dropped his radio, raised his gun in both hands, and fired, his face full of fear.

Jeremiah's stunned gaze finally found the man who was moving toward the younger detective at an insane speed, having disposed of his fourth associate with a single slash of his hand.

Except Maddox was no longer a man.

CHAPTER THIRTEEN

The sun beat down relentlessly on Leah as she wandered through the crowded streets. It was a cloudless summer afternoon and folks were out in droves to make the most of the weather.

I should call Dad and let him know I'm okay. Leah gnawed at her bottom lip. *And I need to talk to Grandma about the pendant.*

She'd thought briefly about going to her grandmother's estate last night, when she'd fled her home. It had been her father's face that had stopped her from following through. He'd looked so betrayed that she'd been seeing Barbara Nolan behind his back that she couldn't bear the thought of hurting him further.

Leah exited a park and blinked when she found herself standing in front of the Museum of Contemporary Art. A bittersweet feeling twisted through her as she stared up at the modern building.

It seemed her unconscious mind had brought her to the one place likely to soothe her frazzled nerves. She was about to climb the stairs to the entrance when goosebumps exploded across her entire body.

A cool wind blew across the city. Shadows obscured the sun.

Leah looked up. Panic flooded her when she saw the eerie storm clouds forming above her head.

Oh no! It's happening again!

The beast inside her stirred.

Leah's vision flickered. She gasped, her hand tightening on the handrail. Images flashed in front of her eyes, like a fast-moving film. She saw her father and Tony Goodman enter a bar. They spoke briefly with a group of men before leaving the building through a back door.

A whimper tumbled out of her lips at what she witnessed next.

The images faded. Leah stared at the concrete steps in front of her, her stomach roiling and sweat beading her forehead. Her pendant trembled against her breastbone. Her fingers rose to grasp it, unbidden.

She knew instinctively that what she had just seen was about to happen. *Was* happening.

Leah looked north; she could sense something faint and dark in that direction. A low growl sounded within her. Whatever it was, the beast could feel it too.

She turned and started to run.

∽

HARUKI STROLLED ALONG THE BEACHFRONT TRAIL, Smokey at his side. He ignored the strange stares they were attracting and looked out over the choppy waters of Lake Michigan.

"She's not going to be easy to find, is she?"

I suspect not. The fact that Serena and Nate cannot find any information on her implies her identity has been cloaked, somehow.

Haruki frowned. One fact above all else troubled him whenever he recalled last night's encounter behind the coffee shop. He hadn't sensed anything from the girl. No vestige of divine energy. No resonance with the beast who resided inside her soul.

It was as if she were a blank canvas, as pale and cold as the moon.

The same consternation Haruki had experienced had been reflected on the others' faces when he'd told them this observation.

"It isn't just her identity that's been masked."

He and Smokey had visited River North again that morning. They'd prowled the streets around the coffee shop and explored the surrounding neighborhood for any clues that might lead them to the new Guardian. As expected, their search had proven fruitless.

Since we cannot find any sign of her, how about we get some food at that place you took me to last time we were down here?

Haruki grimaced. "You mean the steak house that serves Kobe beef? The one where the owner is convinced you are some kind of demon and banned us from ever stepping foot inside again? That one?"

Yes. Smokey huffed. *I am sure I will be able to charm that man with my overly cute countenance.*

"I think I'll pass. Nate is making spaghetti and meatballs, so why don't we head back to—"

Haruki stiffened and stopped in his tracks. His head swung to the west. Smokey's eyes glinted crimson as he followed his gaze.

Haruki clenched his jaw.

They could both feel a sudden rise in demonic energy close by.

~

Sebastian examined his reflection critically. "How do I look?"

"Positively dapper," Artemus said.

Sebastian narrowed his eyes at Artemus in the mirror. "I cannot help but discern a dose of sarcasm in your voice."

"I am in awe of your powers of observation."

Artemus glanced around the small, high-end gentleman's boutique Sebastian had dragged him to on the edge of Old Town.

They'd come to the antique shop to pick Otis up for lunch and had been about to make their way home when the Englishman had asked them to accompany him to the newly opened store. Otis had declined his invitation and headed eagerly to the mansion; Nate was making his favorite dish and the last thing he wanted to do was to traipse around town on a shopping trip. Which had left Artemus laden with the unfortunate task of keeping the Englishman company.

He frowned at his watch as Sebastian started perusing the clothing racks once more. "We're gonna be late. You know Nate gets upsets when food goes cold on the table. Besides, we might not get any if we're the last ones there."

"I am sure he has made plenty." Sebastian lifted a pair of cufflinks that cost as much as his rent and inspected the pieces closely. "We will be home before the hellhound gets there." He glanced at Artemus as he tried on the cufflinks. "You forget that I can use rifts."

Artemus sighed. Callie was also infamous for her eye-watering shopping trips. As Serena once remarked after going to New York with her, it was a miracle the widow hadn't blown through her entire inheritance yet.

Like brother, like sister.

He resigned himself to his fate and started walking around the shop.

"May I assist you, sir?"

Artemus looked at the smiling shop assistant who had addressed him. "No, thank you." He cocked a thumb at Sebastian. "Unlike him, I can't afford this place."

The assistant's smile lost some of its shine. A concerned expression replaced it a moment later. "Sir? Are you alright?"

Artemus turned and stared out of the shop window to the south. Sebastian stood frozen a few feet to his right, his face strained as he gazed in the same direction.

They could sense the corrupt energy of a demon in the distance.

Artemus headed briskly for the exit. "Let's go."

Sebastian followed in his steps. He paused in the doorway of the shop and threw a credit card at the bewildered assistant.

"Here, put the suit and cufflinks on my tab!"

∞

Naomi lifted the fine China cup to her lips, sipped her Assam tea, and perused the newspaper resting on the table. The tearoom buzzed with locals and tourists who'd wandered into the leafy park. Located a quarter of a mile from the Museum of Contemporary Art, the place boasted a pretty outdoor seating area and was a popular place to hang out in the summer.

The white cat sitting solemnly at her feet drew some amused looks from the tearoom's customers. Naomi ignored their stares, picked a piece of ham from her sandwich, and fed it to the feline. The cat gobbled it down and licked her fingers with an appreciative rumble.

Naomi's thoughts drifted back to her meeting with Jeremiah Chase last night and her brief telephone conversation with Barbara Nolan this morning.

Though she knew that whatever had prompted Leah to run away from home was but the opening salvo of the deadly supernatural battle that would take place in Chicago in the coming days, she couldn't help but feel on edge.

The only thing she and Barbara had been able to foretell was that they would be involved in this fight, at some level. What exact roles they would go on to play had been less clear. Which was why Naomi had read her tarot cards that morning and had come to her favorite tea shop in North Side.

She'd just finished her second pot of Assam and was about to ask for a third one when a shiver shook the cat. A pale glow danced across the jade beads on Naomi's bracelet. She tensed, her gaze swinging north.

The cat meowed out a warning.

"I know," Naomi muttered. "I feel it too."

She rose, threw some dollar bills on the table, and headed out of the tearoom toward the dark energy throbbing in the distance, the cat scampering ahead of her.

CHAPTER FOURTEEN

Monsters don't exist!

Horror filled Jeremiah as he gazed at the scene of carnage before him. Having attacked Tony, the creature Maddox had turned into had switched his attention to the men he had killed a short while back.

Sirens echoed in the distance as patrol cars converged on the area. Still, Jeremiah knew that help would come too late for the detective lying unconscious and bleeding in his arms. He swallowed convulsively.

I have to get him to a hospital!

"It's okay, Tony. Help is coming!"

The monster made hungry noises as he gorged on the entrails of a dead drug dealer farther down the alley. Bile rose in Jeremiah's throat at the sickening sounds.

Tony moaned weakly.

The creature's head whipped around. He focused his grotesque attention on the pale-faced detective before raising his gaze to meet Jeremiah's. The look in the monster's eyes and his macabre smile told him neither he nor Tony would make it out of that alleyway alive.

The creature released an almighty roar before twisting and bounding toward them, powerful muscles moving fluidly under his skin, a killing machine bound for his prey.

Jeremiah's panicked gaze swept the alleyway for a sharp weapon. He found none.

The monster's shadow swallowed him.

Jeremiah crouched over Tony and raised his arm defensively, knowing the gesture was futile. Something drew his petrified stare through the gaps between his fingers.

An object dropped down from the sky and struck the monster in the back of the head. The creature rocked to a stop, his claws scraping across the blacktop a scant few feet from Jeremiah and the unconscious detective.

The item fell to the ground. Jeremiah and the monster stared at it.

It was a backpack. A red one with stickers all over it. Jeremiah blinked. He recognized the bag.

Terror wrapped an icy hand around his heart at the same time a voice he knew all too well shouted a warning that reverberated against the dirty walls around him.

"*Get away from them!*"

Jeremiah's stunned gaze found the figure at the opposite end of the alleyway. His stomach twisted.

No!

∽

LEAH GLARED AT THE DEMON POISED BEFORE HER FATHER and Tony. Alarm darted through her when she clocked the younger detective's injuries. He lay ashen faced and motionless in her father's arms, his eyes closed and his chest moving shallowly with his breaths.

"Are you okay, Dad?!"

Fear darkened her father's eyes as he stared blindly at her. He came to his senses with a jolt. "*Run, Leah!*"

Leah fisted her hands. "I'm afraid I can't do that."

She headed into the alley, her steps resolute despite the dread filling her to the bones. The monster turned to face her, his expression curious.

Leah snatched the pendant from her neck.

A blustery wind swept through the back alley. The shadows thickened as the sky grew dark.

The storm cloud had followed her as she ran through the city.

A deadly light glimmered in the demon's eyes when he sensed the change in the air. He sank closer to the ground, muscles bunching as he prepared to spring.

The pendant grew warm in Leah's hand. She clenched her jaw. "Let's do this, beast."

An excited growl rumbled up within her soul. Power blossomed inside her, hot and potent. The golden glow returned to her flesh, an ethereal film that coated her skin like armor. Her hair became thick and heavy.

The monster moved.

Her father shouted her name once more, his voice full of agony. He moved Tony onto the asphalt and struggled to his feet.

Leah started running, her gaze focused unflinchingly on the monster bounding toward her with open jaws and razor-sharp teeth, his intent to tear out her throat all too clear.

Static danced across the pendant as the energy roaring through her veins poured into it. It changed into the silver spear.

She leapt just as the demon swooped down on her, somersaulted over his head, and landed smoothly behind him, feet skidding backward on the asphalt and one hand dragging across the blacktop to slow her slide.

Her father's shocked gasp reached her from behind. Leah grimaced.

I bet he's gonna have questions about this. Like, a lot *of questions.*

The demon twisted around, his obsidian eyes full of surprise.

Leah glared at him. He would not get past her defense and reach the men she was protecting. Not while she had breath left in her body.

The monster charged, his angry shriek ringing in her ears. Leah braced herself.

Talons slashed the air toward her face. She blocked the attack with the spear, swept the demon's legs out from under him, and brought him to the ground. The spear glinted in her grip as she dropped on one knee and aimed it toward his heart.

The demon rolled at the last minute and jumped out of harm's way. Sparks exploded where her weapon struck the blacktop.

Leah climbed to her feet. "He's fast."

We are faster.

The monster came at her again. She deflected his clawed fists with the spear, swooped beneath an attack aimed at her chest, and landed a powerful roundhouse kick on his left temple.

The impact jarred her leg.

The demon sailed across the alley and smashed violently into the wall. Bones snapped. Cracks exploded outward from the crater his body made in the concrete. He howled in rage and pain.

"Whoa," Leah whispered.

She could feel how much stronger she was now that she'd accepted the power flooding her body.

You have an interesting fighting style.

"Thanks. It's called Taekwondo."

The demon attacked a fourth time.

Leah avoided his punches, grabbed his shoulder, and flipped him up and over. A grunt left the creature as he slammed into the ground once more. She turned, one hand still gripping his arm, and sensed the beast poking around her mind.

I see. A combat technique from the East. I approve.

"Beast?"

Yes?

"You're distracting me."

Ah.

The demon snarled and clawed at her leg. Leah stared. Though his talons shredded her jeans, they did not pierce her skin.

She filed this startling observation away for future reference and broke his limb in two places. The monster screamed.

"Time to finish this," Leah muttered grimly.

She stepped on the demon's chest and pierced his heart with the spear.

Black blood bubbled past the monster's lips. He stared at her blankly for a moment, as if he couldn't believe what had just happened. A choking noise rattled out of his lungs. The ochre light filling his gaze started to fade. His body went limp seconds before he started assuming a human form.

Leah removed the weapon from the dead man's corpse and gazed at his pallid face and sightless eyes. Though she felt regret at what she had done, she knew she had been justified in killing him.

The evidence of his crimes was scattered all around her.

An unexpected sense of calm washed over her as she came to terms with these new emotions. She turned and headed toward her father.

He took a step in her direction before faltering, his face gray with shock and his gaze locked on something past her shoulder.

Leah frowned. "Dad, are you—?"

A ripping sound erupted behind her, drowning out the rest of her words. She stiffened when she felt the corrupt energy blasting through the alley.

Leah twisted mechanically on her heels, fear throbbing through her once more. Black lines rendered the air some thirty feet from where she stood, wavering threads that danced and twisted macabrely above the ground. She looked toward the other end of the back lane.

More were materializing there.

Darkness started to fill the boundaries of the passage, blocking out the sight and sounds of the streets flanking the alleyway. A crimson light pulsed from the cracks in space as they widened. Shadowy shapes stepped out of the ghastly portals, yellow eyes gleaming in the gloom.

Oh crap.

The air tore above Leah's head. She looked up and froze.

A demon was dropping toward her, all claws and fangs and glistening gaze full of malice.

"*Leah!*"

Leah gasped as her father shoved her out of the way of

the monster's path. She tumbled to the ground, rolled, and rose on one knee. Her heart clenched with horror.

The demon was on top of her father.

No!

Something large and black sailed above her head and slammed into the monster, casting him violently to the ground.

Leah's eyes rounded.

It was an enormous dog some four feet tall and as black as midnight. Muscles moved sinuously beneath his glossy hide as he took a couple of steps toward the demon climbing to his feet, a growl rumbling out of his throat. But it wasn't his formidable appearance that captured Leah's attention and that of the beast within her. It was the unholy, red light filling his eyes and the energy she could feel thumping out of him with every mighty beat of his heart that caused her own to race.

It was the same power she'd sensed from the man who'd saved her in the alley behind the coffee shop the day before. A power that felt strangely akin to the one coursing through her own veins.

Her beast murmured a name that rang through her skull. *Cerberus.*

Leah climbed unsteadily to her feet, her pulse thundering.

"Now would be a good time for you to do that thing you did yesterday with your spear," someone said grimly behind her.

Leah turned.

A man was walking toward her. Except, he wasn't quite a man. He was a dragon with glowing, orange, vertical pupils, ivory horns, and a large, spiked tail.

CHAPTER FIFTEEN

Haruki glanced past the girl called Leah to the man sitting up shakily behind her. "Who is that?"

Leah gulped. "My—my father!"

Though Haruki detected fear in the girl's eyes, he could also see determination in the way she held herself. Black blood coated one end of the spear she held. He observed the dead man with the stab wound to the heart and the savaged bodies scattered around him, his vision crystal clear despite the shadows around them.

He didn't have to be a genius to figure out what had happened in that back lane.

"Take cover next to those dumpsters," Haruki told the girl's father curtly. "And bring your partner with you."

The man stiffened. He glanced at the wounded figure lying on the blacktop several feet behind him. "How did you know I was—?"

"A cop?" Haruki grimaced. "I can smell you guys a mile away." He gazed steadily at Leah. "I'll take the south. You and Smokey take the north."

Confusion clouded the girl's face. "Smokey?"

Haruki indicated the hellhound. "That's Smokey." His beast's life force swarmed his blood as he turned to face the horde of demons crowding the south end of the alley. "This is only his second form. If he turns into a giant, three-headed hound with golden eyes, that's a sure-fire sign we're in deep shit."

The continuous snarl rolling out of Smokey intensified as he squared up to the monsters gathering at the opposite end of the passage. A thrill danced through Haruki as the hellhound's energy resonated with his own. Alone, each of them was fearsome in his own right. Together, they were twice as strong.

He'd realized this during their most recent battle with Ba'al, in Rome. The more divine beasts joined their ranks, the more intense the synergistic effect of their powers became.

Haruki grasped his fiery sword and wondered briefly what this new Guardian would bring to their holy alliance. Then, there was no more time to think.

∽

THE SOUND OF A BATTLE EXPLODED IN SEBASTIAN'S EARS as he stepped out of the golden rift ahead of Artemus and into the midst of a group of yellow-eyed fiends.

He blocked an attack to his face, grabbed the watch in his suit pocket, and unleashed the weapon within. Divine flames roared along the lashes of the triple-thonged whip a second before it sliced two demons in half.

Artemus swung his blade, the sword singing as it carved the air and cut into corrupt flesh. A clap sounded as he unfurled his wings. He rose, white feathers stark against the twilight filling the passage.

Sebastian cast several lightning balls at the demons around them before joining the angel, his eagle wings striking the air with equally powerful beats.

They would gain a better sense of the battleground from above.

Artemus pointed. "There!"

Haruki, Smokey, and a girl with copper hair and golden skin stood in the middle of a swarm of demons halfway up the alleyway.

Sebastian frowned. "That must be Leah."

Surprise echoed across his bond with Artemus. He glanced at the angel, heedless of the monsters leaping beneath their feet in a vain attempt to attack them.

"What is it?"

"That guy." Artemus was staring at a man sheltering next to a row of dumpsters a short distance from the divine beasts and the girl. He was holding a wounded figure in his arms and looking at them with a shell-shocked expression. "I know him."

"You do?"

Artemus's mouth became a grim line. "Yeah. He's a cop. A detective, to be precise."

Sebastian's ears popped as the atmospheric pressure around them plummeted. He tensed, his gaze sweeping the alley for the demonic source. But it wasn't demons causing lightning-charged clouds to thicken and swirl menacingly above them.

His gaze found the girl standing by Smokey's side.

"It's her," Artemus said quietly. "She's the one doing this."

∼

Dread filled Naomi as she observed the thunderstorm spinning in the sky above a high rise. She cursed her decision to wear heels and willed herself to run faster.

The white cat scurried ahead of her and disappeared around the corner of the building. Naomi scowled.

"Gemini, wait!"

Her bracelet flashed with a green glow. Goosebumps erupted on her arms and the back of her neck as power swelled inside her, the insidious, dark energy tempered by the light that always flowed through her soul.

Naomi skidded to a stop in the mouth of an alley, her breaths coming in short, sharp pants. Her eyes rounded at what she saw.

Shit! This is even worse than I imagined! She gritted her teeth. *Goddammit, Barbara!*

~

"Look out!"

Sebastian startled at Artemus's warning. He caught a glimpse of a dark shape leaping off the side of the building next to them, extended his wings, and shot backward.

The demon shrieked as he missed him by scant inches. He landed on the rooftop of the opposite building, his talons scoring grooves in the shingles.

"Damn." A scowl darkened Artemus's face. "I forgot these bastards could climb walls."

Sebastian looked around. Demons were scaling the buildings crowding them.

A muscle jumped in Artemus's cheek. "Here they come."

The demons sprang, a dark mass of writhing shapes

and ochre eyes arcing through the air and converging on them from every direction.

A grunt whooshed out of Sebastian as the creatures plowed into him and pressed upon his wings, driving him toward the ground. Artemus cursed as he too started falling under the combined weight of the monsters atop him.

Sebastian clenched his teeth. His attackers were too close for him to use his whip effectively. White light bloomed on his hands. He snarled and shoved exploding lightning balls straight into the demons' bodies. The creatures screeched in rage.

He crashed down into the alley, kicked several demons off him, and started to rise. Something white and limber jumped lightly onto his left arm.

Sebastian froze in a half-crouch. He swiveled his head to stare at the creature perched atop his elbow where he rested a hand on his knee, the demons around him all but forgotten. The white cat looked away from the battle and blinked at him slowly, one eye blue and the other yellow. The feline's pupils flashed green.

Sebastian's pulse stuttered as he felt the power throbbing through the creature. *This is—!*

A beautiful woman with dark hair and blue eyes ran past him and Artemus, a glowing jade bracelet on her right wrist. She stopped before the wall of demons and brought a hand up with her palm facing them, her expression fierce.

"Gemini!" she yelled.

The cat leapt from Sebastian's arm and landed nimbly on the woman's right shoulder.

"*Shield!*"

The air shimmered and writhed around her in response to her command.

Several demons tried to attack her. Their talons scraped uselessly against the invisible bubble protecting her and the cat.

The woman squared her shoulders, gripped her right wrist with her left hand, and closed her eyes. Archaic words tumbled out of her lips, low and urgent. A shiver raced down Sebastian's spine as her voice danced in his ears.

A pale light engulfed the cat and the woman, pulsing in tandem with the shimmering bracelet.

"*Release!*" she roared.

Thunder boomed in the sky above them.

CHAPTER SIXTEEN

Leah fended off a blow to her head, kneed a demon in the groin, and stabbed another one in the thigh.

A grunt sounded behind her. She looked over her shoulder. The Dragon had blocked an attack aimed at her back.

"It's okay!" Leah said. "They can't injure me!"

The Dragon batted the demon away with a powerful swing of his tail before narrowing his eyes at her. "You're not invincible, kid."

Leah stiffened at his tone. "I'm not a kid. And I meant my skin. They can't damage it. That demon before—"

Dark shapes slammed into her and carried her across the alley. Air locked in her throat as she struck the wall with her back. Black spots swarmed her vision. She heard her father shout her name.

"Stay back!" Leah wheezed, alarmed.

She struggled to her feet amidst the blows raining down upon her. Though the demons' claws failed to cut her flesh, they were still overpowering her with the weight of their attack.

The hound called Smokey growled ferociously as he came to her aid, his powerful jaws and paws tearing and batting at the monsters who stood between them. Across the way, the Dragon defended her father and Tony from the horde, his anxious gaze flickering to her.

Dammit! He's right! Leah gritted her teeth and pushed back against the monsters. *More! I need more power than this!*

The beast inside her spoke. *The seal must be broken before that can happen.*

Leah scowled. "Seal? What seal?!"

Can you not feel them? The shackles holding you back? They were necessary for your protection until now, but they are no longer needed. They must be undone.

Leah blinked. She hadn't been aware of what it was she'd been sensing until the creature inside her mentioned it. Her skin felt as tight as a drum. So did her jaws, scalp, and belly. It was as if something were trying to burst out of her body but couldn't.

"I don't understand!"

Now is not the time for explanation. The witch is here.

A light-headed feeling swept over Leah. This was too much.

"Witch?" she squealed. "What witch?!"

"*Shield!*" someone shouted somewhere to her left.

Leah swiveled her head with some difficulty and managed to peer between her raised arms. Her breath froze on her lips.

There, standing a mere twenty feet from her and looking as incongruous as a fish out of water, was Naomi Wagner.

The professor's pale blue eyes had turned the color of jade, as had those of the white cat on her shoulder. A sphere of pale light encircled them where they stood surrounded by demons who were trying to attack them, their efforts in vain.

Heat pierced Leah when she met Naomi's gaze. The professor's lips moved, forming words Leah couldn't hear but experienced in the very marrow of her soul.

"*Release!*" Naomi bellowed an instant later.

Leah gasped as something scorched the back of her neck. Her mother's face flashed before her eyes a second before her voice echoed in her ears, steady and strong.

It is time, Leah.

～

A DEAFENING CRACK SPLIT THE SKY. THE TWILIGHT shrouding the alley intensified as the storm clouds swelled, dark billows writhing agitatedly.

Haruki stared.

Something was happening to Leah.

She stood frozen for a timeless moment, heedless of the fiends trying to tear holes in her body. She raised a hand and touched the back of her neck tentatively, her expression full of grief and longing.

It changed into fierce determination a second later.

Heat throbbed through Haruki. He sucked in air as he finally sensed Leah's divine energy. The shock reverberating across his bond with Smokey, Artemus, and Sebastian told him they'd felt it too.

Her hair thickened and lengthened until it was a riot of long, heavy curls that framed her head and extended halfway down her back. The light covering her skin grew sharper. The whites of her eyes turned gold. Her arms and legs swelled slightly, all muscle and sinew.

She is strong.

The Dragon's words echoed in Haruki's consciousness.

Leah crouched, as if she were about to launch into a full sprint. Her figure blurred in the next instant.

Haruki gasped.

She charged the demons in her path, her body moving through the alley so fast he barely managed to follow her progress. Shrieks rose in her passage as she landed powerful strikes on the wretched creatures with her fists, elbows, knees, and feet, her spear dealing the fatal blow that killed them with lethal speed and efficiency.

Haruki's heart trembled as Leah's energy resonated keenly with his own. In that moment, he saw her for what she truly was.

She was brave. Fearless. Bold.

An indomitable spirit bound in the body of a girl who was still to come into her full powers. A warm feeling blossomed in Haruki's belly as he gazed at her.

Static sparked across his scales, distracting him. He looked around and stiffened when he spotted the tiny flashes of electricity flickering across the alley. Alarm shot through him. His stomach dropped when he looked up and saw the expanding glow in the dark heavens.

Shit!

Instinct had him yelling out a warning. "Smokey, come to me! Sebastian, shield yourself and Artemus!"

"Damn," the woman with the cat muttered. She stared at the sky, the blood draining from her face.

A golden haze materialized behind her as Sebastian manipulated the divine energy in the air to create a barrier around him and Artemus, a skill he'd recently learned from Otis. He grabbed the woman's arm and yanked her inside the dome.

Smokey sprang toward Haruki, his gaze wary and his

shape shrinking into that of the Rex rabbit a moment before he landed in his waiting arms. Haruki hugged him to his chest, turned his back to the alley, and crouched above Leah's father and his wounded partner, his powerful tail wrapping protectively around them.

"What's—what's happening?!" the man mumbled, his face ashen as he glanced at the barbed spikes inches from his skin.

Haruki clenched his jaw. "Your daughter is about to show us what she can really do."

CHAPTER SEVENTEEN

Demon blood dripped from the spear in Leah's hand and splashed onto the asphalt. It coated her face and clothes where it had splattered onto her, the drops still warm on her skin.

She stood in the midst of a circle of yellow-eyed fiends, her chest heaving slightly with her breaths as she glared at the monsters. They'd ceased their attacks and crouched hesitantly a few feet from her, their expressions cautious.

So, they do have a self-preservation instinct after all.

Though she'd felled dozens of the monsters, Leah sensed she could go on to kill many more.

The feeling of righteousness overwhelming her heart and soul was echoed by what she could sense from the hound-turned-rabbit and the three men who had come to her assistance. She could tell they were the same, to an extent. But she also knew she was something other. And she had a pretty good hunch it had to do with her mother and Barbara Nolan.

Leah's gaze found the one woman who likely knew the answers to the questions storming her mind.

"Don't," Naomi mumbled where she stood behind a golden barrier. "You haven't mastered it yet! You'll only hurt—"

Leah clenched her teeth and did what her beast had just told her to do. She raised the spear to the sky.

Static flashed along the length of the weapon.

A breathless stillness descended upon the alley.

Blinding light exploded in the sky. An enormous bolt of lightning streaked down toward her within a single beat of her thudding heart. It struck the spear so hard the weapon vibrated violently in her fingers. She clasped it with both hands and clung on for dear life, her skin tingling.

The power of the storm swept over her. Her hair lifted around her head like a halo, the red strands bright with electricity. She took a deep breath.

The air in the alley contracted in response to her inhalation.

Leah breathed out and let the lightning loose.

~

Artemus watched in wonderment as demon after demon burst into a cloud of fiery ash under the power of the electric storm raging through the alley, their bodies disintegrating even as they turned to flee. The rifts that had brought them there were closing, the fiends evidently sensing the threat posed by the Guardian whose powers had just manifested themselves.

A dumpster detonated to his left.

It bounced harmlessly off the divine barrier Sebastian had erected around them and crashed into the high rise.

"Good God," Sebastian said hoarsely. "She is harnessing lightning!"

"Trust me, God has little to do with this," the woman with the white cat said grimly.

Artemus glanced at her. He knew what it was that had shaken Sebastian a short while back, when she'd first appeared. Her power was different to theirs.

In fact, if I had to make a comparison, it's like that of a—

A soft meow rose at his feet. The white cat was twining herself around his legs, a throaty rumble vibrating through her chest as she bumped her head against him.

"Is your cat marking me?" Artemus asked the woman leadenly.

The woman sighed. "No. She just likes you."

The storm started to abate. A shout reached them a moment later.

"Leah!"

The man Artemus had recognized rose to his feet and barged past Haruki. He stumbled to a stop in the middle of the alley and placed a tentative hand on the shoulder of the girl who had sunk to her knees on the blacktop.

Leah was gazing at the spear in her hand with a shocked expression. The weapon transformed into a silver pendant in the shape of a compass.

Artemus stared. *Interesting.*

The clouds above them began to clear. A cacophony of police sirens and shouts arose from the surrounding streets, the sounds finally breaking through the dissipating shadows.

Sebastian removed the divine barrier shielding them.

Haruki met them halfway up the alley.

"You okay?" Artemus asked.

Haruki grimaced and put Smokey on the ground. "I'm good. The lightning bounced off my scales."

"How did you know that was going to happen?" the woman asked Haruki.

The white cat slinked toward Smokey. They eyed each other warily before taking careful sniffs of one another.

"I had a gut feeling." Haruki glanced at Artemus and Sebastian. "Who is she?"

"That's what I'd like to know." Artemus turned to Sebastian. "Can you rift us to the mansion?"

"Yes."

"Good."

Artemus headed over to Leah. He squatted and offered her his hand. "Think you can stand?"

She blinked at him, startled. Some of the color returned to her cheeks at his gentle tone.

"Stay away from my daughter!" the cop barked, his knuckles whitening on the girl's shoulder.

Leah flinched.

Artemus took a firm hold of her wrist and helped her to her feet. "It's Detective Chase, right?"

He studied the cop steadily.

"And you're Artemus Steele," the man ground out in the tone of one addressing a child murderer.

Artemus sighed. "Look, I know you have questions about the crazy stuff you just witnessed, but here and now are not the right place and time for that discussion."

The man opened his mouth to say something.

"He's right, Jeremiah," the woman with the white cat said quietly. "Let Leah go with them. She'll be safe."

"How can you be sure of that?!" The detective's expression darkened. "And this is the last place I thought I would ever see you! Are you really a professor, or are you—" he glanced at Artemus, "like him and his friends?!"

The woman made a face. "There's no need to be insulting. I'm nothing like them."

Artemus narrowed his eyes. Sebastian frowned. Haruki's lips grew pinched.

"Relax," she drawled. The white cat leapt into the woman's arms. "Sheesh, men and their egos," she murmured to the feline below her breath.

The cat meowed and licked her chin.

Smokey gazed longingly at the creature from where he sat at Artemus's feet, having seemingly formed eternal bonds of friendship with her in the five minutes they'd known each other.

"Now, go," the woman told Artemus briskly. "I can help slow Tony's bleeding. We'll just tell the other officers I happened to be passing by."

She glanced toward the ends of the alley. Crowds of confused-looking cops stood at the mouths of the passage.

"Did you do something to them?" Sebastian said stiffly.

"No. I just cloaked this place." The woman's gaze swept Sebastian from his head to his toes. "Your suit is ruined. It's a good thing you paid for it. I doubt that shop assistant would have accepted it if you'd returned it in that state."

Sebastian blinked. Horror filled his face as he looked down at the clothes he was wearing and noted the tears and rips shredding the expensive material. "Bugger."

The woman smiled faintly. "It's a bit premature for that. We've only just met."

Sebastian made a choking noise. Haruki and Smokey's eyes rounded.

Suspicious lines furrowed Artemus's brow. "How do you know he just bought that suit?"

The woman smiled enigmatically. "That's for me to know and for you to find out." Her expression turned serious. "Now, go. I'll bring Jeremiah to your mansion later."

CHAPTER EIGHTEEN

Daniel studied the two boys before him. Their eyes were red and swollen, and fresh scrapes covered their arms and legs from their recent fight. Connor, the boy with dark hair, sniffed and wiped his nose on the back of his hand. Justin, the one with blond hair, glared at him.

"I don't even want to know who was in the wrong," Daniel said in a firm voice. "The two of you are best friends. Now, apologize to one another."

The boys looked at him as if he'd asked them to commit a grave sin.

"It's either that, or I'll ask Cook to make you spinach for dinner," Daniel added, his tone sharpening.

The boys gasped, their mouths rounding. Daniel suppressed a smile at their identical expressions of horror.

"We hate spinach," Connor mumbled hoarsely.

"It's the most disgusting vegetable in the world," Justin stated with an emphatic nod.

A strangled sound came from the doorway of the dining hall. Daniel narrowed his eyes at Sister Martin. The nun ignored his disapproving look and beamed at him, unabashed. A group of wide-eyed children lurked behind her, the littlest ones gripping her habit with their tiny hands while they peered around her legs.

They were watching him with open awe.

Daniel wasn't sure why the children at the orphanage seemed so fascinated with him. He remembered the first day he'd come to the church and been shown around the rambling, brownstone building that sat within its grounds. He'd been full of apprehension at the prospect of meeting the children who lived there and who would be in his care from that day forth; he recalled all too well what he had suffered at the hands of the ones he'd grown up with, in various orphanages in his birth country of Ukraine.

A hesitant voice reached his ears.

"I'm sorry," Connor whispered to Justin.

Justin's lower lip wobbled. He burst into tears and flung himself at his best friend. "I'm sorry, too!"

The two boys hugged each other tightly. A warm feeling of contentment blossomed inside Daniel's chest.

"There, there," he murmured, stroking their heads gently.

This only made them bawl louder. They buried their faces in his legs, their tears and snot soaking into the material of his trousers. Daniel masked a wince. Callie had just bought him those pants. Though she hadn't told him how much they'd cost, he could tell they were expensive.

A car horn honked outside. Daniel looked out of the windows lining the east wall of the dining hall. A black Porsche had pulled to a stop in front of the building's main porch.

Callie stepped out of the vehicle and removed her sunglasses, her pretty summer dress billowing slightly in a breeze. A grin split her face as a bevy of small children raced across the yard to where she stood, their excited squeals piercing the air. They'd become used to seeing her over the past couple of weeks.

"I'll be off," Daniel told the two boys. "Be good. I'll see you tomorrow morning at mass."

Connor and Justin glanced at one another, their eyes sparkling.

"Can we come see Callie's car?" Justin asked eagerly.

Connor nodded vigorously beside him, his head bobbing so fast it was a wonder he didn't give himself whiplash.

"Only if you make yourselves presentable," Daniel said drily.

The two boys jumped up and down with high-pitched squeaks before bolting out of the hall.

Daniel chuckled, bade the other children goodbye, and made his way toward the building's entrance. Sister Martin fell into step beside him.

"Thank you for coming in to help on your day off, Daniel. I truly appreciate it."

Daniel waved a hand lightly. "It's quite alright. I hope Father Abbott feels better soon."

They walked in silence for a while.

"You still haven't figured out why they like you so much, have you?" the nun said.

Daniel startled. He hadn't realized his innermost thoughts were so easy to read.

"Father Nelson let it slip one day that you were appointed to this post by Pope DaSilva herself." The nun's grave expression gave way to a serene smile. "But that's only one of the reasons they revere you so."

Father Nelson was the head of their church.

Daniel bit back a sigh. *That man talks too much.*

He hesitated. "What's the other reason?"

Sister Martin's smile broadened. "It's simple, really. They can sense the goodness in you. All of us can."

∽

Callie looked up from the children gathered around her when she heard the front door open.

Daniel stepped out of the orphanage with Sister Martin. His cheeks were flushed and he looked somewhat embarrassed. The nun grinned at him, murmured something, and patted his back.

A happy feeling danced through Callie as she gazed at the priest. They'd all been worried about how he would adjust to his new life in Chicago after being forcefully relocated there from Rome. Despite the fact that he was the host to one of the most powerful divine beasts to join their ranks, he'd led a relatively sheltered existence within the walls of the Holy See up until a few weeks back.

To their relief, he'd adapted to life at the mansion—and them—pretty quickly. It helped that his lackluster attire and unobtrusive personality hid a sharp tongue and an equally fierce nature. Having explored the unflattering contents of his wardrobe upon his arrival, Callie had taken it upon herself to gradually transform the priest into someone who didn't look like he belonged in the Crusades.

I did have to practically bribe him to get him that haircut though.

"You ready for lunch?" she called out lightly after greeting Sister Martin.

Daniel nodded as he descended the steps, his limp

barely perceptible. The infirmity that had afflicted him since his childhood had started to improve in leaps and bounds ever since his full awakening in Rome.

"I heard Nate was going to make spaghetti and meatballs?"

Callie grinned at his longing tone. "Yeah. He knows it's everyone's favorite." She patted her belly and grimaced. "But I did put my foot down when he said he was going to make tiramisu. I'm starting to get fat."

Daniel's face fell comically. "There's no dessert?"

Callie bit her lip to stop herself from bursting out laughing.

A little girl with pigtails and freckles came flying around the side of the church and bolted toward them. "Father Lenton! Father Lenton! Come see!"

"What is it, Emily?" Daniel murmured, bemused.

The little girl grabbed his hand and tugged.

"You come too, Callie!" she said excitedly as she started dragging the priest toward the church.

Daniel and Callie glanced at each other before following her, Sister Martin watching them curiously from the porch of the orphanage. The smell of pinewood engulfed them as they circled the building and entered the shadows of the trees that dotted the graveyard at the back.

Emily guided them to the far end of the cemetery, where the oldest tombstones stood. Callie tensed when they rounded a headstone and came upon the little girl's find.

"Look!" Emily pointed, her innocent face full of delight. "The man is gone!"

Callie and Daniel exchanged a nervous look before staring at the grave. All that remained of it was a gaping hole in the ground and an empty coffin at the bottom. Callie frowned.

The dirt piled unevenly around the burial site looked fresh.

Daniel laid a hand on Callie's arm, his fingers cold. She followed his frozen gaze. Her stomach twisted.

CHAPTER NINETEEN

Otis sniffed the air and sighed. "I swear to God, you make the best spaghetti and meatballs in the world."

Nate smiled faintly where he stood stirring the large pots on the cast-iron range. He glanced at the antique clock on the wall. "They're late."

"I'm sure they'll be here soon."

The front door opened just as Otis finished setting the table. Footsteps sounded in the corridor leading to the kitchen. Serena and Drake strolled inside the room, their arms laden with bags of groceries.

Drake stopped and raised an eyebrow. "Where's Artemus and Sebastian? I thought they went to get you."

Otis made a face. "Sebastian wanted to check out a new shop that opened close by."

"He's buying clothes?" Serena placed the grocery bags on the counter. "Again?"

"There's nothing wrong with a man wanting to dress nicely," Nate mumbled somewhat defensively.

Serena rolled her eyes. "You're only saying that 'cause he's Callie's older brother."

"Let's face it," Drake observed, "Nate is the next best dressed guy in this place after Sebastian." He paused. "Although Daniel may soon give them both a run for their money."

Serena grinned.

Otis glanced surreptitiously between the two of them. He wasn't the only one who'd noticed the general mellowing in the relationship between the super soldier and the dark angel.

A series of faint clucks sounded from the rear porch. Something tapped on the back door. Drake crossed the kitchen and opened it.

Three chickens stood on the threshold. Two of them backed away when they saw him. The third one stayed put and gave the dark angel a jaundiced look.

Otis brightened. "I didn't know you guys were keeping chickens."

"They are Nate's chickens," Drake muttered while Nate got some feed from the larder. "Although most of us have reservations about Gertrude's true origins."

Two of the hens waddled happily after Nate as he led them into the backyard and cast their food on the ground. The one who'd eyeballed Drake followed slowly while casting pointed stares their way.

Otis blinked. "Oh wow. Is that Gertrude?"

"Yeah." Drake grimaced. "You can literally feel her scorning you, can't you?"

"Kinda."

The roar of a sports engine came from the driveway at the front of the mansion. A squeal of tires and the sounds of doors opening and slamming briskly followed.

Callie and Daniel rushed into the kitchen a moment later. Otis straightened when he saw their expressions.

"Where's Artemus?" Callie asked grimly.

"He went shopping with Sebastian." Serena stared. "What's wrong?"

Callie and Daniel traded anxious looks.

"We found something at the church," Callie said.

"It was in the graveyard," Daniel added. "There's a—"

He stopped abruptly, his eyes rounding. Otis blinked. Drake inhaled sharply. Callie stiffened.

Even Serena and Nate froze where they stood.

"What is that?" Otis mumbled.

He could feel something resonating with the power of the seraph who lived within his soul. From the troubled faces around him, so could Drake, the Guardians, and the super soldiers.

A crimson light flashed in the dark angel's pupils. "It's Artemus and the others. They're fighting demons!"

He stormed into the yard, Otis and the others on his heels. They stopped and gazed out over the city.

The sky had gone dark, the sun obliterated by a gray mantle that had sprung out of nowhere.

Nate pointed. "There."

Otis's eyes widened. "What on earth?"

A mass of ominous, dark clouds was spinning and roiling to the south.

Serena frowned. "It's that weird storm again."

Alarm filled Otis. "That's close to where I left Artemus and Sebastian!"

Warmth blossomed inside his chest. He clutched at his heart and gasped. Drake, Callie, and Daniel mimicked his movement, their expressions reflecting his own shock.

"What is it?" Serena asked tensely.

Otis swallowed. Though Serena and Nate shared some of the divine energy that flowed through him, the two angels, and the divine beasts, they did not possess the holy bond that bound them.

"There's another beast with them." Otis's gaze locked on the storm cloud once more. "It must be the girl my mother mentioned in her journals!"

The hairs on his arms rose as the atmospheric pressure dropped. The heat inside his body swelled.

The chickens scattered in the direction of the graveyard, Gertrude squawking loudly.

Thunder boomed in the distance, the sound so loud it rattled the windows of the mansion. Dazzling light burst through the storm and arrowed down toward the city.

They all felt the new beast's energy escalate.

Otis gulped. "She is—"

Unease danced across Drake's face. "Powerful."

The tempest started to dissipate. The clouds dispersed, letting in beams of warm sunlight. The city was soon awash with brightness once more.

The back of Otis's neck tingled. He twisted on his heels and stared at a spot behind him. He could sense something drawing close.

Drake frowned. "Otis?"

"They're coming."

The air trembled some fifteen feet from where they stood. A rift appeared, golden lines shimmering ethereally. It thickened and split.

Sebastian, Haruki, and Smokey stepped out of the portal.

Artemus followed, his hand wrapped around the wrist of a pale-faced girl with copper hair and hazel eyes. An elegant, silver pendant dangled from her neck.

Otis stared at it. *Oh.*

Shadows darkened the sky. He looked up.

Dozens of ravens were swarming the estate, silent but for the rustling of their shiny wings. They dove past them and landed on the tombstones and trees edging the graveyard.

"Okay, that shit is seriously starting to freak me out," Artemus said dully.

The ravens turned their heads as one, their beady eyes arrowing unerringly in on the girl.

CHAPTER TWENTY

"How fascinating," the demon commander murmured.

The man studied the scattering storm clouds from where he stood beside his master. They'd witnessed the uncanny phenomenon in depth from their location in the luxurious condominium at the top of a high rise next to the lake.

"Did you see them, my liege?"

The commander smiled faintly. "Indeed, I did. The fiends who perished provided me with a first-hand look at Artemus Steele and the new Guardian." The demon's expression sobered. "I fear they will be as troublesome to deal with as I anticipated they might be."

"Can we defeat them?"

The commander looked at him sideways.

For a moment, the man feared he had overstepped his bounds. He bowed, contrite. "I'm sorry, my liege. I should not have questioned—"

He froze when gentle fingers took hold of his chin and tilted his head up.

The commander brushed the man's lips with a featherlight touch. "I believe we can, my beast."

The man swallowed. The demon commander's eyes darkened.

The man gasped as his master took his hand and led him back to the disheveled bed.

"Come. We have much to do. I believe I know where to find the Guardian. But first, let me feed on you."

The commander smiled sensuously and undid the ties of the man's robe before pushing him down on the bed and climbing atop him. The man welcomed his master's heated kisses and scorching touch, his heart swelling with love just as it had the first time they had melded their bodies together all those years ago, when he had first been granted his human form.

∼

Leah glanced around the formal drawing room. The furniture crowding the hardwood floor looked old, as if it belonged in a museum, as did the antique pieces and furnishings dotted around and atop it. She could tell the oil paintings on the walls were originals too. Though she itched to take a closer look at them, she stayed put where she perched on the edge of a large, gold and red damask sofa.

She steeled herself before meeting the curious stares of the room's other occupants once more.

"Feeling better?" Artemus Steele murmured.

He was the man who knew her father.

For some unknown reason, Leah sensed that he was also the leader of the strangers who were watching her as if she were a rare item on display. She nodded and glanced at the empty pasta bowl on her lap.

"Yes," she murmured, feeling strangely shy all of a sudden. "That was delicious, thank you."

"My Nate makes the best spaghetti and meatballs, doesn't he?" Callie Stone said good-naturedly, her arms wrapped around the waist of the colossal man sitting next to her.

Nate Conway's ears reddened.

A slurping noise broke the awkward silence. Leah gazed at the rabbit inhaling his third serving of pasta on the floor next to her, his jaws chomping busily. Smokey sensed her stare and huffed.

"He says he's not always such a pig, but he can't help himself," Haruki Kuroda murmured.

Leah did her best not to blush under his intense gaze. She still felt self-conscious around him, despite everything that had happened between them in the last two days.

"So, you are Detective Chase's daughter?" Artemus said.

Leah hesitated before dipping her chin.

"Who was the woman with the white cat?" Sebastian Lancaster asked gravely.

Serena Blake arched an eyebrow. "There was a woman with a white cat?"

"Indeed, there was. She seemed to know Leah and the policeman. And her abilities were—" the Englishman's eyes narrowed slightly, "—interesting."

Leah swallowed. "That was Naomi Wagner."

Drake Hunter frowned faintly. "That name rings a bell."

"It should. She's a famous artist. She's also my professor at college."

"College?" Otis Boone asked.

Leah dipped her chin. "I'm an Arts major at the Art Institute."

"Ah." Drake looked around the room. "Hence your interest in the paintings. FYI, they're the real deal."

"Trust him," Serena said wryly. "He's a world-class thief."

Leah's eyes widened.

"That's rich coming from a merc," Haruki muttered.

"Oh yeah? Speak for yourself, Yakuza boy."

Leah sucked in air.

Haruki grimaced. "Great. We scared the kid."

Leah stiffened. "I'm nineteen." Lines wrinkled her brow. "And I'm not scared."

"Don't pay any attention to them," Callie told her indulgently. "They may bicker, but they love each other, really."

"The only love happening under this roof is between you and your super soldier boyfriend," Artemus said leadenly.

Callie grinned. "I can't exactly deny that."

Nate flushed. Daniel Lenton sighed and pinched the bridge of his nose. Leah spied a crucifix tucked inside the man's shirt.

"By the way, since when have you had that mark on your neck?" Otis asked curiously.

Leah blinked. "What mark on my neck?"

∽

Naomi glanced worriedly at Jeremiah as she drove along the private road winding up a dark hill. They'd just left the hospital where Tony Goodman had been admitted.

The detectives' superior had turned up minutes before Tony had gone into surgery. He'd taken one look at Jeremiah and told him to take the night off and come in to give his statement in the morning. He'd said the same to Naomi.

Jeremiah had been quiet ever since they'd climbed inside her car.

Although Naomi suspected he was desperately worried about his partner and his daughter, she had a hunch as to what was preoccupying his mind the most right now. It wasn't every day a human witnessed what he had seen today.

After all, the supernatural war that had been playing out over the last two decades across almost every continent wasn't one that was openly advertised or reported upon. Only those who lived in the shadows and on the edges of this world knew of it.

Like me and my kind.

A pair of majestic, wrought-iron gates appeared in the headlights of her classic Mercedes Benz convertible. Naomi braked next to the metal post on the side of the lane and pressed the buzzer on the security box atop it.

A voice came through the speaker a moment later. "Yes?"

"It's Naomi Wagner and Jeremiah Chase. You're expecting us."

"Come in."

The gates opened with a soft, electronic whir. Naomi's skin prickled with a mild, stinging sensation as she pulled onto the driveway and headed up the slope. The road cut through thick woodland and undergrowth. She spotted the pale shapes of tombstones between the trees. The outlook cleared a moment later.

An immense, three-story Gothic mansion loomed on the crest of the hill up ahead. Lights blazed through most of the first-floor windows.

Naomi slowed the car to a stop. She folded her arms across the steering wheel, rested her chin on top, and gazed admiringly at the manor house. "This is something else, huh?"

She'd seen pictures of the LeBlanc mansion before, in some of the Nolan family albums. It was even more impressive in real life than she'd imagined it would be.

Jeremiah remained tight-lipped where he sat beside her. Naomi sighed and stepped on the gas. A soft meow came from the footwell next to her legs.

The front door of the mansion opened just as she pulled up next to a black BMW superbike. Artemus Steele walked out onto his front porch. Leah appeared behind him.

Jeremiah was out of the car before Naomi had stopped the vehicle fully. He headed briskly toward his daughter.

"Dad," Leah whispered, her face crumbling.

They met on the steps, their arms twining tightly around one another.

"Thank God!" Jeremiah buried his face in his daughter's hair, his voice hoarse with emotion. "You're safe!"

Tears streaked down Leah's cheeks. A low sob escaped her.

Jeremiah pulled back and gazed at her hotly. "Are you okay?"

His gaze darted accusingly to the man who stood watching them from the top of the stairs.

Leah wiped her eyes and sniffed, her chin bobbing. "Yes. I'm fine."

Naomi stepped out of her car and headed toward

them, Gemini at her side. Leah glanced at the cat before looking at her with a leery expression.

"Who are you?" she said stiffly.

Naomi winced. "Ouch. Going straight for the jugular, huh?"

"I'm surprised you got through the barrier," Artemus drawled.

Naomi observed him guardedly. *He really is sharp. And I suspect he isn't the only one who noticed.*

"It did smart a little," she admitted candidly.

A man with dark hair and eyes came out of the manor house. Naomi met Drake Hunter's impassive stare.

"There's a woman at the gate," he told Artemus. "She says she has business with us."

"Ah," Naomi murmured. "That would be Barbara."

The color drained out of Jeremiah's face. "Barbara?"

Leah's expression hardened. "She means Grandma."

CHAPTER TWENTY-ONE

"Wow," Serena said. "You could literally cut the air with a knife."

"So, it isn't just me?" Callie whispered.

"No," Sebastian replied.

"I feel like a spectator at a boxing match," Nate murmured uneasily.

"I call dibs on the old lady," Haruki stated.

"I don't know," Otis muttered. "The cop looks pretty tenacious."

"We shouldn't be taking bets," Daniel admonished. "This is a grave matter."

"I'm sorry, but I can't take you seriously when you're wearing those slippers," Drake said bluntly.

Daniel glanced at his furry rabbit footwear. "They were a gift from Persephone."

The real rabbit sat next to the priest, his fascinated gaze locked on the cat snoozing beneath the formal dining table. An old, gray-haired terrier was curled up next to the feline.

Artemus cut his eyes to them where they lurked in the doorway of the dining room.

"If you're going to spy, do it properly!" Barbara Nolan snapped.

"Yes, ma'am!" Drake resisted the urge to salute and herded the others inside the chamber.

Artemus sighed. He sat at the head of the table, mediating the tense discussion taking place between the man and the three women seated around it.

"You're my aunt?" Leah asked Naomi, her expression shocked.

"Well, technically, I'm your first cousin once removed," Naomi murmured. "I took my mother's maiden name. Barbara and my mom are sisters. I even came to your parents' wedding."

Jeremiah blinked. "You did? I don't recall that."

"Well, you wouldn't. You were too busy making googly eyes at Joanna."

Jeremiah flushed.

"Were you sent to the college to spy on me?" Anger darkened Leah's face. Her heated gaze moved to Barbara. "Did you plan this whole thing from the beginning?" She grasped the pendant nestled against the base of her throat. "Even this?!"

Something went crunch on Drake's right.

Daniel froze in the act of removing a second biscuit from his pocket, the subject of their stares. Smokey gulped and swallowed happily next to him.

"You know he gets grouchy if he misses a snack," the priest said defensively.

"He's right," Serena murmured. "I swear the hellhound was going to eat me last week."

Smokey huffed, abashed.

"I'm sorry," Artemus told the people at the table leadenly. "There's something wrong with them." He narrowed his eyes at Drake and the others. "All of them."

"Hey!" Callie protested.

"That's mean," Otis said, crestfallen.

"Dude, you're breaking my heart," Haruki muttered.

Barbara Nolan sighed and rubbed her temples.

"Are they always like this?" Naomi asked Artemus.

"More often than you'd think."

Barbara turned to Leah.

"The answer to your first question is yes," the older woman said quietly. "I asked Naomi to take up a tenured post at the Art Institute so she could watch over you. She'd been invited to take on that position several times. She just needed a good reason to accept it."

"And the pendant?" Leah paused and swallowed. "Did it—did it really belong to mom, or did you lie about that too?"

Jeremiah startled. "What?"

Barbara closed her eyes briefly. "No, it wasn't a lie. The pendant truly is a Nolan family heirloom. And your mother was meant to pass it to you, just as I did to her."

Silence fell across the dining room. Jeremiah broke it a moment later.

"I don't understand any of this." His voice hardened. "What went down in that alley. What—what Leah and you guys did. I want someone to tell me what the hell is going on here!"

His words echoed in their ears.

"What you saw today was a glimpse of the war taking place on Earth right now," Artemus said calmly. "It's been going on for a while. And the Vatican has had knowledge of it for a number of years."

"A war?" Jeremiah repeated guardedly. "What kind of war?"

"A war between Good and Evil," Barbara replied in Artemus's stead, her voice weary. "Between Heaven and Hell." She glanced at Artemus and Drake. "And between angels and demons."

Jeremiah went slack-jawed. "That's—that's impossible!"

"You saw the evidence with your own eyes," Sebastian said. "And you witnessed what your own daughter is capable of only hours ago."

Jeremiah froze for a moment before raking a trembling hand through his hair, his expression frustrated.

Drake felt a flash of pity for the detective. He was someone who worked by the rigid rules of the law and saw the world in black and white. He was also a man who was used to being in command. That control had slipped from his hands tonight.

"The incident at Elton LeBlanc's auction house last winter," Jeremiah finally said, his face wary. "Was that part of this—this war too?"

"Yes," Artemus said. "That was the first time I found out about it. Elton and his men have been working as agents of the Vatican for a number of years, so they knew about the existence of demons. That was also the night I met Drake, Callie, Serena, and Nate." Artemus looked over at Smokey and smiled faintly. "As for the pooch, we'd met before."

Smokey's eyes gleamed with a crimson light.

Jeremiah paled. "So, the men and women who were behind that incident were like—like Maddox?!"

Artemus stared. "Who's Maddox?"

"He's the one who attacked Tony and killed those drug dealers in that alley."

"Oh." Artemus grimaced. "Then, yeah. From what Elton's said and from what we've observed ourselves, it takes a while for newly awakened demons to appease their hunger for human flesh."

"Tell him." Leah looked from Artemus to Jeremiah, her expression determined. "Tell my father what you guys told me."

In the hour that followed, Artemus recounted everything that had happened since the night Callie turned up at Elton's auction house with the cane her husband had charged her with selling after his death. He told the dazed detective about the battle in New York and how they had ultimately uncovered the name of the demonic organization the Vatican had been fighting for decades. Haruki pitched in and chronicled the deadly events that had taken place in L.A., starting with his brother's murder. Sebastian and Daniel narrated the tales of their own awakening and their conflicts with Ba'al in England and Rome.

"That meteor shower at the Vatican was you guys?" Jeremiah mumbled, now as white as a ghost.

"Yeah." Serena made a face. "Although it was mostly Daniel's fault, Persephone stuck Artemus with the bill for the damages."

A guilty expression washed across the priest's face.

"I still have a bone to pick with her about that," Artemus said darkly.

Leah stared at Serena. "You call the Pope Persephone?"

Serena shrugged. "She insisted."

"Otis's mother wrote several journals recording the visions she'd seen about the upcoming war the Fallen Angels intend to bring to Earth," Artemus continued. "Her writings were heavily encrypted. Otis and Sebastian are only halfway through deciphering them, with the help of a group of Vatican experts and a new friend. She predicted that there would be a Guardian awakening in Chicago soon."

"That Guardian is Leah," Sebastian told a stunned Jeremiah. "She is the host to a divine beast. And somewhere in Chicago is a gate of Hell that only they can open."

CHAPTER TWENTY-TWO

Jeremiah suddenly felt dizzy. He clutched at the table, seeking an anchor in a world gone mad. A world he no longer recognized. Gentle hands landed atop his clenched fists. He looked around into his daughter's pale face.

"It's the truth," Leah said. "Everything you've just heard. It really happened. *Is* happening right now."

"I—" Jeremiah stopped and swallowed. He couldn't find words to express what he was feeling.

"I know it's a lot to take on board," Artemus said in a sympathetic voice. "And I expect it'll take some time for all of this to sink in. But we have to deal with what's happening to Leah and what Ba'al are up to."

The man's words focused Jeremiah's attention like little else could. He took a deep breath.

I'll deal with my feelings later. I need to concentrate on Leah right now.

"Tell me more," he said.

Although she was hearing the account of how Artemus and the others had met and the battles they had fought for the second time, the reality of it all still rocked Leah to the bones. Drake's possession by the demon who had sired him. The identity of Drake and Artemus's mothers. The super soldiers and the Immortals. All of it was ludicrously fantastical. But there was never a moment when she'd doubted their narrative.

She knew instinctively that they would never willingly lie to her, just as the beast who lurked inside her did too.

"The pendant Leah is wearing is her key," Artemus said. "It is also a weapon that she can wield to kill demons."

"What we saw today wasn't its full form," Haruki added. "Both she and the key will only achieve their full potential once they are in the presence of their gate and they utter the divine words that will unlock the sigils that can open it."

Leah's pulse stuttered.

There were many things she found daunting about what she'd learned that afternoon. Of all of them, this was by far the worst.

"May I see it?"

Leah blinked at Artemus. He was indicating the pendant. She hesitated before taking it off and handing it to him.

Artemus examined the necklace for a moment before passing it to Sebastian and Otis.

"You guys sensing the same thing I am?" he asked quietly.

Otis nodded, his expression wary.

"Yes. This artifact is demonic in origin." Sebastian's

cool gaze moved to Barbara and Naomi. "As are your energies."

∼

Naomi swallowed a sigh as palpable tension filled the room. *Oh boy.*

"What do you mean, it's demonic?" Leah stared from Sebastian to the pendant and back, confused. "I thought the keys were meant to be holy items."

Callie's face cleared. "Oh. So *that's* what we can feel from Naomi and the old lady!"

A puzzled look dawned on Daniel's face as he studied the two women. "But they are not demons. We'd know if they were. And our beasts would be poised to kill them."

Naomi grimaced. *I'm glad we're on their side.*

"The pendant is a holy artifact," Barbara told Leah. "Or it was. Its nature changed after the angel it belonged to was driven into Hell by Michael and Heaven's Army."

Otis's eyes widened. "So, you know what the artifact is?"

"No," Barbara replied. "I do not know the identity of Leah's weapon. All I can tell you is that it is the Nolans' most valuable family asset and has been handed down from mother to daughter ever since our family's inception."

Artemus stared at Barbara. "Are you saying that a Grigori, a Fallen Angel, deliberately left his weapon on Earth before he was cast to Hell?"

"That is exactly what I'm saying," Barbara asserted calmly.

Artemus exchanged startled glances with his companions.

Serena frowned. "This would imply what, exactly?"

Drake's expression grew guarded. "It would mean—"

"That not every Grigori wants the upcoming war," Sebastian concluded pensively.

"You are correct," Barbara murmured.

A stunned silence descended upon them.

"Are you telling us that there are demons out there who wish to help us?" Callie said in a dubious voice.

Naomi scratched her cheek lightly. "Well, I wouldn't stretch things that far. But a lot of them wouldn't stand in your way. And they won't help Satanael's forces either."

"Can they even do that?" Daniel narrowed his eyes. "Go against his orders?"

Naomi and Barbara exchanged a cautious look.

"The powerful ones can," Naomi said.

Sebastian studied her with an intense expression that almost had her squirming in her seat. "Does this mean that the demon who bestowed his powers upon your bloodline is one of those willing to rebel against Ba'al?"

"Yes," Naomi replied reluctantly.

Another hush followed.

"My beast said—" Leah faltered, her face ashen as she gazed at Naomi. "He said you were a witch."

Artemus's surprised stare swung between Leah and Naomi. "He did?"

Otis drew a sharp breath. He glanced at Sebastian, understanding dawning on his face. "Then, the one whose energy we can feel within you is probably—"

"Azazel, the Third Leader of the Grigori," Sebastian concluded in a self-assured tone. "The angel most skilled at wielding magic in all of Heaven. And the one who taught humankind the forbidden secrets of sorcery and witchcraft."

Barbara looked at him steadily. "You are correct, once more."

CHAPTER TWENTY-THREE

Leah's heart slammed wildly against her ribs as Sebastian and her grandmother's words sank into her consciousness.

"Wait," she mumbled. "My mother was a witch?!"

Jeremiah jumped to his feet. "That's nonsense!" He glared at Barbara. "There's no way Joanna was a—*a witch!* For God's sake, can you even hear yourself?!"

"I can hear myself just fine, Jeremiah," Barbara said sharply. "Now, sit!"

A low bark sounded beneath the table. The terrier rose and waddled over to Barbara while Jeremiah slowly took his seat again.

She picked up the dog and gently stroked his head. "There, there, Thorn. It's quite alright, old friend."

The white cat leapt onto the table and took a possessive stance next to Naomi.

Barbara cleared her throat. "The Nolans are but one of a large number of families of witches and sorcerers descended from Azazel. Joanna walked away from that world the day she married you." She frowned at Jeremiah.

"You can rest assured in the knowledge that she never performed any spells or used any magic while she was your wife."

"Well, except for that one time," Naomi muttered.

Jeremiah scowled. "What do you mean?"

A flash of intuition shot through Leah.

"It's the mark on my neck, isn't it?" she said hoarsely. "Mom placed a spell on me to hide it." Her gaze switched to Naomi. "And you broke it today. That's why I heard her voice in that alley. And that's why the mark is now visible!"

"What mark?" Jeremiah asked, looking utterly baffled.

Leah twisted in her chair and raised a shaky hand to her nape. She pulled her thick locks aside, exposing the dark lines imprinted at the base of her skull. The ones that hadn't been there a few hours ago.

Her father gasped. "Is that a—?"

"Well, I'll be damned," Naomi said. "It's a lion."

Leah swallowed and straightened in her seat. She'd needed mirrors to see the symbol of the beast that marked her skin. It was different from the lion imprinted on Callie's nape.

Barbara gazed at Leah, her eyes glistening with unshed tears. When she spoke, her voice trembled slightly. "She never did tell me what it was she saw on your body the day you were born."

Naomi passed the older woman a hanky.

The lingering anger Leah felt toward her grandmother finally faded. It was clear to her that Barbara had had little choice but to act in accordance with what had already been preordained. What was unfolding in the city was beyond the control of the Nolans and very much in the hands of a higher power.

And our own, to a certain extent.

Leah's thought was echoed by what she could sense from her beast. Though her fate and that of Artemus and his companions seemed predestined, she couldn't help but feel that they still had some measure of influence over it.

"Your mother's spell did more than mask the mark of your beast," Serena said.

Confusion darted through Leah. "What do you mean?"

"I have skills that mean I can find anyone in the world." Serena ignored Jeremiah's pointed frown. "But I couldn't find you, despite scouring every database on the internet and all the street cameras in this city. It's like you don't exist in the digital world."

"We couldn't sense your powers until Naomi released the spell," Sebastian added. "We've been looking for you for weeks." He glanced at Haruki. "Haruki has been to the coffee shop where you work numerous times. He should have detected the divine energy of your beast."

A tight feeling squeezed Leah's chest. *Was Mom really that powerful?! And were Artemus and the others searching for me for that long?!*

"Joanna did it to protect you, Leah," Barbara said. "I think she suspected long before I did that the prophecy foretold by our ancestors was about you. That's why she refused to keep the pendant with her and why she distanced herself from me and the rest of our family. And it's why she made your father promise to never have anything to do with the Nolans after they got married. She was running away from the truth."

"You knew?" Jeremiah murmured. "About the promise?"

Barbara's expression grew tired. "I am aware there was never any love lost between us, Jeremiah. But I am also conscious that you are not the kind of man who would have kept Leah from seeing me unless you had a good reason to."

Leah's stomach twisted. All this time she'd blamed her father for keeping her away from the Nolans and it turned out it was her mother's wish to protect her that had been behind it all.

Fear slowly darkened Jeremiah's eyes as he stared at Barbara. "You said there was a prophecy about Leah?"

He reached over and grasped Leah's hand. She squeezed his fingers gently.

"Yes," Barbara replied. "The descendant of Azazel behind our bloodline crossed paths with a divine beast thousands of years ago. They formed a pact which meant that the beast would awaken inside the body of a Nolan in the future, when his powers would be needed to fight the forces of Hell."

"Does—does this mean I'm a witch too?" Leah mumbled.

"If you have the Grigori's blood inside you, we cannot sense it." Sebastian switched his attention to the terrier on Barbara's lap and Naomi's cat. "Are they your familiars? The same energy running through your veins is inside them too."

"Familiar is as good a word as any, I guess." Naomi smiled and rubbed Gemini under her chin with a knuckle. The cat purred. "They are creatures that can augment our powers. We are bound together by contracts we form with them upon the awakening of our powers."

"And the bracelet and the ruby pendant?" Sebastian queried insistently.

Leah stared at Naomi's jade bracelet and her grandmother's necklace.

"They are our weapons and a medium for our magic,"

Naomi explained. "They allow our spells to take form in this dimension."

"So, I was right." Sebastian's eyes glittered. "The words you spoke in the alley were an incantation."

"You're pretty sharp," Naomi murmured.

"I am the Sphinx," Sebastian said, as if that explained everything.

"Hmm, do I—have a familiar too?" Leah asked hesitantly.

"I'm afraid you don't," Naomi replied. "You have something even stronger."

The beast rumbled appreciatively inside Leah. *The witch is correct.*

∼

HARUKI WONDERED IF THE OTHERS COULD FEEL THE subtle shifts in Leah's divine energy. Something told him it had as much to do with her state of mind as that of the creature inside her. He frowned faintly.

I'm not normally this sensitive to the others and their beasts.

The Dragon was being unusually quiet where he lurked inside Haruki's soul. He couldn't help but feel that the creature was sulking, for some unfathomable reason.

Leah stared at her hands for a moment before taking a deep breath and turning to her father, her expression resolute. "Dad, I have something tell you."

Jeremiah visibly stiffened.

"It's about last night," Leah mumbled.

Jeremiah's face started to clear. "If you mean our fight, there's nothing to—"

"I killed someone yesterday," Leah blurted out.

Her words reverberated loudly around the room.

Jeremiah blanched. "What?"

"She means she killed a demon." Haruki's frown deepened. "It was a guy who worked at the coffee shop. He followed her into the alley behind the building and attacked her."

Jeremiah's knuckles whitened on the table. He opened and closed his mouth soundlessly, too stunned to speak.

Leah met Haruki's gaze, her expression tortured. "Still, Patrick was—"

"He was a monster," Haruki interrupted coolly. "Just like the man who tried to kill your father and his partner tonight."

He caught Callie and Artemus's puzzled glances out the corner of his eye and swallowed a grimace. *Great. Even they think I'm acting like an asshole.*

Leah chewed her lower lip, her eyes on him. "You said something to Patrick yesterday, just before he transformed. You told him he could fight the demon inside him. What did you mean by that?"

An awkward hush fell over them.

It was Drake who replied. "He meant that, in some instances, a human with a strong will power can suppress the monster inside him."

A troubled expression flitted across Artemus's face as he looked at his brother. From the guarded way Naomi and Barbara observed Drake, Haruki suspected they too could sense the demon within his soul.

Artemus sighed and rubbed the back of his head. "With everything else that happened this afternoon, I forgot to tell you guys about Elton's visit today."

"Elton dropped by?" Otis said.

"Yeah. And he had a doozie of a story to tell." Artemus made a face. "Apparently, the dead are going missing around the city. And we think it has something to do with Ba'al."

Jeremiah blinked "Oh. A couple of detectives at my precinct were just assigned that case."

"Why on Earth would Ba'al be stealing dead bodies?" Sebastian said.

Serena's face hardened. "Maybe they mean to experiment on them, like they did with the first-generation super soldiers."

Nate clenched his fists. Their recent clash in Rome with the genetically enhanced super soldiers created by an Immortal and a rogue branch of the U.S. Army, and subsequently imbued with demonic powers by Ba'al, was still fresh in all their minds.

"I can't quite see how a horde of demonic undead are meant to stop us," Drake said dubiously. "I mean, they're probably bone dry. All it'd take is for the Dragon to sneeze and they'd turn into walking torches."

"Thanks," Haruki muttered.

A worried look passed between Callie and Daniel.

"They should start checking graveyards," Daniel said grimly. "We found an empty burial site behind the church today."

Lines wrinkled Artemus's brow. "Elton didn't say anything about cemeteries."

"The grave wasn't just empty," Callie elaborated. "There were handprints and footmarks next to it."

Haruki tensed at Callie's nervous expression.

"You mean, like a trail the perpetrators left behind when they stole the body?" Artemus said, mystified.

Daniel's reply had Haruki's stomach clenching in dread.

"No." A muscle jumped in the priest's cheek. "Like someone climbed out of their coffin and dug their way out of their own grave."

CHAPTER TWENTY-FOUR

ARTEMUS GAZED BLINDLY AT THE CEILING OF HIS bedroom, his hands folded behind his head. It was gone 2 a.m. and he still couldn't sleep.

Well, a lot of stuff went down this afternoon. And fighting Ba'al always leaves me on edge.

Barbara Nolan had taken her leave just after 10 p.m. Naomi, Jeremiah, and Leah had followed shortly after. Although Artemus would have personally preferred it if Leah had stayed at the mansion that night, he'd known there would be no arguing with her father. He'd briefly considered telling Jeremiah that the divine barrier shielding the LeBlanc estate would offer more protection to Leah than anything the detective could ever do, but he had chosen to remain silent.

He could tell Leah needed to be with her father that night as much as Jeremiah yearned to be with his daughter.

Haruki had surprised Artemus by pulling him aside and volunteering to go and guard the Chases' home after the detective and his daughter had left.

"Why? Do you think they're still in danger?"

Haruki had hesitated in the face of Artemus's puzzled stare. "No. It's just—" He'd stopped abruptly, his expression growing embarrassed. "Forget about it."

Artemus pursed his lips. *I hope he's wrong and Ba'al doesn't pull any more stunts tonight. Chase will blow a fuse if anything else happens to his daughter.*

Lines wrinkled his brow as he recalled Callie and Daniel's gruesome findings behind the church where the priest worked. A dark foreboding had swept over him when he'd heard their account, one he'd sensed the others shared too.

Of all the things that happened today, that is by far the creepiest. A grimace twisted Artemus's lips. *That, and those ravens.*

He'd wanted to call Elton to update him about recent developments and to ask if he'd found out anything about the dead people going missing around the city. In the end, he'd decided to wait until the morning to contact his old friend and mentor.

A soft snore sounded by Artemus's feet. Smokey was sprawled on his back on top of the covers, his legs in the air and his mouth slightly open. Artemus gazed wryly at the hellhound.

At least one of us is getting some shut-eye.

He plumped his pillow, turned on his side, and closed his eyes determinedly.

The next thing he knew, someone was calling his name.

"Artemus!" a voice hissed close to his ear. "*Artemus, wake up!*"

"What is it?" Artemus grumbled. He blinked fuzzily.

Sebastian's pale features appeared in the gloom next to the bed. He was holding a poker in one hand and staring toward the opposite end of the room.

Smokey was in his dark hellhound form in front of the

leaded windows. He was gazing intently through the glass, his body as still as stone.

Artemus bolted upright, fully awake and senses on high alert. "What's wrong?"

"There are people outside the house," Sebastian said grimly.

"What?!"

Artemus pushed the covers off his legs, climbed out of bed, and headed swiftly over to the windows. Sebastian joined him.

Clouds drifted slowly across the sky, obscuring the moon and stars.

Artemus frowned. "Are you sure? I can't see any—"

A shaft of moonlight pierced the night. He froze, his pulse spiking.

Something was moving in the shadows beneath the trees.

The others were in the foyer when they got downstairs.

"Anyone sensing demonic energy?" Drake asked stiffly, his eyes on the front door.

"No." Haruki frowned. "I got nothing."

Otis hovered close to Haruki. He'd decided to spend the night at the mansion and was wearing a set of the Yakuza heir's silk pajamas.

"I thought I heard the chickens a few minutes ago," Nate murmured. "They sounded agitated."

A click came on Artemus's left. Serena had loaded a bullet into the chamber of her Sig.

A soft gasp escaped Callie. She clutched Nate's arm, her tense gaze riveted to the front door. Artemus's knuckles whitened on the switchblade in his right hand.

A shadow had just moved across the glass.

Wood creaked softly on the porch. They followed the sound with their gazes.

"They're headed for the back," Serena said in a hard voice.

They entered the kitchen in time to see the rear doorknob slowly twist. Ghostly figures shifted in the darkness beyond the windows.

Daniel made the sign of the cross and mumbled a short prayer, his crucifix in hand and his ring alight with the divine glow that was the precursor of his weapon. Sebastian took his pocket watch out of his gown and unleashed the flaming whip within.

Artemus's heart thudded dully against his ribs. He could tell why everyone was on edge. Whatever was out there wasn't generating any kind of life force that they could detect, good or bad. Which was inconceivable in itself.

The doorknob turned again.

They all jumped when a soft tapping came a moment later.

"They can't be that bad if they're knocking, right?" Callie mumbled.

"Open it!" Serena hissed at Artemus.

Artemus scowled. "Why me?"

"It's your house."

Artemus rolled his eyes before glancing around the kitchen. "Everyone ready?"

There were nods all around. Haruki and Drake were holding their swords in hand, while Callie wielded her spear.

Smokey padded over to Artemus's side, his eyes gleaming with a crimson light. Artemus released his divine blade and grasped the door handle, the hellhound's energy twining with the golden threads of his own holy life force. He took a shallow breath and yanked the door open.

The tall figure of a man filled the doorway. Huddled behind him, their silhouettes swaying slightly as they shuffled their feet on the porch steps and across the backyard, was a mob.

Artemus reached inside his soul to the power that had been gifted to him by his father and mother and braced himself for battle. Smokey growled and bunched his muscles, preparing to spring.

But no attack came.

An eerie sense of the familiar swept over Artemus as he gazed at the indistinct features of the man before him.

The cloud cover broke. Pale radiance washed across the woodland and the cemetery encircling the yard. Artemus's world tilted sideways as the light illuminated the silent mass who stood watching them. Smokey whimpered by his side, the fight draining out of him as effectively as if someone had flipped a switch.

Artemus's heart lurched painfully inside his chest, his eyes locking on the one face he'd thought he'd never see again in this lifetime.

The man in the doorway flicked a withered hand at the rat who'd just darted out of his tattered morning suit, adjusted the knot in his tie in a move Artemus had witnessed dozens of times before, and glowered at him.

"What the devil is going on, Artemus?!" Karl LeBlanc growled.

CHAPTER TWENTY-FIVE

Drake fisted his hands as he felt bone-deep shock reverberate through his brother across the bond that linked them.

A gasp broke the frozen hush.

"Gertrude!" Nate exclaimed.

Drake's gaze dropped to the limp form in the grasp of the man who stood framed in the doorway of the kitchen. Nate rushed forward and took the lifeless body of the chicken in his large, gentle hands.

"Oh." The stranger's expression turned contrite. He scratched his cheek absentmindedly with his long nails, oblivious to the sliver of parchment-like flesh that peeled away. "I'm sorry about that. It was an accident. Aunt Bessy got peckish."

An indistinct mumble rose from the short figure with the bowed back next to the man.

Artemus finally snapped out of his daze. "*Karl?!*"

Drake stiffened. *Wait. That's Karl LeBlanc?!*

The others were similarly staring in astonishment at

the man facing Artemus. Drake scrutinized the stranger's features.

Now that I look closely, I can see the family resemblance to Elton.

Although the mansion was filled with paintings and photographs of several generations of the LeBlanc family, there weren't any pictures of Elton and his deceased brother. It was as if Artemus hadn't wanted any painful reminders of the man he'd long considered to be his true father.

Artemus leaned a shaky hand against the doorjamb. "I don't—I don't understand!"

Karl peered at him. "Hmm. Contrary to my initial thoughts on the subject, it seems this was not of your making after all. You were never a good liar."

"Why the hell would I lie to you?!" Artemus snapped, some of the color returning to his face. "Or bring you back from the dead, for that matter?!"

"Because you're a born troublemaker," Karl replied bluntly.

"He's not wrong," Serena muttered.

The others nodded wisely.

Artemus scowled at them before indicating the crowd of silent people behind Karl. "Who the hell are they?!"

The elderly and somewhat desiccated dame with the bowed back grumbled something in a distinctly threatening tone.

"It's alright, Aunt Bessy," Karl said soothingly. "He didn't mean anything by it."

Further grumblings ensued.

"No, you can't put him over your knee and smack his bottom. He's twice your size." Karl sighed. "Besides, your arms would fall off."

"Hey, anyone else think that old lady looks familiar?" Callie said in a loud whisper.

"Now that you mention it, she does bear a resemblance to the matriarch in that LeBlanc family portrait in the foyer," Serena muttered.

"You mean, the creepy one with the woman who follows you with her eyes?" Haruki asked.

"Yeah."

Karl LeBlanc studied them curiously before arching an eyebrow at Artemus. "Who are these people?"

"It's a long story."

∽

Elton got out of the town car and gazed at the LeBlanc mansion. Relief flashed through him when he saw faint light coming from the side of the property.

Well, it doesn't look like there's a demonic fight going on.

Artemus had called him a short while ago and asked him to come to the mansion urgently. He'd refused to elaborate on the reason why and had hung up on him after issuing his curt demand.

Elton frowned. *That kid needs to learn to be more tactful.*

He'd climbed the steps to the porch and had just grasped the front door handle when something made him pause and look over his shoulder. The uneasy feeling that had swept over him when he was driving up the access road intensified. He stared at the shadowy tombstones scattered through the woodland crowding the grounds.

There was something strange about them.

Elton told himself he was being irrational and used his key to enter the mansion. Gloom filled the foyer. He followed the low murmur of voices coming from the hallway on the left.

Light seeped beneath the door of a room at the far end of the corridor. Elton opened it and entered the mansion's formal drawing room.

Artemus was sitting on the large, red and gold damask sofa to the right. Drake, Otis, and the other Guardians stood behind him.

"What's so important that you had to call me at 3 a.m.?" Elton said tersely.

A man was seated in the armchair opposite Artemus. He stiffened at the sound of Elton's voice and slowly twisted around.

A buzzing noise filled Elton's ears. His knuckles whitened on the doorknob as he gripped it hard. "K—Karl?!"

There was movement on either side of him. Elton felt the blood drain from his face when he registered the other figures in the room.

"Aunt Bessy?! Uncle—*Uncle Winston?!*"

A very dead looking Aunt Bessy grumbled something. The slightly mummified figure next to her dipped his chin with an ominous creak of bone and dried flesh.

Artemus sighed. "Come sit down, Elton."

Elton's feet remained rooted to the ground. *This is a dream. No, a nightmare! I'll wake up any second now and this will all be—*

"No, this isn't a dream, Elton." Karl frowned. "And if it's any consolation, I am as much at a loss as the rest of you as to what is going on here."

Elton swallowed, his heart thumping erratically against his ribs. He hesitated before making his way across the room to the damask sofa. He sat down heavily next to Artemus.

Something stirred next to his feet. Elton looked down. Smokey was gazing anxiously out between Artemus's legs in his rabbit form, his fur on end.

"I think we may have solved the mystery of those missing bodies your medical examiner friend told you about," Artemus said grimly.

Elton gazed numbly at his older brother and the bevy of dead LeBlancs around them. A figure shuffled past the windows of the drawing room. He stiffened.

"Is that—?"

"Yeah," Artemus muttered. "There's more of them out there."

Elton ran a shaky hand down his face. "This is—"

"Impossible?" Sebastian said pensively. "After everything that happened yesterday, I am inclined to believe in the implausible."

Elton gave him a bewildered look. "Why? What happened yesterday?"

"I was going to call you first thing this morning and tell you," Artemus said ruefully. "But it seems events are progressing even faster than I expected."

He indicated Karl and the other LeBlancs with a vague wave of his hand. Awkward silence fell across the room.

Elton stared at his brother, his mind and heart in turmoil. *I can't believe he's really here. That he's sitting across from me and Artemus right now.*

The memories of the day he'd found Karl in the alley behind the antique shop washed over him all over again, bringing with them the usual flood of anger at the demons who'd killed his brother, and the pain and regret at not having been able to save him.

Karl's face softened. "You couldn't have saved me, Elton. It was my time to go."

Elton's vision blurred. He blinked away the film of tears clouding his eyes and smiled faintly. "You always could read my mind."

"Well, I am your brother."

Elton took a deep breath and squared his shoulders. Now was not the time for reminiscing. "What happened to you?"

Karl wiped away some flakes of dead skin from his knee. "From what I've gathered from the other members of the family, I believe we started waking up a few days ago. It took a while for everyone to navigate their way out of their final…resting places."

"Graves," Callie elaborated, slightly pale-faced. "They climbed out of their graves. Just like that guy behind the church."

Elton startled. *The tombstones! They'd moved slightly. That's what was odd about them!*

Callie's words finally registered.

"Wait." Elton frowned. "What guy behind what church?"

∼

BY THE TIME ARTEMUS HAD FINISHED RECOUNTING THE events that had taken place the previous afternoon and evening, the sky was turning pale to the east.

"The new Guardian is Detective Chase's daughter?" Elton repeated, dumbfounded. "*That* Detective Chase? The one who investigated the incident at the auction house last winter?!"

"Yeah."

"The guy who was like a dog with a bone?!"

"Yeah."

"And his daughter is descended from a family of *witches?!*"

"Yeah."

"I always knew there was something strange about that Nolan woman," Karl mused.

He'd listened with great interest while Artemus had outlined what had happened since the night he'd first confronted demons at Elton's auction house the previous winter. To Artemus's unease, Karl had seemed completely unfazed by the extraordinary situations he and the others had come to face in the past months.

It's almost as if he already knew. He wasn't even shocked when I told him the identities of my and Drake's parents.

Aunt Bessy grumbled something.

"Is that true?" Karl's surprised gaze shifted to the shriveled figure next to her. "You once proposed to Barbara Nolan, Uncle Winston?"

Uncle Winston carefully dipped his chin.

"But she's, like, thirty years younger than you!" Elton blurted out. He glanced at Callie. "No offense."

"None taken." Callie smiled faintly. "And the age gap between me and Ronald was even larger than that."

Aunt Bessy berated Uncle Winston in a sharp but unintelligible voice. Uncle Winston shrugged laconically and nearly lost an arm.

Elton raked a hand through his hair before meeting Artemus's gaze.

"None of this makes sense."

Now that his initial shock had passed, Artemus couldn't help but feel a wave of sympathy for his old friend. They'd gotten used to battling some pretty outlandish enemies in the last six months. Even so, none of them could have anticipated this particular development in their fight against Ba'al.

"The dead coming back to life must have something to do with the demons' interest in our new Guardian," Sebastian said thoughtfully.

"I agree. There's gotta be a connection somewhere." Artemus turned to Otis. "Did your mother mention anything about this in her journals?"

Otis shook his head. "Not that I have seen so far."

Aunt Bessy was staring intently at Sebastian.

He shifted awkwardly. "Why is she looking at me like that?"

The old dame mumbled something.

"She says you look like someone she once saw in an oil painting in England." Karl arched an eyebrow. "A man from a renowned family connected to the royals?"

Smokey's eyes rounded. Artemus bit back a grin.

"I get the feeling she kinda has a crush on you," Callie told Sebastian. "Maybe we should tell her your age. I mean," she glanced around the drawing room, "you're older than her and half the dead people in here anyway."

Serena chuckled. Sebastian scowled.

"There's something I forgot to mention," Karl said. "When we woke up, we could feel something calling to us."

"Calling to you?" Artemus stared. "You mean, like a voice?"

Karl shook his head. Aunt Bessy's brow crinkled loudly as she frowned. She muttered indistinct words.

Karl's face cleared. "You're right. It was like a force pulling at our very bodies."

The faint foreboding Artemus had experienced the night before bloomed inside him once more.

"It came from the city," Karl added, oblivious to the uneasy feeling storming through Artemus. "Uncle Winston and some of the others tried to follow it, but something stopped them at the wall of the estate."

Artemus met Drake's startled gaze.

"It must have been Theia's barrier," Drake said.

The divine shield that protected the LeBlanc estate from demonic intrusions had been erected by their goddess mother, shortly after Artemus had come to live at the mansion. It also guarded all of them from detection by demons when they were out and about.

Artemus frowned. *And it can apparently also stop whatever it is that is making the undead disappear from their resting places.*

CHAPTER TWENTY-SIX

A DULL ACHE POUNDED JEREMIAH'S TEMPLES AS HE exited the precinct. He paused on the steps of the building and took a deep breath of the cool morning air before heading over to the parking lot.

He'd just finished giving his statement about the incident that had taken place in the alley in North Side yesterday and had been placed on paid administrative leave until the investigation was complete. It was routine practice and what he'd expected, but it still stung. No one bar he and Tony had survived the deadly attack by Shane Maddox.

Jeremiah clenched his jaw. *And whether Tony pulls through or not is still a topic up for discussion.*

He acknowledged the sympathetic greetings of the detectives and officers whose paths he crossed with curt nods and heaved a sigh when he reached his car. Jeremiah got inside, shut the vehicle's door after him, and dropped his head back against the headrest.

He'd closed his eyes and was enjoying the reprieve from the curious stares when he heard the passenger door open. He blinked and looked around.

Naomi Wagner dipped her head beneath the roofline of the car and flashed a smile at him. "Hey."

She climbed in, closed the door, and reached for the seat belt.

Jeremiah snapped out of his stupor. "What the hell do you think you're doing?!"

"Hitching a ride to the hospital." Naomi arched an eyebrow. "That's where you're headed, right?"

Jeremiah frowned. "Is that a question or a statement?"

"Relax, Jeremiah," Naomi drawled, clipping her seat belt in. "I'm not a mind reader."

Some of the tension started to ease out of him.

"I use tea leaves and tarot cards for that."

Jeremiah stiffened.

Naomi grinned. "It's scary how easy you are to tease."

Jeremiah considered kicking her out of his car for all of ten seconds. His shoulders sagged.

There was no denying that the primary reason he'd not been arrested by Internal Affairs was Naomi's testimony yesterday and the statement she'd given to the police that morning.

He started the engine and pulled out onto the avenue. The hospital where Tony had been admitted was only a ten-minute drive from the precinct. He'd been there once already that morning, before he'd given his deposition.

A surprisingly comfortable silence fell between them as he made his way through traffic.

"Is it true that you were at my wedding?" Jeremiah said after a while.

"I was. I wore a sapphire-blue dress and silver heels. Your Uncle Bob made a pass at me over the punch bowl."

Jeremiah startled. "He did?"

"Yup. He even tried to cop a feel."

He grimaced. "I'm sorry."

"Why?" Naomi glanced at him. "It wasn't your fault."

Jeremiah stayed silent.

"You know, I had quite the crush on you back then," Naomi mused. "I couldn't believe Joanna had bagged herself such a catch."

Jeremiah's foot slipped from the gas pedal.

An amused light danced in Naomi's eyes. "Careful there."

He gripped the steering wheel and concentrated on the road, his heart pounding for some unknown reason.

"Don't worry," Naomi added in a reassuring tone. "I got over it a long time ago."

Something that felt suspiciously like disappointment darted through Jeremiah.

"You did?" he murmured in a neutral voice.

"Yeah." Naomi smiled. "My taste in men has changed over the years."

Jeremiah found himself struggling not to frown.

"Aren't you gonna ask what kind of guys I'm into these days?" Naomi teased.

"It's none of my business," Jeremiah retorted coolly.

Naomi chuckled. "It isn't really, is it? But, for your information, it seems I quite like a man with an accent."

Her expression grew thoughtful as she gazed out front.

They reached the hospital and pulled into the underground garage.

Naomi hummed a tuneless song under her breath while they rode the elevator. Her handbag rustled as they stepped out onto the floor where Tony's private room was located.

Jeremiah spied the white cat peering at him through the opening.

"I don't think animals are allowed in here," he said gruffly.

"Gemini isn't just any animal. Besides, her powers will help me make Tony better."

The cat meowed softly in agreement.

Surprise jolted Jeremiah. "I thought he was out of danger."

"He is. But I can accelerate his healing with my magic."

Jeremiah wasn't sure he liked the sound of that, even though he knew it was Naomi's intervention in the alley that had saved Tony yesterday.

He hesitated. "Aren't you going to be late for your appointment?"

"What appointment?"

Lines furrowed Jeremiah's brow. "The one you have with my daughter this lunchtime."

Naomi stared. "I don't have an appointment with Leah today."

~

Leah secured her bike, tucked her Chicago Cubs hat firmly on her head, and headed into the Art Institute building on South Columbus.

I wonder what Naomi wants. She frowned faintly. *I mean, we only saw each other a few hours ago.*

Leah had slept fitfully last night, the incredible events and revelations of yesterday too fresh in her mind for her to rest properly. She was still struggling to come to terms with the fact that Naomi was her first cousin and that her mother Joanna was descended from a powerful family of witches and sorcerers.

If I told any of my friends about this, they'd think I'm crazy. She grimaced. *Ken, on the other hand, would be thrilled. Particularly if I told him Haruki was the Colchian Dragon.*

Heat warmed Leah's cheeks as she thought of the Yakuza heir. Despite the battles they'd fought together, his very presence still made butterflies dance through her stomach.

She knew her father disapproved of the young man's links to a powerful Japanese crime syndicate, even though Callie had told them the Kuroda Group were very much engaged in legitimate business activities these days.

Leah chewed her lip. She had a feeling her father would object to any guy she was interested in romantically.

She was approaching Naomi's office when her cell phone rang. It was her father.

Leah took the call, puzzled. "Dad?"

"Where are you right now?!"

Her eyes widened at the palpable fear in her father's voice. "I'm just about to go in for my meeting with Naomi. Why? What's wrong?"

"Naomi didn't set up that appointment! She's with me at the hospital right now. We're coming over. Stay put!"

Leah's heart lurched as she listened to the call end tone. She backed up against the wall and scanned the people navigating the corridor nervously, her senses on high alert.

What's going on? Is this a trap? But I can't see or feel anything demonic close by!

The beast inside her stirred.

"Hello, Miss Chase."

Leah's head snapped around.

Director Patel was standing to her left. The couple Leah had seen with him in Naomi's office two days back were with him.

"We were looking for Professor Wagner." Patel smiled affably. "Have you seen her?"

"Er, no," Leah mumbled.

"Oh." The blonde studied Leah curiously. "Is this Professor Wagner's star pupil?"

"Yes, it is." Patel made the introductions. "Miss Chase, this is Jane McMillan and her assistant, Travis Calderon."

"It's a pleasure to meet you." Jane McMillan smiled and shook Leah's hand. "I saw some of your artwork in the student gallery the other day. You are extremely talented."

Leah's pendant trembled under her T-shirt. She met the blonde's steady gaze and the stare of the dark-haired man who stood behind her and knew instinctively that they weren't human.

"It's a pity we missed Professor Wagner, but I am sure Miss Chase would be equally interested in the consignment of paintings we brought to the institute today," the blonde said sedately.

Patel brightened. "I'm sure she would. Why don't you come with us, Leah?"

CHAPTER TWENTY-SEVEN

Barbara drummed her fingers on the armrest of her chair, her brow furrowed in an almighty frown as she gazed at the old-fashioned desk phone before her. "What are you saying, Armand?"

The man on speaker sighed. "I am only expressing the views of some members of our esteemed community, Barbara. These incidents in Chicago have alarmed many of them. They want answers and reassurances."

Barbara scowled. *No. What they want is information that they can use as leverage over the Nolans in the future.*

"There are only two things I am willing to say on this matter, Armand. Please relay the following messages to our...concerned members. First, this has nothing to do with the main focus of interest of our society of late. Secondly, this matter concerns the Nolans and the Nolans alone. If there are any ramifications for our community, I will take responsibility for the actions of my family."

A short silence fell across the line.

"I believe this might not be sufficient for some of the

people who've expressed their concerns to the council," Armand said diplomatically.

Barbara swallowed a curse. This was her old friend's code for *"Give me a better reason to silence the curious bastards."*

"Alright, then tell them this. If they poke their noses in this matter, they won't just have to answer to me and the entire Nolan clan. They will be accountable to Michael's heir and Samyaza's son."

An audible gasp sounded from the speakers. "Oh. So, you've met them?!"

Some tension eased out of Barbara. She knew Armand was asking the question privately and not as a representative of their council.

"Yes, I have."

"And?!" Armand said with all the excitement of a child on his birthday.

Barbara thought back to the time she'd spent in the company of Artemus and his friends last night. "They are as formidable as I expected them to be."

This seemed to satisfy Armand. They exchanged pleasantries and ended the call a short while later.

Barbara sat still for a moment before twisting her chair and looking out of the library windows. It was a beautiful summer day and the sky was a perfect blue. It was hard to believe that a momentous battle was about to unfold in the city.

Still, Barbara understood that what had been preordained would come to pass, even though some of the details were still unclear to her. Just as she'd known her daughter Joanna would die and that her own time was running out. She met the wise gaze of the gray-haired terrier lying on a pillow next to her feet and called for her butler.

William entered the room. "Yes, mistress?"

"Gather the family," Barbara commanded in a steely voice.

~

Artemus and Karl stepped out of the rift ahead of Sebastian and Smokey. The golden portal closed behind them with a soft hiss.

"I shall be in my shop," Sebastian murmured tactfully before exiting the room.

Karl watched him leave with a pensive expression. "His powers are quite something to behold. Divine energy manipulation, was it?"

"Yes. If it weren't for his rifts, we would have been in some pretty sticky situations during our fights with Ba'al."

Karl looked curiously around the office that used to belong to him. "You made some changes."

Artemus followed his gaze and grimaced. "Do you hate it?"

Karl smiled faintly. "On the contrary. I think it suits you."

Artemus stared. He'd almost had to pinch himself when he'd come downstairs and seen Karl sitting in the kitchen that morning, as if the older man had done so every single day for the past six years. He swallowed.

There was so much he wanted to tell the man who had saved him. And so much he wanted to ask him.

"Are you okay?" Karl asked.

"I've never been better."

"Let's go to the smithy. I'm intrigued to see what you've done with it." Karl glanced at Smokey. "Come along, rabbit."

The hellhound seemed more comfortable with Karl today.

It was Sebastian who'd pulled Artemus aside that morning and explained why Smokey was so apprehensive around the revived LeBlancs.

As the beast who once guarded the gates of the Underworld, Cerberus's relationship with the undead was one of confrontation and subjugation. He was at a loss as to how to deal with the present situation, especially considering Artemus's close relationship with Karl.

They entered the workshop where Karl had taught Artemus his metalsmith skills. The older man paused in the middle of the room and trailed a hand over the anvil that had been there for as long as there had been LeBlancs in Chicago.

"Let's see what you can do," Karl said quietly. "Make me something."

This wasn't the first time Karl had said those words to Artemus. It had been their routine throughout the years he'd been his apprentice, whenever Karl had wanted to test him.

A bout of nervousness danced through Artemus. He felt like an awkward teenager all over again.

Karl's eyes bore into him. "Make me...a sword."

∼

Callie finished patting the soil down with her hands, took her gardening gloves off, and rose to her feet. "There, all done."

She turned and swallowed a sigh.

Nate stood forlornly in front of the small dirt mound in the front garden.

"It was an accident, Nate." She slipped her fingers through the super soldier's hand. "Besides, Gertrude wasn't going to live forever."

Nate dipped his chin heavily and laid a bunch of chrysanthemums on the tiny grave. The remaining two chickens stood a short distance away, as if they could sense the presence of their dead brethren beneath the ground. Callie masked a grimace.

Great. Now even I am having depressing thoughts.

"Why don't we go for a drive?" she suggested brightly. "I'll go get my bag."

Serena and Drake were having lunch when Callie entered the kitchen and grabbed her handbag from the countertop.

"How'd the ceremony go?" Serena asked.

"It was fine, no thanks to you two." Callie narrowed her eyes at them. "You could at least have made an effort to attend it. Even Daniel said a short rite before he went to work."

Drake made a face. "Having a funeral for a chicken is ridiculous."

"Yeah, well, my parents had one when my goldfish died. You and Serena will have to do the same for your kids one day."

Drake froze with his sandwich halfway to his lips.

Serena's expression grew cool. "Who the hell said we're having kids?"

"Oh." Callie stared. "Well, it's good you're using protection. Family planning is important."

The atmosphere in the kitchen became glacial.

Callie rolled her eyes. "Oh, come on! Everyone bar Artemus knows you two have been playing hide the salami since you came back from Rome."

Drake put the sandwich on his plate and groaned.

Serena glared at Callie. "How did you guys find out?"

Callie started counting on the fingers on one hand. "Nate saw Drake come out of your bedroom one morning; Haruki spotted your lingerie in Drake's laundry; Sebastian reported seeing bite marks on Drake's neck; Daniel thought you were playing footsie under the dining table one night; and Smokey spied you two kissing in the larder. And I can sense these things." She made a moue. "The only one oblivious to what's been going on is stupid Goldilocks."

Drake dropped his head in his hands. "I said we shouldn't kiss outside our rooms." He frowned at Serena through his fingers. "And I told you to go easy on the biting."

"Well, we couldn't keep it under wraps forever," Serena muttered, flushing.

Callie shrugged. "I don't know why you two bothered to hide the fact that you got together. Artemus isn't a child. He knows you like each other."

The way Serena and Drake avoided each other's eyes made Callie pause. *Ah. They haven't admitted their feelings for one another yet.*

She grinned impishly. "So, the sex is hot, huh?"

Drake and Serena scowled at her.

Callie's grin widened. She waggled her eyebrows. "We talking monkey-hot sex or demon-hot sex?"

Serena pointed to the door. "Get out!"

Callie chuckled and headed for the foyer. She retraced her steps a moment later and popped her head around the doorway. "By the way, have you guys seen Haruki?"

"He headed into town a short while ago," Drake muttered. "Said he was going to check something out."

CHAPTER TWENTY-EIGHT

I'M PROBABLY OVERREACTING.

Haruki stepped out of the brand-new Ford Mustang his father had gifted him the previous month and studied the complex of buildings across the road.

He ignored the curious stares of the students and passersby milling along the avenue, popped his shades on, and headed over to one of the rear entrances of the Art Institute.

He hadn't told anyone at the mansion about his decision to visit the college where Leah was a student. He suspected she would be there, despite everything that had happened in the last two days.

The new Guardian was not only devoted to her studies, but also stubborn as hell.

Haruki frowned. *Besides, she's a trouble magnet. God only knows what sort of calamity will befall her if someone doesn't look out for her.*

Why he felt it was his personal duty to perform such a task was not something he was prepared to explore right now. And, guessing from his beast's silence, neither was the Dragon.

~

Leah's pulse pounded as Director Patel led her toward the Art Institute's basement. She could feel Jane and Travis's stares on her back.

I still can't sense any dark energy from them, though.

Her beast prowled agitatedly behind her eyes, his turbulent emotions resonating inside her soul. His reaction and that of her pendant confirmed her suspicions about the museum's latest benefactors.

They're definitely not human. Leah recalled something Artemus had said yesterday. About how Ba'al's commanders could mask their auras. She swallowed. *Does that mean they're both high-level demons?*

Patel finally stopped in front of a pair of metal doors beneath the museum. Leah blinked. It was the first time she'd been down there.

The director entered his biometric data in the security panel on the wall, punched in a code, and unlocked the storeroom with a complex key. "Watch your steps."

The chamber they entered was split into two levels. Access ramps framed the staircase that led to the vault-like space some fifteen feet below. Secured in orderly, vertical metal racks suspended from the ceiling were rows of paintings of varying sizes. They extended toward the rear of the building as far as the eye could see, silent soldiers frozen in an endless march of time.

Thump.

Leah startled at the sudden, heavy throbbing inside her chest.

"Come." Patel descended the stairs. "The new shipment is being unloaded at the back."

Thump-thump.

Leah followed slowly, her heartbeat matched by the forceful one of her beast. Her pendant twitched violently where it rested against her breastbone. She gripped it through her T-shirt.

It was hot to the touch.

Patel led them farther inside the storeroom.

Thump-thump. Thump-thump.

A queasy feeling swept over Leah as they approached an area where several museum workers were removing framed paintings from crates on a pallet. She could sense a corrupt force coming from somewhere close by. Whatever it was, it was causing sweat to bead her forehead.

This is more than just demonic energy!

"Some of the artwork Jane has donated has been damaged and needs to be restored to its former glory, hence why she chose our institute for that great privilege." Patel puffed his chest out proudly, as if the honor had been personally bestowed upon him. "I hope you and Professor Wagner can be involved in the refurbishment project that we'll be—" He stopped and stared at Leah. "Are you okay, Miss Chase? You have gone quite pale."

No, I'm not! I'm gonna be sick!

Leah's stomach churned violently. Evil was spreading through the air around her, thick and pungent. Panic swamped her body as the oily tendrils filled her throat.

I—I can't breathe!

Her beast's voice jolted her. *Calm yourself, child. Hysteria will lead to nothing. We must face this situation head on.*

Leah swallowed. "How?"

Patel blinked, confused. "Excuse me?"

Leah cursed internally. She hadn't realized she'd spoken out loud.

"Aren't they pretty?" Jane ignored their awkward exchange and strolled past them, her gaze on the paintings being unveiled a short distance from where they stood. "Don't you think, Miss Chase?"

The woman turned and focused her pale stare on Leah. Her pupils glowed ochre for an infinitesimal moment.

Leah bit back a whimper. She could feel the demon's energy now. It was as if the woman had just flipped a switch that revealed her true nature.

Oh God. This is the power of a demon commander?!

It pressed down on her, so heavy she feared it would crush her bones. Her legs threatened to give way beneath her.

Get ready.

Leah gulped, sweat rolling freely down her face. *Wait! Do you mean to fight them? Here? Now?!*

No. We are not strong enough yet. I meant get ready to run.

"There you are," a voice said behind them.

Leah whipped around so fast her head spun.

Haruki was striding across the vault toward her. He looked as striking as always in a dark blue T-shirt and jeans, his expensive sunglasses tucked neatly at the base of his throat.

Leah had never been so happy to see anyone in her life.

Patel bristled. "Who are you? This place is off limits to—"

Haruki flashed him a disarming smile and slowed to a stop. "I'm sorry. I'm here for Leah. I'm afraid there's been a family emergency. We must attend to it ASAP."

Patel blinked, the fight draining out of him. "Oh. Of

course." He paused, his expression growing puzzled. "But how did you know she was down—?"

"Come." Haruki glanced impassively at Jane and Travis before extending a hand to Leah. "We must leave. Now."

The eyes of the dragon on his bracelet glinted with a crimson light.

Leah took Haruki's hand. His skin seared her flesh where he clasped her fingers. She shivered, as overwhelmed by his touch as she was by the corrupt forces swirling around them.

Haruki turned and practically dragged her toward the exit.

"Be ready to make a run for it once we're outside this place," he murmured in a hard voice. "They will not let us get out of here easily."

Leah nodded jerkily. She glanced over her shoulder and flinched when she met the demons' stares.

∽

Naomi raced alongside Jeremiah as they crossed the skywalk that connected the building on South Columbus to the museum, blood thundering in her veins.

God, I can't believe I was so stupid. Of course Ba'al will be after Leah now! They've witnessed what she's capable of!

"Where could she be?" Jeremiah shouted in a frustrated voice. "She wasn't in your office!"

"I don't know!"

Naomi gritted her teeth and cast a prayer to the Heavens. *Please let her be okay! I won't be able to face Joanna in the afterlife if something happens to her daughter.*

They reached the foyer of the main museum building.

"Wait!" Naomi grabbed Jeremiah's arm and pulled him to a stop. "Let me see if I can sense her!"

Gemini returned from where she'd been running ahead of them and leapt into Naomi's hold. She hugged the cat to her chest, closed her eyes, and mumbled a revelation spell under her breath.

The hairs rose on her arms seconds later. "The basement!"

Naomi turned and bolted down the split-level stairs.

Jeremiah followed closely on her heels.

CHAPTER TWENTY-NINE

Haruki cursed and swung his fiery blade at the mantle of shadows closing in around them. They hadn't gotten thirty feet from the storeroom before an oppressive wall of darkness had erupted before them, cutting off their exit. It was clear Ba'al was intent on trapping them.

Shit! This is like London all over again!

He'd suspected Ba'al wouldn't let Leah go after discovering her existence. The same thing had happened to him in L.A., after the demons had found out he harbored a divine beast. He realized now that it was this intuition that had had him subconsciously seeking out the new Guardian.

Leah stood next to him, her spear in hand and her eyes aglow with holy light. Static danced along her weapon. Though they were beneath the museum, Haruki could feel the electric charge in the air.

"Together!" he shouted. "I'll take the front, you take the rear!"

Leah nodded, her expression determined despite the dread he could see reflected in her pupils. She placed her back solidly against Haruki's, the energy of her beast echoing through his flesh. He welcomed it, his own power swelling as the golden threads that linked their souls combined.

They fought their way out of the demonic murk, inch by slow inch.

∾

Travis took a deep breath and exhaled. Inky vapors rushed out of his jaws and joined the billowing, black blanket filling the corridor. Fire and electricity flared through the thick pall where the Dragon and the girl fought against the demonic barrier.

Jane's words rang in his ears. *You know what to do.*

Travis frowned, drew on his powers, and prepared to inhale again, his master's command resonating inside his damned soul. Faint footsteps rose behind him. He looked over his shoulder, his beastly gaze piercing the gloom and augmenting his vision.

Jeremiah Chase and Naomi Wagner were headed toward him.

Wait. Jane's delighted voice danced through Travis's skull. *This is even better than I anticipated.*

His master and commander could make out what he was seeing through his eyes. He discerned her intent with his next heartbeat.

Let the girl and the Dragon go.

∾

Trepidation engulfed Naomi when she spotted the dark fog filling the end of the passage. Faint flashes of fire and lightning pierced the churning darkness.

She could sense Leah and the Dragon's divine energies beyond it.

A man with dark hair and yellow eyes stood before the shadowy wall. Though he'd maintained his human form, Naomi could tell he was anything but.

∽

Leah panted, heart thumping and face damp with sweat. The barrier blocking their escape was not getting any thinner. Haruki's breaths shuddered against her back, his skin scalding where he touched her.

She tensed. "Wait! Is the darkness subsiding?!"

Haruki grabbed her hand and darted for a narrow break in the pitch-black wall. "There!"

Shadows engulfed them as they entered the fog.

∽

Jeremiah skidded to a stop some dozen feet from the inky veil blocking the corridor. His instincts told him Leah was close. He glared at the man who stood in his path.

"*Jeremiah!*" Naomi shouted warningly behind him.

Something thick and heavy struck him in the chest. Jeremiah gasped as he was thrown violently across the underground passage. He slammed shoulder-first into the wall and heard bone crack.

He blinked, too stunned to move for a moment. Green light lit the gloom. The white cat leapt onto Naomi's shoulder, the feline's eyes the color of jade.

Something moved sinuously in front of Jeremiah.

His eyes rounded when he saw the enormous, black, barbed tail dancing through the air. He followed it to the man with the eerie, sulfurous gaze.

Impossible! That's—

～

Leah glanced over her shoulder as Haruki tugged her toward the fire exit at the end of the passageway.

"What is it?" he said tensely.

Leah hesitated, her gaze on the roiling darkness behind them. "I—I thought I heard something."

They barged through the metal doors and approached the base of a murky stairwell. Haruki had his foot on the first step when Leah yanked him to a stop.

She stared at a dark shape huddled in the shadows on her left. "There's someone there!"

A muscle danced in Haruki's cheek as he followed her gaze. "Stay behind me."

He raised his fiery sword and closed in carefully on the figure hunched up on the ground. The light from the flames washed across the body of a man.

The figure raised his head from where he rested it atop his knees and stared at them, his face full of fear and confusion.

Leah's heart stuttered.

～

Heat pierced Naomi's belly, sudden and fierce. She gasped and froze in her tracks. Gemini hissed where she perched on her shoulder, her rage echoing through Naomi's very soul.

Naomi looked down numbly. The wicked spike of the demon beast's tail was embedded inside her abdomen.

Shit!

A cold smile curved the demon beast's mouth.

Naomi bit down hard on her lip as he slowly extracted his tail from her body, her blood coating his dark scales thickly. She fell to her knees, her hands clamped over her jagged, bleeding wound.

Shots exploded across the corridor.

Jeremiah fired his gun where he slouched against the wall, his face ashen and his left arm limp at his side.

The bullets bounced off the beast's scales. The demon opened his jaws and inhaled, his chest swelling to monstrous proportions. A cold wind rushed through the corridor. The darkness started to dissipate.

By the time the glow of the overhead lights washed over Naomi, the demon beast and Jeremiah were long gone. She sagged where she knelt on the ground. A crimson pool was forming around her. She was hemorrhaging heavily.

Dammit. This sucks.

Naomi collapsed onto her side with a soft thud. Gemini's white shape blurred before her eyes. The cat's warm tongue lapped anxiously at her face. She raised a weak hand and grasped the animal's body, her fingers tainting the white fur with blood.

Just a little bit. Lend me your strength for just a little bit more!

Naomi closed her eyes and drew on her fading powers. She murmured an archaic incantation and felt heat bloom through her soul.

The face of a man rose in her mind.

See me!

CHAPTER THIRTY

Sebastian perused the shelves of his bookstore. He found the tomes he was looking for, headed over to the leather armchair by the window, and piled them on a side table. He picked up the first one and started reading, elegant fingers turning the pages at a leisurely pace.

China rattled next to him. He looked up from the fresh cup of tea someone had just placed on the table.

Otis was standing by the armchair.

"Thank you," Sebastian murmured. "Are you not busy in the shop?"

"Not really. It's kinda quiet today." Otis peered at the volume in Sebastian's hands. "What are you reading?"

"It is an anthology about witches."

"Oh." A nervous expression flitted across Otis's face. "Is this about the Nolans?"

"Indeed. I wish to educate myself about our new allies. The history of England and Salem is rife with tales of witchcraft and sorcery. There must be an element of truth to them after all."

"Ah. Hmm, I'll leave you to it then." Otis scurried back toward the antique shop.

Sebastian frowned faintly as he stared after the young man. It still astonished him how much of a scaredy-cat Otis seemed to be in his human form, when he was the most powerful seraph currently walking the Earth.

Ah, well. He did gain some confidence after the battle with Ba'al in Rome. I hope he realizes his own worth soon.

Sebastian had finished his tea and was a quarter of the way through the book when his skin prickled. His watch vibrated in his vest pocket. He stiffened and swept the room with his gaze.

Both he and his weapon had just sensed a faint demonic energy.

The air trembled in front of him. A pale shape materialized, its form blurry and insubstantial, as if he were looking at it through water.

A voice came to Sebastian from afar, weak and desperate. *See me!*

Green eyes flashed. The shape became clearer. A high-pitched meow reached his ears.

"Gemini?" Sebastian murmured, perplexed.

The cat's fear was tangible.

Another figure became visible behind Gemini.

Sebastian's eyes widened. He rose, the book falling from his lap and thudding onto the floor. He drew on his divine powers, opened a rift, and stepped through it.

∽

A FAINT RIPPING NOISE SOUNDED SOMEWHERE CLOSE BY. Naomi blinked sluggishly and spied the indistinct shape of a man crouching over her. Gemini meowed loudly.

The cat seemed relieved.

Naomi slumped where she lay on the ground. *Thank God!*

A pair of powerful arms lifted her up. She moaned, her head flopping against a strong chest. A heartbeat echoed against her cheek, forceful and steady. She ignored the hot pain stabbing through her body and focused on the mesmerizing rhythm.

There was warmth and light and a feeling of weightlessness.

Softness enfolded her. A wave of dizziness swept over her.

Naomi drifted in and out of consciousness, dimly aware of gentle hands undressing her and pressure being applied to her wound. A sharp stinging lanced through her flesh.

She came to in time to see Sebastian finish securing a bandage to her abdomen.

Naomi licked her dry lips and glanced around. Gemini was curled up on the bed next to her. "Where am I?"

"In my room, at the mansion." Sebastian picked up a glass of amber liquid from the nightstand and brought it to her mouth. "Taking you to a hospital would have invited too many questions. I thought it best to bring you here."

Naomi pulled away. "What is that?"

"Whiskey. It will help with the pain. I had to stitch you up."

He cradled her nape and brought the glass firmly to her lips once more. The alcohol burned a fiery path down Naomi's throat. She finished the drink and sighed as Sebastian lowered her back onto the bed.

She could smell his scent all around her.

He arched an eyebrow. "How is that?"

"It's not bad. But I know something that will make me feel better faster." Naomi hesitated. "I need some of your energy to augment my healing ability."

Lines wrinkled Sebastian's brow. "And how do you propose we go about doing that?"

She met his steady stare and felt the pull of destiny once more, just as she had done in the alley yesterday, upon their first meeting. "Bear with me."

Naomi wrapped a hand around Sebastian's nape, lifted her head off the pillow, and drew him toward her. He stiffened as she pressed her lips to his.

Gemini yawned and jumped off the bed.

Naomi drew back slightly. The man she desired tasted of tea and mint and a power that would melt her senses.

"How is that?" she breathed.

Sebastian's eyes darkened. The air crackled between them. "I can work with it."

He dipped his head and took her mouth in a none-too-gentle kiss.

~

IRRITATION DANCED THROUGH ARTEMUS AS HE STEPPED inside the mansion. "I wonder where he went."

Karl entered the foyer after him, Serena and Smokey in his wake. The super soldier had given them a ride back home.

Artemus observed the older man's strained expression anxiously. They'd chosen to leave the LeBlanc estate through a rift so it would be less taxing on Karl. The building housing the antique shop and Otis's apartment was also protected by a divine barrier, this one erected by Artemus's archangel father Michael.

It had become inherently clear to Serena and Artemus during their drive over that, without the protection of these holy shields, Karl would have no choice but to follow the call of the invisible force drawing the dead into the city.

The front door opened behind them. Callie and Nate walked in.

"Oh. You're back." Callie stared. "What's wrong?"

"Sebastian disappeared from the bookstore," Artemus said, disgruntled. "He was supposed to return us to the mansion."

"Hence why I had to play chauffeur." Serena narrowed her eyes at Artemus. "You really should take that driving test and get yourself a car. The rest of us are getting tired of ferrying you around as if you're some kind of young master."

"He still hasn't renewed his driving license?" Karl said.

"Like I've said a million times before, cars are tools of the devil," Artemus stated militantly. "Besides, you guys don't have a choice. It's in your tenancy agreement."

Drake entered the hallway from the back of the house. He slowed to a stop when he saw them. "Something happened?" He raised an eyebrow at Artemus. "Why do you look so pissed?"

Motion on the stairs drew their gazes.

Artemus scowled at the man coming down the steps. "Where did you go?"

"I apologize," Sebastian said gravely as he joined them. "There was an emergency."

Callie sucked in air. "Is that blood on your vest?"

Artemus's irritation drained out of him when he saw the crimson stains on the Englishman's clothes. Smokey scuttled over to Sebastian.

"Yes. But it is not mine." Sebastian lifted the rabbit in his arms and ruffled his head. "Thank you for your concern, brother. I am quite alright." He met their wary gazes. "Naomi got hurt. She is in my room, resting."

Artemus's pulse spiked. "Was it Ba'al?!"

"I believe so. I only witnessed the aftermath of the fight."

A flash of intuition darted through Artemus. "Leah." Trepidation swamped him. "She must be in danger!"

An engine gunned up the driveway. Tires squealed to a stop outside the mansion seconds later.

Callie stiffened. "Haruki!"

Artemus exited the house at the head of their group, Haruki's agitation resonating through the bond that linked them.

The Yakuza heir stepped out of his car, a pale-faced Leah in tow. A third figure climbed out of the back and hovered by the vehicle, his expression wary.

"What happened?" Artemus's gaze swung to the stranger. "And who is that?"

Leah's throat worked convulsively.

"That's Patrick," Haruki said grimly. "He's the guy who attacked Leah two days ago, behind the coffee shop."

"You mean, the one she killed?" Serena said skeptically.

"Yes," Haruki replied curtly. "He is one of the undead who has risen again."

"He—he doesn't remember any of it." Torment filled Leah's eyes. "And it's like he's a totally different person!"

"What is this place?" Patrick's gaze flicked fearfully from Leah to Artemus and the others. "Who are these people?" His mouth trembled. "I wanna go home."

To Artemus's surprise, Karl stepped forward and laid a

hand on the young man's shoulder. "Come with me. I shall explain everything."

Patrick hesitated before following Karl's lead, his distress clear to see.

"Where did you find him?" Sebastian asked as they watched the two dead men head around the corner of the mansion.

"In the basement of the museum." Haruki clenched his jaw. "Ba'al laid a trap for Leah. She met a demon commander. A woman called Jane McMillan. Apparently, McMillan has made substantial donations to the Art Institute recently."

Artemus gritted his teeth and berated himself. He should have seen this coming.

"There was a man with her." Lines creased Haruki's brow. "It was strange. Although he emitted demonic energy, he was…different."

"That's because he's a demon beast."

Artemus whirled around. Naomi stood in the mansion doorway, her complexion pale. She was wearing Sebastian's peignoir and was barefoot.

"I'm sorry, Leah." Her lips grew pinched as she met Leah's stare. "I couldn't stop him."

Confusion clouded Leah's face. "What do you mean? Stop whom?" She looked behind Naomi. "Where's my dad? He said he was with you."

Remorse filled Naomi's gaze. "We came to find you. Jeremiah was—" She paused and drew a shaky breath. "He was taken by the demon beast."

Leah gasped, her hands rising to cover her mouth. "*No!*"

Tears spilled over and ran down her cheeks. Haruki hesitated before laying a hand on her back. She turned and buried her face in his chest, her shoulders trembling as she cried. He hugged her to him, heedless of their surprised stares.

A faint sound from the garden drew their attention. Artemus turned. His gaze landed on a small mound of fresh dirt some dozens of feet away.

The flowers atop the soil were moving.

"Now what?"

The mound grew, as if something were forcing its way up through the ground. The earth sagged and gave way at the top of the inverted cone.

A shape flew out and landed in the garden with an angry squawk.

"Oh God," Callie mumbled.

"Is that—?" Drake started, horrified.

Nate rushed over and cradled the chicken in his arms. "Gertrude!"

She pecked viciously at his hand, a chrysanthemum spinning slowly atop her head.

"I thought she was dead," Serena said leadenly.

"She *is* dead." Some of the color drained out of Sebastian's face. "Her neck is broken."

They gazed at the chicken's lopsided head in consternation.

"Oh," Naomi murmured, surprised. "It's you."

She was staring at Leah.

Leah wiped at her eyes. "What—what do you mean?!"

"The reason the dead are coming back to life. It's because of the pendant. I can hear it humming."

CHAPTER THIRTY-ONE

Jeremiah came to with a jolt.

Pain throbbed through his left arm. He groaned and tried to move. Steely restraints tightened around his body. He froze and looked down slowly.

Dark bands held him captive to a chair. Nausea twisted his gut when he saw the inky strands coiling and twisting next to his flesh.

He could feel evil oozing from them.

Jeremiah swallowed the lump of fear in his throat and scanned his surroundings.

Shadows filled the space around him. Though he could barely make out a thing, he nonetheless had the impression that he was in some kind of cavernous chamber. A faint, rectangular shape was suspended from the ceiling some thirty feet ahead of him.

Where the heck is this place?

"I see you are awake."

Jeremiah's head snapped to the left. A woman in a white pantsuit stepped out of the gloom. She was pretty, in a cool, corporate kind of way. Her red stilettos clicked on concrete as she strolled toward him, the color of the shoes matching her crimson lips.

A man appeared behind her. Jeremiah tensed. It was the monster who had attacked them in the basement of the museum.

Naomi's face flashed before his eyes.

Oh God! Is she okay?!

"I see you are worried about the witch," the blonde drawled at his alarmed expression. "Do not be concerned. I believe she is still alive."

Relief flooded Jeremiah. It was followed by dismay.

Is this woman reading my mind?

He glared at his captors. "Who the hell are you? And what do you want with me?"

The blonde smiled, her white teeth glinting faintly in the murk. "What an interesting choice of words."

She stepped behind the chair and trailed a hand across his shoulders, her scarlet nails scratching the material of his suit lightly. Jeremiah shuddered.

The woman leaned down and brought her lips to Jeremiah's left ear.

"Hell is where I'm from, Detective Chase. As is my beast."

The man who had hurt Naomi shifted where he stood opposite Jeremiah. His pupils brightened to two sulfurous spots of light. A giant, black tail covered in shiny scales and silver barbs sprouted from the base of his spine. Horns tipped with dark flames protruded from his temples. A foul mist curled out of his lips and nose, the inky tendrils moving with his every breath.

Bone-deep terror echoed through Jeremiah where he sat rooted to the chair.

"Not many people in this world know of us," the

woman said lightly. "After all, I was not always a Great Duke of Hell." She moved out from behind Jeremiah and crossed the floor to the monster with the ochre gaze.

"Is he not wonderful?"

The blonde caressed the monster's face. The man shivered and closed his eyes briefly, his expression one of pleasure.

"It took a long time for me to find a suitable host so that my beast could walk this world in a human form." The blonde dragged her hand down the monster's chest and rested her palm over his heart. "He is the only thing I have left in this cruel world. My one and only possession."

Despite the disgust coursing through him, Jeremiah witnessed the loving look the two demons exchanged.

"Why are you after Leah?" he murmured numbly.

The woman's gaze lingered on her lover's face before shifting to him. "Alas, I am bound by an oath which means I cannot defy a direct order from Ba'al's leader, however much I despise that arrogant fiend. Unfortunately for you, he instructed me to find your daughter and her key, and to bring her before her gate." Her mouth stretched in a smile. "Now that I have you in my grasp, it is inevitable that she will come to me. To be fair, this is a much better turn of events than I originally planned for. I want to avoid a war with Artemus Steele and the other Guardians. I have no wish for gratuitous bloodshed."

Jeremiah's pulse thrummed in his veins at the demon's words. "Leah isn't that stupid. And neither are Artemus and his friends." His voice hardened. "They won't fall into your trap just because you took me prisoner."

"Oh. You misunderstand my intent." The blonde's smile widened. "I apologize. I did not explain my strategy properly."

The demon beast crossed the floor to where Jeremiah sat.

"You see, I intend to send your daughter your living, beating heart."

Jeremiah's stomach dropped. The monster's nails were extending into deadly claws.

"Don't worry, you won't die," the blonde continued in a conversational tone. "I will put the heart of a demon inside your body so that you may live."

She lifted a careless hand. The shadows next to her tore open. Crimson light pulsed out of the portal that appeared several feet above the ground. A demon stepped out of it and bowed to the woman.

Sweat broke out across Jeremiah's forehead. *I'm going to be sick!*

The blonde made a face. "Mind you, I say live, but that is a debatable term. Being the host to a demon's heart means you yourself will slowly turn into a fiend."

Horror engulfed Jeremiah as the demon beast ripped his suit and shirt open. He struggled violently against his restraints and felt the corrupt bands sting his flesh.

Talons scraped his skin. The beast's eyes flashed yellow. He drew his arm back and stabbed at Jeremiah's chest.

Heat bloomed on Jeremiah's skin. He closed his eyes tightly and waited for the agonizing pain to roar through him.

It never came.

A breathless moment ensued. Jeremiah blinked his eyes open.

The blonde was frowning. "How...interesting."

A faint glow caught Jeremiah's gaze. He looked down.

A circle of pale blue light filled with intricate lines and

symbols spun slowly over his chest. It hummed as it resisted the talons aimed at his heart.

Shock reverberated through Jeremiah. *What—what is this?!*

The demon beast scowled and straightened.

"It's a spell." The blonde came closer, her expression curious. "A powerful one."

Confusion filled Jeremiah.

"Your wife was a formidable witch," the blonde mused.

Jeremiah startled and stared at the glowing charm that had protected him from being torn apart. *Wait. Joanna did this?!*

The blonde looked at her companion. A silent exchange passed between them. The demon beast nodded before bending close to Jeremiah's chest and sniffing at the barrier shielding his heart.

"Fortunately, someone of her bloodline should be able to break that spell." The blonde smiled again. "And my beast can hunt down such a person."

A shuffling noise came from all around Jeremiah.

Something was moving in the shadows.

CHAPTER THIRTY-TWO

Artemus's words rang out across the kitchen. "What we really need to figure out is what the undead have to do with Ba'al's plans."

Leah stared at the pendant in her hands. Though she was appalled by the revelation that it could resurrect the dead, she had been unable to part from it.

She had asked Sebastian to check her mother's grave through a rift. He'd reported back that it was undisturbed. Leah wasn't sure whether it had been relief or disappointment she'd experienced when he'd told her this. Her beast was silent where he lurked inside her. Leah frowned. She had a feeling he was unsurprised by this latest discovery.

Aunt Bessy grumbled something where she sat at the head of the table.

"I doubt it's because the demons want to eat us, Aunt Bessy," Karl murmured.

"Yeah, they prefer fresh meat," Drake said.

"Maybe it has something to do with the gate?" Leah suggested.

Artemus leaned against the counter and studied her

with a faint frown. "I don't think we can rule out anything at this point."

A troubled expression danced across Serena's face. "What kind of weapon can bring the dead back to life?"

Otis and Sebastian shared a glance.

"There is one Grigori who was said to possess the power of resurrection," Sebastian said.

"He was also famous for having visions and for his mastery over the weather, especially storms." Otis paused. "Which would explain Leah's ability to control lightning."

Artemus frowned. "What's the name of that Grigori?"

"Ramiel, the sixth leader of the Watchers," someone said on Leah's left.

Leah startled and gazed at her cousin.

"The angel who was once known as the Thunder of God." Naomi frowned. "He was said to carry a formidable spear."

Sebastian acknowledged the witch's statement with a nod. "Indeed."

"So, this—Ramiel left his spear on Earth for Leah before he was driven to Hell, like Barbara claimed?" Callie asked dubiously.

"That's what it sounds like," Haruki said.

"What I don't understand is why Jane McMillan approached me in the first place," Naomi muttered. "She couldn't have known about Leah at the time or else she would have attacked her directly. Did she just guess the Art Institute would be a good place to try and lure out the Guardian Ba'al suspected was in Chicago?"

"We may never find the answer to that question," Sebastian said. "But it could be that Ba'al is aware of the abilities of your family and has been keeping an eye on you."

A lull fell across the room.

"How's Patrick?" Artemus asked Karl.

"Still shell-shocked. Uncle Winston is keeping him company in the mausoleum." Karl paused. "They appear to have bonded, for some peculiar reason."

"We should talk to him," Drake said. "He might have an idea of the location of the dead people who've been disappearing across the city."

The front door opened and shut in the distance.

Nate walked into the kitchen ahead of an agitated looking Daniel.

"It's getting worse," the priest blurted out. "Practically every grave in the cemetery behind the church is empty. The children saw some of the undead heading south last night." He clenched his jaw. "The ones old enough to understand what's going on are really upset."

"We should follow them," Drake said, adamant.

"I get the feeling they're not exactly strolling around in broad daylight," Artemus said. "I think we—"

A humming sound interrupted him.

They all stared at the glowing bracelet on Naomi's wrist. It was pulsing out green light and emitting a low whine. The witch blanched.

Gemini rose from where she and Smokey had curled up around each other on the window seat. The white cat leapt onto the table and hissed at the light throbbing from the jade beads, back arched and fur on end.

"The Nolans," Naomi mumbled. "They're in danger!"

∼

"What is this about, Barbara?!" Floyd Nolan barked as he stormed inside the formal drawing room of the Nolan family mansion, a parrot on his shoulder.

"Steady on, Flo-flo," Carmen Nolan murmured to her cousin. She sat sipping tea, an iguana on her lap. "You only just got here."

"Yeah, calm the heck down, Uncle Floyd," Miles Nolan said.

He sat on the floor next to Carmen, a ball of golden light spinning above one palm while he stroked the boa constrictor coiled around his waist with his other.

Barbara sighed and pinched the bridge of her nose. *Why did I ever think this was a good idea?*

She felt her butler direct a sympathetic gaze at her from where he stood by the drinks trolley and took a steady breath. Her gaze was sharp as she observed the bevy of Nolans crowding the parlor.

There were still more making their way to Chicago from all over the country.

"The time has come." Barbara paused. "The Nolan family heirloom has claimed its rightful owner. It is my granddaughter, Leah Chase."

Esther Nolan choked on her coffee. The ginger cat on her lap meowed loudly and leapt onto the floor. Barbara's second cousin once removed put her cup down, dabbed her mouth with a napkin, and gave her a wide-eyed look.

"Your granddaughter is the host of the divine beast?!"

Barbara nodded grimly. "Yes. And her initial clash with Ba'al has already drawn the attention of the magic council."

"Those busy bodies," Amir Nolan muttered, feeding cake to the frog on his lap.

"Bunch of old farts," Daniela Nolan added. The

chihuahua at her feet growled. A contrite expression washed across the young woman's face as she glanced around the drawing room. "No offense."

"I fear some members of the council may decide to involve themselves in matters that do not concern them, hence why I called upon you to come here today." Barbara's tone grew steely. "We must not let them intervene in the battle between Ba'al and Leah, and her Guardian friends. Too much is at stake."

Carmen frowned. "Are you saying what I think you're saying?"

Miles's eyes shone brightly.

"We can kick the council's ass?" he said with bloodthirsty eagerness.

An excited hiss escaped his snake.

Barbara swallowed a tired sigh. *Why is my family full of such hot-blooded fools?*

"We must not harm members of the magic council," she said sternly. "Our task is only to stop them from interfering with the Nolan family prophecy."

"So, what's Leah like?" Miles arched an eyebrow. "Is she hot?" Someone slapped him sharply on the back of the head. "*Ouch!*"

He glared at his mother.

Carmen sniffed, unrepentant. "I wish you'd get over this sex-craved phase of yours. And she's your cousin."

"I was only asking out of friendly interest," Miles protested. "Besides, I am a healthy twenty-two-year-old. I need to sow my wild oats."

"The way you're sowing your oats, it's a miracle you haven't impregnated some poor girl yet," Violet Nolan said acerbically. "Or caught a sexually transmitted disease."

Miles cut his eyes to the teenager with colorful, dyed

hair slouching on the window seat behind him, a white rabbit on her lap.

"Just because you haven't had your coming-of-age ceremony yet and can't have sex doesn't mean you should rain on my mating parade," he sneered.

Violet flipped a finger at him.

Barbara made a mental note never to leave Leah alone in Miles's company. Haruki Kuroda's face danced before her eyes. She couldn't help but smile faintly despite the gravity of their present situation.

She had a feeling Miles would have his work cut out for him if he ever tried to flirt with Leah.

"So, what's our plan of attack?" Floyd grumbled reluctantly.

Barbara studied her eldest cousin steadily. By rights, he should have been the head of the Nolan clan. But as the oldest female alive at the time of the passing of their previous leader and the latter's sole heir, that responsibility had fallen on her shoulders. Though there were many powerful sorcerers among the Nolans, their family was very much a matriarchal one when it came to the succession of power.

"For the time being, I believe we should keep a close eye on Leah and—"

The air trembled across the parlor. A loud buzzing filled the room. They froze, their gazes gravitating to the precious stones set in their distinctive jewelry pieces.

Their weapons were screaming in alarm.

The pressure inside the mansion plummeted. Barbara's breath misted in front of her face.

Violet cursed and leapt from the window seat, her gaze locked on something outside. Barbara rose from her armchair and joined her swiftly, the other Nolans crowding behind them.

Dark lines were splitting the twilight across the grounds of the estate. They thickened and parted, forming wavering, glowing crimson doorways.

"What are those?" Violet said, aghast.

"Those are rifts." Barbara narrowed her eyes and reached for the ruby pendant around her neck. "They are how demons travel through space."

Yellow-eyed fiends spilled out of the portals. And at their head, the tips of his jet-black horns smoldering with the blue glow of a dark fire and an enormous, barbed tail sweeping the grass in his wake, was a giant beast.

CHAPTER THIRTY-THREE

They saw flashes lighting up the sky above the wooded hill when they were still half a mile from the Nolan estate. Ominous, winged shapes swooped through the air, their backlit forms dark against the intermittent flares of magic.

"Can't this thing go any faster?!" Leah yelled, one hand on the dashboard of the Mustang and the other braced against the roof.

Haruki dropped gears, skidded around a corner, and floored the pedal. "The aim is to get there alive!"

The sports car responded with a roar at the same time a thud came from behind him. He glanced in the rearview mirror.

"I told you to put your seat belt on!"

"I *have* the damn belt on!" Artemus snapped, straightening from where he'd slammed into a door shoulder-first. "It's you who's driving like a goddamn maniac!"

Nate's SUV was twenty feet behind them, the super soldier keeping up effortlessly with the Mustang.

"By the way, was it a wise idea to separate us?" A

muscle twitched in Haruki's cheek as he met Artemus's gaze in the mirror. "It would have been faster if we'd rifted to this place."

"Naomi's suggestion was worth exploring. After all, she has more to lose than any of us if she is proven wrong."

They reached the Nolan estate moments later. Leah entered the security code for the gates and fidgeted impatiently as they shot up the winding driveway. An imposing, rose-vine-and-ivy-covered, three-story brick mansion came into view at the end of the road.

Leah's eyes widened. "Oh God!"

Haruki's knuckles whitened on the steering wheel of his car.

The place was swarming with demons on the ground and in the air.

Standing inside and hovering above the forecourt in front of the manor house, their eyes and weapons aglow with various colors, were a group of witches, sorcerers, and familiars. Barbara Nolan stood at their head, her gaze filled with the same scarlet light that emanated from the ruby embedded in the pommel of her sword and the eyes of the elderly terrier at her feet. Black blood splattered her dress and face as she cut down a demon, her expression furious.

Haruki braked to a stop. The SUV screeched to a halt inches from his rear bumper. He jumped out of the car and morphed into his divine beast at the same time as Callie and Daniel. Artemus assumed his angel warrior form and unleashed his holy sword, the blade brimming with the divine fire spilling from his ring-turned-gauntlet, a power gifted to him by the Flame of God, the weapon that Daniel wielded.

Nate released the liquid-armor combat suit from inside the disc he'd slammed onto his chest and took out his dagger, a faint radiance dancing in his pupils and across his skin as the nanorobots inside his body responded to the divine energy flowing through his veins.

Storm clouds erupted above the hill. Leah's eyes and body lit up with a golden light. Her hair thickened and extended halfway down her back. Her pendant shifted into the spear.

"Let's go save some witches!" Artemus said with a grim smile.

He joined Daniel where the latter floated above him, the giant, fiery wings of his Phoenix form harmlessly brushing the tops of the trees. They charged the demons diving toward them.

~

Awe filled Leah as she witnessed the aerial battle taking place above the gardens. Daniel's flaming weapon changed at will, from a bow to an ax to a lasso to a sword. No demon could get close to him, yet he felled a dozen in half as many seconds. Artemus flitted around him, his divine blade humming as he slashed and stabbed and carved demons, his movements so fast his body blurred.

Beneath them, Callie roared out a sonic jet that paralyzed a group of ochre-eyed fiends. She cast her scepter at them, batted away the demons springing toward her flanks with a powerful sweep of her snake tail, and reduced them to clouds of burning ash with the stream of liquid fire that ripped from her jaws, her flamed-tipped horns shining brightly. Her weapon winged through the air and returned to her grip, the staff slick with the blood of the frozen demons it had impaled.

It was Leah's first time seeing Daniel and Callie in their beast forms and witnessing Artemus fighting at full power.

"Watch out!" Haruki shouted.

Leah caught movement out of the corner of her eye and blocked the talons headed for her head with her spear. The demon who'd pounced on her shrieked. She backfisted him in the face and roundhouse-kicked him in the chest, sending him flying into some bushes.

"Pay attention to your surroundings," Haruki said sharply. "I don't have time to protect you!"

Leah deflected another attack, stabbed a demon in the chest, and glowered at the Dragon. "I didn't ask you to protect me!"

Callie glanced at them over her shoulder, her eyes flashing jade. "Now is not the time to be having your first lovers' tiff, you two. Those witches and sorcerers look like they're starting to tire."

"We are not having a lovers' tiff!" Haruki growled.

Guilt shot through Leah. *Callie is right. We don't have time for this!*

Lightning exploded and thunder boomed overhead. The power of her beast and her holy weapon surged through her veins. Static danced across her skin and hair.

She bolted into the forecourt, her gaze focused on her grandmother.

There was motion in the gardens. Leah's eyes widened when she registered the monstrous shape charging toward the old woman.

"Grandma!"

CHAPTER THIRTY-FOUR

"What the—?!"

Artemus gaped at the gigantic beast thundering through the grounds of the estate, great clods of dirt and plant debris flying in the air in his wake.

It was a black dragon some forty feet long and twenty feet tall, with inky wings and a shiny, spiked tail. Dark flames tipped the curved horns on the creature's head. A corrupt mist coiled out of his massive jaws and nostrils.

Artemus shot down toward the creature, alarmed. *The demon beast Naomi described to us was still a man! That was obviously not his final form!*

The dragon turned his head and glared at him.

A jet of blue-black flames roared through the night, straight as an arrow. Artemus swore and flicked his wings, rocking to a halt mid-air. The fire warmed his skin and armor as it shot past, missing him by scant inches.

Something flashed in front of Barbara Nolan as the black dragon refocused his attention on the witch. Leah skidded to a stop before her grandmother.

"*Leah, no!*" Barbara shouted.

Leah gritted her teeth and braced herself as the demon beast charged them.

Artemus scowled. "That idiot!"

He tucked his wings and dove.

Daniel moved in behind him and warded off the demons who would have attacked him, his flames casting an orange light on the battlefield below.

Leah grunted as the dragon slammed head-first into her. Her sneakers slid backward across the ground, leaving rubber marks on the stone. Sparks erupted near her hands.

Her spear was locked under the creature's horns.

Muscles bunched in her arms and legs as she pushed back against the dragon, a ferocious expression on her face.

Admiration darted through Artemus. *She really is fearless. That, or she's a moron!*

The dragon flapped his powerful wings. The gust of wind he generated sent several witches and sorcerers to the ground.

Leah barely moved.

The beast growled and inhaled deeply, his ribcage swelling to twice his size.

"*Shit!*"

Artemus accelerated.

Haruki bolted across the ground beneath him, his flaming sword carving through the demons in his path with deadly accuracy as he too aimed for the dragon.

The beast exhaled.

Black flames engulfed Leah.

Barbara cried out her granddaughter's name.

The storm clouds froze in the sky.

Artemus slammed into the dragon's flank at the same time as Haruki. The beast roared in outrage as they carried him across the forecourt and into a hedge. His cry became one of pain as Artemus stabbed his left wing with his sword and Haruki struck his flank with his own barbed tail, piercing his dark scales.

Obsidian blood pooled on the beast's wounds. He drew back some dozen feet and licked at his injuries before glowering at them. Surprise rounded his slit-like pupils a second later.

"Your little trick didn't work!" someone panted behind Artemus.

Artemus and Haruki whirled around.

The black flames engulfing Leah were dissipating. She emerged unharmed from the fading inferno, her body aglow with a golden sheen and her chest heaving with her breaths.

Artemus stared. *How did she—?!*

The storm clouds started spinning furiously above them. Electricity charged the air.

Crap! She's gonna do that lightning thing again!

Crimson light flared behind Leah. Two demons stepped out of a rift, grabbed Barbara by the arms, and retreated inside the portal.

The gray-haired terrier growled and barked before biting one of the demons on the leg. The fiend snarled and kicked him away. The dog struck the ground with a whimper.

Barbara's anguished voice traveled faintly through the rift as it closed. "*Thorn!*"

Leah darted toward the fading, red light. "Grandma!"

Her fingers closed on empty air.

"Your father is waiting for you at the same place we're taking your grandmother. They both have only hours to live.'

Artemus turned.

The black dragon had assumed the form of a man once more. He clamped a hand to the wound on his ribcage and studied Leah with a frown.

"We will call for you soon, Guardian."

The demon beast twisted around and disappeared inside a crimson portal. The other demons similarly vanished inside the rifts opening up across the estate.

A hush fell upon the forecourt when the last doorway closed.

Callie joined them, her Chimera form and scepter shrinking. "Was this a trap?"

"I don't think so." Artemus clenched his jaw. "It looks like they were after Barbara."

Daniel landed beside him, his fiery wings fading and his gauntlet resuming the shape of a ring once more.

A girl with dyed hair and rings of bright purple magic around her wrists touched down nimbly on the ground and gazed at them in awe, a white rabbit atop her shoulder. "Whoa. It really *is* them."

A young man sporting a boa constrictor and spheres of golden magic alighted beside her and watched them warily.

A man with gray hair and a beard made his way briskly across the forecourt, a parrot on his shoulder. "Are you Leah?"

Leah nodded. She blinked as the Nolans gathered around her. A gasp escaped her lips when the man wrapped her in a fierce embrace.

"It is nice to finally meet you. I'm Floyd Nolan, Barbara's eldest cousin. Your mother Joanna was my favorite niece." The man pulled back and examined Leah with warm affection. He looked over at Artemus. "Thank you for coming to help us."

Artemus shrugged at his grateful tone. "You guys weren't doing too badly. We just speeded things up a little."

"Do you know why the demons were after Leah's grandmother?" Daniel asked the Nolans. "They already have her father."

They glanced at one another and shook their heads.

Floyd's expression hardened. "Whatever the reason, it appears they intend to use both Jeremiah and Barbara as pawns in their game."

A woman with an iguana stepped forward, her eyes glittering with anger. "Although many of us have dealt with demons before, our society has so far not been involved in any large-scale conflicts with Ba'al. *This* was a declaration of war. Please, let us help you." Her face softened slightly as she glanced at Leah. "After all, we are Leah's family."

The air tore asunder in the gardens. A doorway opened. The Nolans tensed, magic brightening their eyes and weapons.

"It's okay." Artemus stared at the warm, golden light spilling onto the lawn. "That's one of Sebastian's portals."

A message came through on Nate's smartband. He frowned. "They found something." He studied the portal. "That's our rift in."

CHAPTER THIRTY-FIVE

"THIS PLACE IS CREEPING ME OUT," OTIS MUMBLED.

He gazed anxiously at the murky gallery around them.

Sebastian had to concur. The Art Institute at night was not exactly a pleasant place.

Serena had bypassed the security cameras and was tracking the locations of the museum's night guards on her smartband. She cast a faintly suspicious look at Drake.

"Please tell me you're not thinking of making the most of this situation and stealing one of these art works?"

Drake shrugged. "I can't deny that it's crossed my mind."

Naomi frowned at him over her shoulder. "Kindly refrain from doing so. I'm already twitchy enough about the fact that I've brought a world-renowned thief to this place."

The witch's cat was a pale shape up ahead, where she padded alongside Smokey's dark hellhound form.

"Is it—is it really okay for us to be here?" Patrick stammered.

The young man's eyes flicked uneasily around the passageway.

"Yes, it is," Naomi murmured reassuringly.

It was she who had suggested they bring Patrick to the Art Institute while Artemus and the others went to the Nolans' aid. She'd wanted to test her theory regarding the reason why Leah's pendant had summoned the dead from all over the city.

Sebastian frowned faintly. *She has a point, just as Drake did. Shadowing one of the undead is the fastest way to figure out where they have gone, especially since we believe their disappearance may be linked to Leah's gate in some way.*

They followed Patrick down into the basement of the museum and navigated a series of corridors. He finally stopped in front of a pair of metal doors.

"This is where I found Naomi this afternoon," Sebastian murmured.

"Is this where you want to go, Patrick?" the witch asked the young man.

"Yes." He hesitated. "I think this is where I was meant to come when Leah found me in the stairwell."

Naomi clenched her jaw and looked at Serena. "Can you take care of the biometric lock on this door? I could use magic but the circuits are sensitive and I might trigger the alarm."

"Sure."

Serena removed her dagger from the sheath on her thigh, lifted the security panel open, and went to work, her fingers moving nimbly. The lights on the display flashed green after a minute.

The door remained locked.

"Looks like that keyhole isn't just for decoration after all," the super soldier muttered.

"I got this." Drake slipped a lockpick set from his back pocket and squatted in front of the door.

A soft click sounded a moment later. Drake straightened.

Serena sighed. "Is it bad that I find that seriously hot?"

Drake grinned and dropped a kiss onto her lips.

Otis gasped and clutched his chest, his eyes round with shock. "Wait?! *You guys are going out?!*"

"It appears Goldilocks is not the only one who has failed to notice that the two of you are copulating," Sebastian said.

Serena grimaced. "Can we not use that word? It's kinda…depraved."

Drake arched an eyebrow. "Well, we've done some pretty depra—*ouch!*"

Serena had stepped on his foot.

Naomi muttered something under her breath and opened the doors. They entered a gloomy chamber.

"This is one of the museum's storage facilities." The witch frowned. "I don't really see what could be drawing the undead—"

Sebastian laid a hand on her arm. Patrick was walking down the stairs, his expression strangely glazed. They headed quietly after him.

Rows of artwork secured in metal grilles lined the central corridor cutting through the storage room. Sebastian could feel the weight of time pressing down on them as they traversed the chamber.

They reached the far end and drew to a halt.

"There's nothing here," Otis said, puzzled. "I can't sense any demonic energy."

Patrick turned left and followed the wall, unheeding of their presence.

"Where is he—?" Drake started.

Patrick stopped and walked straight through the concrete, vanishing from their sight.

They froze.

"What the heck?" Serena muttered.

Sebastian narrowed his eyes. "There is a barrier there."

"I feel it too." Naomi glanced at her cat. "Gemini."

The feline leapt onto her shoulder. Green light emanated from Naomi's bracelet, her eyes and those of her familiar glowing the same shade as they drew on their magic.

The hairs rose on Sebastian's arms. A shiver raced down his spine, one that had as much to do with admiration as it did with desire. The latter emotion still shocked him to an extent. After all, he wasn't a man used to being ruled by his feelings. But there was no denying the connection between him and Naomi. All it had taken was a single kiss to convince him of it.

She was his, as much as he was hers.

The wall shimmered. The concrete dimmed. Wavering dark and crimson lines appeared. A complex pattern of demonic scriptures took shape where a ten-foot-wide section of the wall once stood.

Sweat beaded Naomi's forehead. "I don't think I can break through it."

Sebastian drew on his powers, placed his hand against the barrier, and closed his eyes. A frown furrowed his brow a moment later.

"I could try rifting through, but I am unsure what lies beyond," he admitted reluctantly.

Wings clapped behind him. Sebastian looked over his shoulder.

Drake had changed into his dark angel form. "How about we try a demon's weapon instead?"

His eyes flashed crimson-gold as he stabbed his inky blade into the demonic shield. It cut through it like a hot knife in butter.

"Tell the others where we are," Sebastian instructed Serena grimly while Drake carved out an opening large enough for them to navigate.

He created a golden rift behind them and followed Drake and the others through the demonic doorway.

∼

Trepidation churned Jeremiah's belly as a crimson portal opened on his left. A pair of demons exited the rift. They were dragging a limp figure between them.

"Barbara?!" Jeremiah mumbled.

He stared aghast at his mother-in-law. Dark demon blood marked her dress and skin, the stains still fresh. Her face was pale and her eyes glassy.

The demon commander stepped out of the shadows, her expression satisfied. "Good."

She took the older woman's arm and guided her to the chair next to Jeremiah.

"What have you done to her?" he asked stiffly.

The blonde smiled. "Oh, nothing much. It's just a charm to keep her docile."

She snapped her fingers in front of Barbara's face.

The older woman blinked. Awareness returned to her eyes. She tensed and looked around. Her guarded expression transformed into one of relief when she saw Jeremiah.

"Thank goodness you're okay!"

Jeremiah swallowed. He had never been so grateful to see his mother-in-law in all his life. "Is Leah—?"

Another portal opened.

The demon beast stepped through it, his form that of a man once more.

The blonde's eyes widened when she saw the blood on his body. "What happened?!"

She closed the distance to him and pressed light fingers to his wounds.

"It's nothing," the man murmured. "They are already healing."

Anger darkened the blonde's face. "Who did this to you?!"

The man lifted a hand to the demon commander's face and stroked her cheek gently. "It is alright, my love. Do not look so pained."

She clutched his fingers and pressed a kiss to his knuckles, her expression a mixture of fury and distress.

The two demons suddenly stiffened. They twisted around, their gazes locking on a spot somewhere in front of Jeremiah.

"Jeremiah?" Barbara murmured. "What are those?"

The older woman was staring at the moving shadows around them.

Jeremiah clenched his teeth. "They are—"

A sound like a thousand pages being torn to pieces rang out across the chamber. A point of pulsing, crimson light pierced the darkness some fifty feet ahead of where they sat. It extended, forming a jagged doorway filled with writhing, inky billows.

"That's impossible," the blonde said in a hard voice. "Nothing can break my shield." She narrowed her eyes. "The only weapons that could tear through it are—"

A man stepped through the boiling mantle of darkness.

Jeremiah's heart lurched in his chest. *That's not a man.*

The angel's wings were the color of midnight, as was the armor that covered his body. Flames danced on his fingertips and along the serrated edges of his immense sword. A shield covered in scarlet runes sat on his left arm. His strong gaze gleamed red and gold.

He was the opposite of Artemus Steele. The Yin to the other man's Yang. The darkness to the white angel's light.

"Samyaza's heir!" the blonde hissed.

CHAPTER THIRTY-SIX

Waves of corruption danced across Drake's skin where he stood at the edge of a gloom-filled chamber. He kept his gaze on the blonde and the dark-haired man across the way. Though the woman was in human guise, he could tell she was an incredibly powerful demon. More powerful even than the commanders they had faced thus far.

He could feel the devil inside his soul fighting against the divine restraints that bound him. Eager to fill his veins with wicked bloodlust. Hungry for death and chaos. Dying to drag him to the pits of Hell.

Sebastian and the others emerged next to him. The Englishman had changed into the Sphinx and held his triple-thonged whip in hand. Otis's skin and gaze emitted a silver radiance as he half-transformed into the seraph, his right palm and the third eye on his forehead pulsing with divine power.

The doorway closed behind them.

"Barbara!" Naomi exclaimed. "Jeremiah!"

Sebastian took hold of the witch's arm as she started

toward where the two sat a short distance from the blonde and the dark-haired man.

The Englishman was staring intently at something in the air up ahead. "Wait."

Otis's eyes were similarly locked on the murky, rectangular shape suspended from an invisible ceiling.

"Are you okay?" Serena murmured to Drake.

He nodded stiffly, grateful for her presence.

She had helped ground him more times than he'd cared to admit in the weeks they'd been together, her touch and her kisses pushing back the darkness growing inside his heart and soul. Because one thing had become clear to Drake after their battle with Ba'al in Rome.

The demon inside him was getting stronger.

"Is that what I think it is?" Serena said grimly.

Drake could tell she too sensed the evil energy roiling off the object hanging from the ceiling. "Yes. That's a gate of Hell." He glanced at Sebastian. "How about you make it a bit brighter? These shadows are getting on my nerves."

Twin balls of dazzling light flared in Sebastian's hands, the glow matching that of his eyes. He cast them upward. The gloom shrouding the chamber faded under the brilliant, spinning spheres.

Otis sucked in air.

"Well, now we know where all the dead people went," Serena said leadenly.

∾

ARTEMUS EXITED THE GOLDEN RIFT AHEAD OF THE Guardians and the Nolan clan. They found themselves in a dimly lit, vault-like storeroom.

Haruki frowned. "This is the place I helped Leah escape from."

Leah looked around uneasily. "Jane and Travis brought me here. I think there was something they wanted me to see. Whatever it was, it made me feel sick to my stomach."

"Then it was quite likely your gate," Callie said.

"It kinda makes sense." Artemus perused the precious artwork filling the depot with a thoughtful expression. "Your gate must be hidden inside a painting."

Nate looked at his smartband. "Serena's GPS tracker says she's behind that wall."

He indicated the end of the storeroom.

"There's nothing there," Leah said, perplexed.

Daniel narrowed his eyes. "No. There is *something* there."

Green light flared next to Artemus. Floyd Nolan walked up to the wall and placed a hand on the solid surface, his ring and eyes glowing with the same radiance Naomi emitted when she wielded magic.

A screen made of black and red lines shimmered into existence where a section of concrete once stood.

Artemus clenched his jaw as he studied the motifs. "That's a demonic shield."

He morphed into his angel form and stabbed his divine blade into the barrier. It held.

Artemus frowned and poured more energy into the weapon, Smokey's life force augmenting his powers as the hellhound joined him.

The shield resisted their attack.

Artemus stared at Michael's sword. *It should be able to cut through this!*

Daniel changed into the Phoenix, his ring stretching

and widening into his gauntlet of divine fire while his wings extended. "Let me try."

The Nolans shifted, surprised. The flames kissed their skin and enveloped their bodies, the blaze as harmless as a light breeze.

"Wait," Haruki said. "We should try another weapon."

Artemus and Daniel looked at him, puzzled. Understanding dawned a moment later. They turned to Leah.

"What?" she said warily.

Callie's expression cleared. "Of course. Her spear is demonic!"

∽

CRIMSON RIFTS BURST INTO LIFE ALL AROUND THE hundred-foot-wide chamber. Naomi gritted her teeth as demons poured out of the portals and joined the undead crowding the floor.

The ones who had risen from their graves shuffled around aimlessly, their expressions vacant. There were several hundred of them packed tightly inside the place.

She could see no sign of Patrick.

"What are they doing here?" Otis said nervously.

Sebastian's face hardened. "It must have something to do with the gate, like Naomi suspected."

He frowned at the gilded frame hanging on chains above the middle of the cavern. The front of the painting was facing away from them.

"Welcome." Jane McMillan's surprised expression had been replaced by one filled with self-assuredness. "I had hoped to avoid a clash with you and the other Guardians but, alas, it seems we are doomed to do battle after all."

Her pale gaze grew cold and her voice deepened. "Now, who was it that hurt my beast?"

Her eyes turned crimson.

Naomi's heart pounded violently as the demon commander grew in size and transformed, her dark wings unfolding with a thunderous clap and her nails extending into talons. A rift opened next to her. She reached inside and withdrew a long spear from the hellish portal. Dozens of black vipers made up the shaft of the weapon, their slit-like pupils glowing with the same light blazing from their mistress's gaze.

Travis Calderon shuddered before metamorphosing into a giant dragon with horns tipped by blue-black flames and a large, barbed tail. Enormous, horned wings rose from his back.

"Shit," Naomi muttered. "He wasn't in his full form when he fought me and Jeremiah?!"

Drake stared at the beast. "This is new."

Sebastian exchanged a tense glance with Otis. "Are you thinking the same thing I am?"

The seraph nodded grimly. "Yes. I'm surprised, though. I didn't know the Great Duke of Hell was a woman."

"What are you guys talking about?" Serena said.

"That demon is Astaroth. But she was not always a fiend. She was once known as the Babylonian goddess Astarte." Sebastian's face grew pensive. "How does a god become a demon?"

"I'm sure the answer to that question is fascinating, but here they come!" Serena warned.

The demons under Astaroth's command charged toward them, their shrieks rending the air.

Gemini leapt on Naomi's shoulder.

"Together!" the witch barked.

The cat's gaze flashed green.

The bracelet on Naomi's wrist shifted into a sword with a jade stone embedded in the pommel. The same glow radiating from the cat's eyes and the precious gem enveloped her entire body.

The light of the first witch flared inside her soul, tempering the dark power of her mate, the fallen archangel who had bequeathed their race the gift of magic.

CHAPTER THIRTY-SEVEN

Nausea slammed into Leah the moment she passed through the demonic barrier. Her eyes rounded when she saw the battlefield ahead.

Drake, Serena, and Sebastian were surrounded by dozens of yellow-eyed demons inside an immense chamber. Naomi stood some fifteen feet to their left, her magic keeping the fiends attacking her at bay while she felled them expertly with a sword, her face fearsome and her eyes and body glowing with magic.

Poised close to her, his gaze radiating divine light, Otis protected Jeremiah Chase and Barbara Nolan from the black dragon and the demon atop the creature.

Relief swamped Leah when she saw her father and grandmother.

Thank God! They don't seem to be hurt!

Her gaze shifted to the enormous figure with the horned wings and the spear made of vipers that sat astride the beast. She knew instinctively that this was Jane McMillan's true form.

A dark miasma wafted from the demon commander's

mouth and her eyes flared scarlet as she cast her weapon at Otis. Her dragon inhaled deeply and roared out a jet of blue-black flames.

Both the spear and the fire bounced off the invisible shield Otis projected.

"Whoa." Violet Nolan observed the demon commander with an awed expression. "That's one scary chick."

"And that's a lot of dead people," Miles Nolan mumbled, pale-faced.

The queasiness twisting Leah's stomach intensified as she registered the tightly packed crowds of undead shuffling around behind the demons.

"She's the first female commander we've come across." Callie frowned where she stood in beast form next to Daniel and Haruki. "I was certain Ba'al hierarchy was patriarchal after what Delacourt revealed to us in L.A."

"It doesn't matter." A muscle jumped in Artemus's jaw. "Let's level this playing field, shall we?"

His figure blurred and vanished. Smokey bolted after him, his shape shifting into that of the giant, three-headed, golden-eyed Cerberus.

Leah's beast roused as the other Guardians and the Nolans rushed into the fray.

Thump.

Her eyes gravitated unerringly to a rectangular shape suspended from the ceiling.

Thump-thump.

The divine creature whose soul was entwined with her own peered out from within her mind. A growl of satisfaction rumbled through Leah's skull.

Finally. It is time.

Leah's pulse spiked. She knew the meaning of her beast's words. Dread seeped through her veins.

"Will we be okay?" she said, her voice trembling slightly.

Yes. Do not fear the gate. You must do as I say.

Leah swallowed. "I will."

She moved toward the gilded frame.

Thump-thump. Thump-thump.

◦

Sebastian leaned out of the range of a wave of talons, lashed the demons who'd attacked him into flaming ash, and looked over his shoulder.

"They are here."

Drake's gaze found his brother. "About time!"

A demon struck him in the flank. He scowled and sliced the fiend's head clean from his neck. Monstrous winged shapes appeared from the rifts above them.

Drake narrowed his eyes and extended his wings. "Time to take this fight to the air."

He shot up toward the ceiling, Sebastian at his side and Artemus and Daniel making their way rapidly toward them. Smokey, Callie, and Nate regrouped with Serena on the ground, along with a band of strangers wielding weapons shining with varied colors.

Drake stared. "Who are they?"

Artemus avoided an attack from a demon and kicked the fiend in the gut. "Magicians!"

The creature struck several of his brethren and carried them across to the distant wall. They crashed into the concrete, their dark blood exploding across the crater their bodies made.

Drake swooped beneath several sets of claws. "As in balloons and party tricks?"

A complex pattern of blazing, purple lines formed around the demons who'd attacked him. The fiends shrieked as the sphere constricted, slicing them to pieces.

"If it weren't for the fact that you're an ally, I would *so* put a hex on you right now," someone muttered behind Drake.

The dark angel turned. A teenage girl with glowing, violet eyes and discs of purple magic around her wrists floated in the air behind him, a white rabbit on her shoulder. The ends of her dyed hair framed her head like a halo.

"We are sorcerers and witches, not cheap-ass conjurors," the guy next to her snapped. Golden spheres of magic floated above his palms and a boa constrictor was coiled around his body. He studied Drake's broadsword with reluctant admiration. "That's a cool sword."

"Thanks." Drake looked down and scanned the crowd beneath them. "Where's Haruki?"

"He appears to be protecting his new girlfriend," Sebastian declared.

Drake's gaze found Haruki where the latter was tailing Leah. He laid a heavy hand on Artemus's shoulder. "Are you and your wife having marital problems? I'm here for you if you want to talk."

Artemus scowled. "Like I've said a thousand times before, Haruki and I are *not* married!"

"I have pictures that prove otherwise."

"Oh wow." The girl with the purple magic pressed her fingers to her mouth, her expression one of horrified rapture. "It's a love triangle!"

The guy with the golden magic rolled his eyes hard.

Haruki stabbed a demon with his sword, batted another two with his tail, and breathed out a jet of liquid fire that engulfed a group of four. The creatures' shrieks echoed in his ears as he turned and headed after Leah.

Though the demons were attacking him and the other Guardians, they stayed clear of the young woman, as if conscious she would soon be opening a portal to Hell for them.

Leah's face was glassy as she navigated the floor of the chamber, her expression telling him she was following a summons only she could hear.

The call of her gate.

Haruki gritted his teeth as he recollected the pull of his own gate the first time he had come into its presence. It was a draw that could not be denied, however terrible it felt. Still, he wished he could shoulder part of Leah's burden for her.

Haruki frowned at the gilded painting hanging from the ceiling. *If I cannot help her with her gate, I can at least protect the people she loves the most in this world.*

He turned and headed toward where Otis defended Jeremiah and Barbara. He had to trust Leah, just as he had trusted his own beast on the day they had fully awakened.

CHAPTER THIRTY-EIGHT

Jeremiah's heart thundered inside his chest as he crouched within the invisible barrier protecting him and Barbara. In front of them, Otis's body radiated a dazzling brilliance, his stance resolute in the face of the deadly monsters attacking him.

"It's beautiful," Barbara murmured. Her gaze was locked on the seraph. "His power is magnificent."

Even Jeremiah could feel the supernatural energy emanating from Otis and the mystical forces swarming the chamber. Though fear throbbed through his veins, he was also full of wonderment.

This was the kind of battle most humans had never witnessed. The fight between light and darkness. The holy war of good versus evil.

He still found it hard to believe that his daughter was a part of all of this. Or that his wife had been a powerful witch who had protected them both even in death.

I'm sorry, Joanna. I'm sorry that you felt you had to hide the truth from me. Jeremiah clenched his teeth and felt tears bloom in his eyes. *I'm sorry you could never tell me about the incredible world you were born into.* His gaze found his daughter through a sea of demons. *And I'm sorry that Leah grew up without her grandmother to guide her.*

"It's okay, Jeremiah."

Jeremiah turned to the woman beside him. As always, it seemed she had read his mind.

Barbara took his hand. "Joanna wanted to protect you and Leah for as long as she could. And she wished for Leah to have as much of a normal life as possible before—" she glanced at the battleground around them, "—all of this. So, don't feel guilty. I am proud of you for bringing up Leah on your own." Her fingers clenched around his. "She is a wonderful young woman. And she will be a most fearsome Guardian."

~

Leah twisted around and finally saw the front of the frame. Surprise jolted her. It was a diptych, a painting taking the form of two hinged, wooden panels. Her eyes widened.

It's Jan van Eyck's The Crucifixion and Last Judgment!

Incredulity turned to horror as she stared at the bottom right wing of the glazed, oil-painted artwork, where Eyck's version of Hell was depicted in petrifying detail.

The figures of the beasts and damned souls who had fallen into the abyss were moving, as if alive. The distant shrieks of the tormented reached her ears as fiends tore into their flesh and ripped their bodies apart.

Death's eyes glowed with a malevolent, crimson light from where he looked down upon them, his skeletal figure enveloping his dominion within his giant, pale wings and limbs.

His eyes moved and his wicked gaze found her. Leah flinched.

A spot of darkness blossomed in the center of the painting. It grew rapidly, corrupt tendrils snaking across the rich surface like a web. The gossamer threads started to merge.

Heat blossomed in the very center of Leah's being.

Golden runes exploded across the surface of her spear.

She listened to the beast, took a shaky breath, and did as he instructed.

∽

THE FOUL ENERGY OF HELL BLASTED ACROSS THE chamber as the gate started to resonate with Leah. Haruki resisted his instinct to go to her and stepped inside Otis's barrier.

"She's going to need you once that gate starts to open," he told the seraph.

Otis glanced at the throbbing rectangle of expanding blackness suspended above them.

"I will protect them when the time comes for you to leave," Haruki said, cocking his head at Barbara and Jeremiah.

The Dragon growled inside him, the beast raring for battle. The seraph dipped his chin at him. A flash of white light drew their eyes.

They stared at the dazzling shapes taking form on Otis's right palm.

∽

Barbara gazed wide-eyed at the three inverted Vs being etched into the seraph's skin by an invisible power.

No, that's not it. They have always been there!

She could see the shock reflected on the Dragon and the seraph's faces.

"What are those?" Haruki said.

"I—I don't know!" Otis mumbled.

The air shimmered around them, forming a haze in the shape of a dome. The Dragon hesitated before raising a hand and trailing it above his head. Sparks erupted where his fingers touched the barrier.

"Your shield," Haruki murmured. "It's visible."

∽

Leah's blood heated up as her beast uttered the holy incantations that would open their gate. The arcane words burned her throat, their power so formidable she felt her very bones vibrate.

The runes on the spear turned crimson one by one.

Movement around the chamber caught her eye. The dead were moving. They gathered around her, their glazed faces focused on the darkening portal above. Shadows writhed and quivered inside the golden frame.

The pressure inside the room dropped as the gate started to assume its full form. The hairs rose on Leah's arms. Something was happening to the dead.

Their bodies wavered and became insubstantial. They rose into the air one by one, their ethereal feet dangling limply above the floor. Their ascent accelerated as they neared the gate.

Leah's eyes widened as they vanished inside the throbbing darkness with faint whooshes. *Naomi was right! The dead were needed for the gate to open!*

Concentrate, child.

Leah startled at her beast's steely command. She hesitated before bobbing her head shakily. She could feel their powers growing as more runes darkened from gold to scarlet.

"*Jeremiah!*"

Leah's heart stuttered at the sound of her grandmother's voice. She whipped her head around.

Fear twisted her stomach.

∼

JEREMIAH STARED AT HIS HANDS. SOMETHING WAS happening to him.

His flesh had begun to shimmer, as if he were looking at it through sunlit water. He drew a sharp breath when the tips of his fingers turned see-through.

Barbara was gazing at him in horror.

"What—what's going on?!" he mumbled.

"I don't know," she replied hoarsely.

Jeremiah touched his face. Nausea churned his gut when his hand passed through his flesh, as cold as ice.

Blue light flared over his chest. Jeremiah looked down and saw his dead wife's spell take shape over his heart. The lines wavered and broke as his body turned spectral.

A bark of laughter reached his ears. He turned his head and gazed at the demon where she sat atop her dragon, panic flooding him.

"What sweet irony," the fiend rasped, her expression amused. "Not even your wife's magic can protect you from this fate, human." She glanced at the growing, dark doorway. "The gate is hungry. It will soon consume you too."

Otis frowned. Haruki's knuckles whitened on his fiery sword. Jeremiah could tell they were powerless in the face of whatever was happening to him.

Something tugged at his body. He gasped as his feet started to lift off the ground.

"*Jeremiah!*" Barbara shouted.

CHAPTER THIRTY-NINE

M<small>OTION</small> <small>IN</small> <small>THE</small> <small>MIDDLE</small> <small>OF</small> <small>THE</small> <small>CHAMBER</small> <small>DREW</small> Artemus's attention. He ducked beneath talons, decapitated two demons, and looked over. Surprise shot through him. He pivoted in mid-air.

"What the hell?" Drake muttered, coming to a hover next to him.

Astonishment echoed across their bond with the other Guardians as they witnessed the flow of dead people rising into the air and vanishing inside the gate.

"Shit." Artemus gripped his sword tightly. "Naomi was right."

"Yes." Sebastian narrowed his eyes. "The dead are indeed crucial to the opening of that gate."

He stiffened. Artemus and Drake followed his gaze.

"Oh." Surprise washed across Sebastian's face. "It is visible."

Artemus glanced at him, confused. "What is?"

"Otis's barrier." Drake stared. "We can see it."

Artemus's eyes rounded when he discerned the misty

dome surrounding Otis. *They're right. We've never been able to see it before!*

"It is more than just his barrier," Sebastian said. "There is something…different about him. And—" he peered closer, "—is it just me, or are there more symbols on his palm?"

Movement came from Artemus's left. He raised his arm instinctively. Claws sparked against his armor. A distant shout reached his ears as he turned to face the demons who'd surrounded them.

"*Jeremiah!*"

Artemus saw a shape rise out of Otis's protective barrier.

Jeremiah had turned ghostly pale and was headed for Hell's gate.

∼

"D*AD!*"

Leah could only watch, terrified, as her father's spectral-like figure soared above her. She turned and scanned the chamber wildly for the other Guardians and the two angels, desperation a living entity threatening to swallow her whole.

Please, someone, help him! Anyone!

Her beast's voice resonated in her ears. *They cannot. It is not up to them to destroy that gate and save your father. It is up to us.*

Shock flared through Leah. "He can be saved?!"

Yes.

Tears blurred her vision as her father vanished inside the growing portal. She had never felt so helpless in all her life as she did in that moment.

Warmth danced inside her body and her heart in the next instant.

She felt her beast's affection wash over her. *I am here for you, child. Now, let us become one so that we may fulfill our destiny and bring your father back.*

Leah swallowed, her distress giving way to gratitude.

"Thank you," she whispered shakily.

With those words, the last of her lingering doubts and fears finally melted away.

All she had ever wanted was a simple life, taking care of her father and grandmother and doing the things she loved to do. But she could no longer deny her fate.

She was meant for something bigger.

Something formidable.

Something sacred.

The final incantation tumbled from her lips. Her weapon transformed into its ultimate form. And as the glorious, holy energy surged through her blood and she fully awakened, Leah finally saw the beast who had been with her for as long as she had been alive.

The Lion's golden eyes glowed fiercely as their souls merged. They opened their mouths and roared as one.

∼

The air trembled as the beast's bellow echoed around the underground chamber.

Haruki stared at Leah, his heart pounding with a heady mixture of awe and excitement. Her hair was a thick riot of rich, red curls extending all the way down to her tailbone. Her nails had lengthened into deadly, curved claws. A thin, flexible armor covered her skin, the metal the same color as her eyes. And in her right hand, static sparking along its length and on its spikes, was a large, three-pronged, double-ended, silver spear.

"The Nemean Lion." Otis's gaze dropped to the weapon in Leah's grasp. "And the Spear of Ramiel."

The seraph's voice made Haruki's eardrums quiver. He blinked, startled.

Though he was yet to fully transform into his winged form, Otis's body was radiating a force powerful enough to make the ground shake beneath their feet.

What's happening to him?

Motion beyond the barrier distracted Haruki. The demon commander and her dragon were moving toward Leah.

∽

Jane studied the newly awakened divine beast curiously. She could feel the power of Ramiel echoing from the spear.

How interesting. It seems I was not the only demon who wished to defy Hell's forces.

Though she wanted nothing more than to step out of this battle and return to the place she now called her home, Jane knew she could not go against the wishes of Ba'al's leader. To do so would mean an immediate death warrant for her and Travis.

She did not personally mind the prospect of death. She had lived an eon, both in Heaven and in Hell. But the centuries she and Travis had spent together on Earth had made her greedy. Though she would welcome eternal darkness, she could not forsake that which was most precious to her.

Jane frowned. *And I can definitely not forgive the ones who've hurt the being I love more than my own life.*

A thin, crimson line split the dark portal that was Hell's gate. Jane extended her wings and rose.

∾

Leah followed the demon commander briefly with her gaze as she shot into the air, her path taking her on a collision course with Artemus. She studied the band of pulsing, red light in the middle of the painting before focusing on the dragon approaching her.

If she had to describe what she was feeling right now, she doubted she could find the words. There were none that could embody the raw emotions coursing through her consciousness or the strength of the bond she could feel forming with the ones who fought at her side.

Their existence shimmered in her mind, points of brightness that would now forever be linked to her own. Leah sensed the Lion's pleasure as the other divine beasts welcomed him. He had been alone for a long time and was home at long last.

The dragon's scarlet eyes were unblinking as he stared at her, dark fire simmering on his horns and at his nostrils. He took a giant breath and unleashed a jet of blue-black flames from his jaws, the blaze erupting from his lungs with a thunderous boom.

Leah stopped the attack with her hands, the inferno dissipating as it struck the armor covering her skin. She suspected nothing could pierce it.

The dragon snarled in outrage and bolted toward her, the ground trembling beneath his enormous, pounding feet. Leah steeled herself and raised her spear. It locked under the demon beast's horns as the monster crashed into her.

They stared ferociously into each other's eyes, gold clashing with crimson, neither of them giving ground.

"Stand down, beast," the Lion growled. "You are no match for us."

"*Never!*" the dragon hissed. "*The only one I obey is my master!*"

Surprise flared inside Leah. She had not thought him capable of speech in this form. The air moved next to her. She grunted as the dragon's barbed tail smashed into her left flank.

His spikes did not cut her flesh.

Leah raised her leg. "So be it."

She kicked the dragon violently in the breastbone.

The beast's eyes rounded as he skidded backward some half a dozen feet, his claws raising sparks on the floor.

∾

"Did she just kick him?" Callie said leadenly.

"Yeah." Serena frowned. "He's gotta weigh at least eight tons. Just how strong is she?"

"Haru had better be careful," Callie mumbled. "I mean, she could easily crush him in beast form."

Serena arched an eyebrow. "Oh, so those two are—"

"Yes," Nate said solemnly. "It appears Haruki intends to cheat on Artemus."

"*For the last time, we are NOT a couple!*" Artemus roared as he flew above them.

"Sure, whatever," Serena muttered.

"Oh." A witch with glowing, golden eyes and a sword embedded with a yellow sapphire scooted over to Callie and Serena. "Leah and the Colchian Dragon are an item?"

Callie dipped her chin.

The witch made a face. "That's a shame. She would have made a great match for a sorcerer. Or my stupid son, were they not related by blood."

"I heard that!" the guy with the boa constrictor snarled before he blasted a couple of demons with spheres of bright magic.

The witch became aware of Callie's stare. She followed her gaze to the iguana on her shoulder. "Oh. His name is Harold. Say hello, Harold."

Harold hissed at Callie, his tongue tasting the air curiously.

Callie shuddered. "I'm sorry. No offense, but—iguanas give me the heebie jeebies."

Serena and the witch looked pointedly at the giant reptile protruding from Callie's tailbone and the hundreds more making up her mane.

She shrugged at their deadpan expressions. "Snakes are different."

CHAPTER FORTY

ARTEMUS GRITTED HIS TEETH AND PUSHED BACK AGAINST the demon commander as they clashed weapons.

Damn. She is strong!

He could not deny the power of the demon. She was clearly on another level compared to the ones they had crossed paths with thus far. And he had a sneaky feeling she was targeting him because of what he'd done to her dragon.

"You will lose this fight." Artemus scowled. "Just as the others lost to us. So, why don't you just give up?"

The demon glowered at him. "Do you really think it is that easy to disobey his command?"

Artemus blinked, surprised. "Wait. You mean, you're here just because you're obeying orders?!"

"I was. I did not long for this battle and neither did my beast." The demon's crimson eyes flared. "But now, it's kinda personal."

The vipers making up her spear coiled around Artemus's hands. They multiplied in the blink of an eye and shot up his arms and onto his torso, their coils tightening as they enveloped his entire body in a blanket of writhing, sinuous shapes.

He sagged, his wings weighed down under their snowballing mass.

Shit!

∼

Leah flipped over the dragon's back with one hand and raked his hide with her spear as she came down the other side of his colossal body.

The demon beast howled in pain and rage, black blood blooming on his wound and dripping onto the slicked-up floor. He was already bleeding from the other cuts she had inflicted upon him. He turned his head and released another jet of blue-black flames in her direction.

Leah stood her ground. The blaze washed harmlessly over her, as it had done time and time again.

Let us finish this.

She narrowed her eyes at her beast's words. "Yes. Let's do that."

Heat flooded her veins as she drew on the divine energy dancing through her soul. Her skin tingled and her armor glinted. Static filled the air around her. The sparks expanded and spread across the chamber.

Leah felt the storm gathering in the sky above the building. She could almost see the maelstrom of churning clouds forming across the city, the giant mass illuminated by flashes of lightning.

She raised her weapon toward the ceiling, aware that her gate was mere minutes from opening and letting loose all of Hell's forces upon the Earth.

We don't have much time!

More demonic rifts exploded into existence above and around her as Ba'al's forces started gathering under the building, their hungry anticipation filling the air with evil so pure it became thick and heavy.

Whiteness bloomed on the tips of the prongs atop Ramiel's spear. The dazzling brilliance swelled and engulfed the weapon.

∽

The loudest explosion Naomi had ever heard boomed behind her. She winced, ears throbbing and jaw vibrating, before whirling around. Her knuckles blanched on her bloodied blade.

A giant hole had been ripped open in the ceiling.

Violent gusts of wind poured through it and arrowed down upon the figure at the very center of the chamber, scattering the falling debris to the four corners of the room.

Naomi's heart thumped painfully against her ribs. She ignored the corruption boiling off the dark portal suspended above her and stared at the divine beast who stood fearlessly facing a growing sea of demons and the black dragon.

The golden glow in Leah's eyes had turned to liquid silver. Her mane lifted around her, framing her head and body like a red halo. Small flashes leapt across her skin and claws.

Her mouth curved in a savage smile as the tempest engulfed her, her hair fluttering wildly in the wind. A gigantic, blinding bolt of lightning followed the storm's passage and struck the spear with a deafening crack.

The demons in the vicinity stumbled and fell under the

force of the detonation. Even the dragon reared away, his crimson pupils wide with surprise.

Naomi stiffened. Instead of dissipating, the lightning was intensifying, as if physically grounded to the spear and the creature who held it.

No. The witch swallowed. *Not just grounded. It's being amplified!*

Leah's gaze flashed. She breathed in, her chest expanding to gargantuan proportions.

Naomi startled as her body was pulled toward the center of the chamber, her feet skidding helplessly across the ground. *It's like what happened in the alley the other day!*

The witch glanced around. Everyone else in the room was similarly being tugged in the direction of the newly awakened beast. Everyone except for Otis, the angels, the other Guardians, and the demon commander.

There was a moment of breathless stillness.

The Lion breathed out and unleashed the storm.

Lightning exploded across the chamber. The demon beast screamed in shock and pain.

∽

Jane spun around, her stomach contracting with fear.

Agony tore through her when she saw the black dragon fall, his head and one of his wings partly severed from his body. She dove toward the Lion, fury bubbling in her veins, the white angel and Hell's gate all but forgotten.

"*No! Run!*"

Travis's desperate voice echoed in her ears.

Jane faltered, her gaze locking with her lover's. She changed direction and landed by the demon beast, the other fiends scattering in the face of her wrath. Black blood stained her skin as she knelt beside the dragon's shrinking form. She put her spear down and pressed her fingers to the gaping wound on Travis's neck.

"It is alright, my love," he murmured, ashen-faced. He lifted a shaky hand to her cheek. "It does not hurt."

Anguish twisted her belly. *Why is he comforting me when he is the one dying?!*

Tears flooded Jane's eyes and spilled upon the demon beast's bloodstained knuckles. She blinked, shocked.

Demons cannot cry. What is—?!

The answer came to her even as the question formed inside her head. Her dark heart was shattering.

The light faded from Travis's eyes. He exhaled his last breath, his face at peace and a tender smile on his lips.

Jane froze as she felt the bond that had linked them for thousands of years quiver and fade to nothingness. In its place came a roaring darkness and a rage so intense she felt she could destroy entire worlds. She pressed her lips to Travis's mouth as his body started crumbling to black ash, grabbed her spear, and climbed to her feet.

She glared at Leah before raising her weapon toward Hell's gate. *"I call upon thee, Belial! You who bound me and my beast with your oath. Lend me your strength so that I may bring you glory!"*

A hush descended upon the chamber as her cry echoed against the distant walls. The black portal suddenly creaked and swelled, as if something were trying to break through it.

A jagged bolt of crimson light arced down from the center of the gate and struck Jane. She growled, the ungodly power of Ba'al's supreme leader filling her veins.

Drake gritted his teeth. The corrupt forces inside the chamber were multiplying exponentially. It was taking everything he had to resist the evil threatening to overwhelm him.

"Stay back."

Drake turned at the sound of his brother's voice. Artemus came to a hover next to him, his gaze on the demon commander.

He glanced at Drake, his expression steely. "Don't get close to her or the gate. We'll take care of this."

Drake hesitated before swallowing and nodding. He could no longer hide the truth from his twin. Artemus could sense what was happening inside him. So could Smokey, from the anxious vibe dancing across their bond.

Drake landed next to the hellhound and leaned weakly against his flank, his sword and shield shrinking as he resumed his human form.

Smokey huffed and butted him gently with a giant head, his power grounding Drake and pushing away the darkness swirling inside his heart.

Warm fingers clasped his left hand. Serena's skin shimmered with divine energy where she stood beside him.

"I'm here," she said quietly.

CHAPTER FORTY-ONE

Leah blocked a blow to her stomach. She winced when the demon commander's spear struck her left flank. Though her armor-like skin protected her from cuts and demon flames, it could not shield her from the brute strength of the fiend's attacks.

She's stronger than ever! What happened to her?!

Her beast answered her question. *We are not just fighting Astaroth. I can smell the energy of another demon coursing through her body. One ten times more powerful than her.*

"What?!" Leah mumbled.

"Why don't you concentrate on your gate and leave the enraged demon goddess to us?" someone said above her.

Artemus landed between Leah and the demon commander, along with Daniel and Sebastian.

The fiend narrowed her eyes at the angel and the two Guardians. "Do you really think the three of you can defeat me?!"

Artemus rubbed his chin thoughtfully. "Well, I don't know about defeating you. But we can kick your ass."

He moved.

The demon commander blocked his sword an inch from her heart. "That's good. But still, not good enough."

She punched him in the face.

Artemus grunted as he went flying in the air. Daniel grabbed him with a lasso of fire, spun him around several times, and hurled him right back at the demon commander.

"Hey! A little more gently please!" Artemus yelled.

∾

Otis turned to Haruki as Artemus crash-landed into the demon commander in a melee of limbs and wings. "It is time."

The Dragon nodded, the flames of his sword brightening as he prepared to do battle. Otis dipped his chin at Barbara before dropping the barrier and heading across the chamber toward Leah.

He glanced at the new symbols on his hand, the power of the seraph keeping the demons who tried to attack him at bay. The inverted Vs now formed a four-pointed star.

He didn't know why they had appeared when they did, or how they had magnified his abilities. He had yet to come across any mention of them in his mother's journals.

Still, he knew, deep down inside, that everything that had happened to him, and to Artemus and the others, had been preordained to a certain extent.

I just have to trust in this new power, whatever its ultimate purpose turns out to be.

Divine energy blasted through his body. His wings fluttered into existence as he took on his full form. Otis realized something then.

It was becoming easier for him to transform with every battle that they fought.

∼

Leah turned when she felt the seraph's presence. Her eyes widened as she looked upon his dazzling hair and armor. To her surprise, the Lion had her lowering her weapon and dropping onto one knee with her head bowed.

She could tell her beast held the being before them in the highest regard.

"*Rise,*" the seraph murmured.

Leah's eardrums vibrated painfully as she straightened, such was the shockwave his voice generated.

The seraph looked up at the gate.

Blackness filled the portal from edge to edge. The crimson band in the center was almost a third of the painting's width, the redness radiating the evil that waited beyond.

Her beast spoke. *We must return the gate to its original form. Only then will the seraph destroy it.*

"How?" Leah murmured.

She gasped when her feet lifted off the ground. Otis was rising and taking her with him, his power moving her body effortlessly.

They came to a hover some ten feet in front of the gate. Otis glanced from the giant hole in the ceiling to Leah, his expression serene.

Leah blinked. "Oh."

Of course!

She took a deep breath to calm her nerves before reaching for the divine light burning inside her. Sparks exploded across her spear and armor as the air became charged with electricity once more. She frowned when she sensed the storm building high up in the sky above them.

More. It needs to be bigger!

Leah clenched her teeth and concentrated, her beast's energy spilling over in her veins. A rumble rose inside her throat as her power surged. It became a thunderous roar that drowned out the noise of the battle beneath them.

Lightning cracked.

Brightness filled the chamber.

∼

JANE BLOCKED ARTEMUS'S HOLY SWORD AND SCOWLED AS the Sphinx's whip wrapped around her left ankle. He tugged on the weapon and sent her crashing into the wall, the lashes burning dark grooves into her flesh.

She grunted, concrete and stone caving beneath her body. Holy flames engulfed her as the Phoenix roared out a river of fire. The rocks melted under the force of the blaze.

Jane clenched her jaw and rose from the molten pool, her furious gaze on the enemy. Her injuries were healing almost as rapidly as they appeared. Had it not been for Belial's power coursing through her veins, she would probably be dead by now.

Artemus narrowed his eyes. "How the hell are you still alive?!"

Jane's mouth thinned into a grim smile. "Let me give you a small piece of advice, little boy. This is but a fraction of the power that Ba'al's supreme leader wields."

Surprise washed across Artemus's face.

Dazzling light engulfed them, the brilliance accompanied by a deafening sound. Jane's pulse stuttered when she felt Belial's energy start to subside. She whirled around and stared at the gate.

The new Guardian stood in the center of a storm, her eyes and skin glowing with power. A bolt of pure electricity arced from the tip of her weapon into the roiling rectangle of darkness that was Hell's portal.

The lightning was destroying the crimson line in the middle.

"*No!*"

Jane extended her wings and bolted toward the Lion. Three figures blocked her path.

"Your fight is with us," Artemus said in a hard voice.

⁓

Leah's body tingled as she poured power into the spear, the elemental forces of the storm filling up her beast's energy stores.

The scarlet line in the center of Hell's gate finally wavered and disappeared. The darkness enveloping the painting started to shrink from the edges in.

Shrieks and howls tore the air. Ba'al's winged demons lunged toward her and Otis, their ochre eyes full of fury.

Leah frowned. "Yeah, I don't think so."

She captured lightning from the tempest raging above the city and brought it down into the chamber. The fiends' screams of rage turned to terror as bolts of electricity streaked through the air and pierced their bodies, turning them into burning clouds of ash. Some made it to the safety of crimson rifts.

Most perished at the hands of Leah, the Guardians, and the Nolans.

THE PORTAL TO HELL VANISHED AND THE PAINTING resumed its normal appearance. Otis met Death's angry gaze before the skeleton's crimson eyes dulled.

The seraph sighed. *He always was a cantankerous soul.*

Ethereal shapes exploded from the bottom right panel of the diptych. The dead who had vanished inside the hellish portal materialized again and drifted gently down to the floor of the chamber, their spectral forms solidifying as their feet touched the ground.

The last person to emerge was an unconscious Jeremiah Chase.

"*Dad!*" Leah lunged toward her father and caught him in her arms.

Otis lowered them to the floor before studying the painting.

A powerful energy exploded behind him. The seraph turned and observed the demon commander floating a few feet from him.

Blood dripped down her arm where she held her spear in a tight grip. Though she was hemorrhaging from her injuries and her chest heaved with her breaths, her eyes still blazed with crimson fury.

Otis glanced at Artemus and the two Guardians winging their way toward the demon. *She managed to get past their guard, even in her weakened state?*

"You should stop, Astarte. You may be a goddess, but I can still kill you."

The demon blinked at her old name. A mirthless smile curved her bloodied lips. "It is unusual for you to show such pity, Seraph. You, who are the Judging Hand of God himself."

Otis gazed into the demon goddess's eyes and suddenly knew what he had to do. "You have suffered enough. I will not make you suffer more."

The demon's eyes widened. Her gaze moved to Otis's right hand.

The four-pointed star was blazing with divine light, as was the third eye on his forehead. A complex sigil formed above Otis's palm. It grew into a giant circle some three feet wide.

"Now, sleep," he murmured.

Something that looked like relief flashed in the demon commander's gaze. The seal of Astaroth swallowed her in blinding brilliance. She vanished with a faint whoosh of air. The symbols and the light faded.

Otis brought his attention back to Hell's gate. He raised his hand and whispered sacred words. The air trembled around him.

The painting slowly crumbled to golden dust under the power of the divine energy flaring from his palm and third eye.

The seraph captured the flakes and closed his hand. Light flared between his fingers. The remains of Hell's gate were gone when he opened them once more.

CHAPTER FORTY-TWO

Elton stood on the rear porch of the LeBlanc mansion, his anxious gaze riveted to the dissipating storm. He had come to the place he once called home on Artemus's instructions, when the latter had called him several hours ago.

"If you're going to fight Ba'al, I want to go with you," Elton had protested when Artemus had briefed him on what had been happening.

"You are staying put," Artemus had retorted stubbornly. "We are not arguing about this, Elton!"

Elton swallowed. He understood now the reason why Artemus had not wanted him to join this fight.

"He always was a sensitive child," Karl said next to him. "Remember that time he almost burned the house down and we grounded him?"

Some of Elton's tension eased as he recalled the incident. "And we found out it was because he was trying to bake a cake for your birthday?"

He smiled faintly at his older brother. Karl nodded, his own mouth curving upward.

Emotion clogged Elton's throat. He knew their time together was coming to a close. Hence Artemus's insistence that he remain at the mansion.

"He's still a terrible cook. If it weren't for Nate, I think they would all have starved to death by now."

"The man does make a mean pancake," Karl murmured.

The sky to the east started to pale.

Elton swallowed. "I'm going to miss you, you old coot."

"Same here, you young scoundrel."

A comfortable silence fell between them. Karl finally turned and laid a hand on Elton's shoulder.

"I'm proud of both of you," he said, his tone no longer teasing. "Artemus, for embracing his fate. And you, for supporting him."

Tears blurred Elton's vision.

"There's something I need to show you." Karl's expression turned troubled. "And something I need to say before I go."

Elton followed him inside the mansion. To his surprise, Karl led him upstairs to Artemus's bedroom. He headed over to a dresser, removed an object swaddled in several layers of oilskin from the bottom drawer, and laid it on Artemus's bed. Elton's eyes widened when Karl pulled the coverings aside and revealed what lay within.

It was a sword. One unlike any Elton had seen before. The metal seemed to glow with an internal light, its pale surface and edges so smooth they were almost transparent.

"Be careful," Karl warned as Elton reached out to touch the blade.

Elton froze and drew a sharp breath. Something had cut his finger a couple of inches from the weapon. He gazed at the drop of blood blooming on the tiny incision, stunned.

He stared at his brother. "What the—?!"

Karl nodded, his gaze grave. "Yes. It is that sharp."

Elton's heart thumped heavily as he gazed at the weapon. "Artemus made this?!"

"Indeed. To tell you the truth, I was quite taken aback. I had not realized his skills had progressed so much." Karl frowned. "But, then again, neither had he."

Shock reverberated through Elton as his older brother described what had happened in the hours he had spent in the workshop with Artemus the day before.

"Wait," Elton whispered hoarsely. "You're saying he can manipulate fire?!"

"Yes." Karl rubbed his chin thoughtfully. "In fact, I suspect he doesn't even need a forge. It gives him comfort to have one and to use the tools he is used to wielding, but the fire on his gauntlet more than matches that of the hottest furnace in this world. And his hands are the only devices he requires to make a weapon." He paused. "No flame could ever burn him."

Elton sat down heavily on Artemus's bed. *What—what does this all mean?!*

He asked the question of his brother.

"I honestly don't know." Karl hesitated. "But I think it has to do with...the future."

Elton stared at him. Karl was gazing blindly into space, as if seeing something Elton could never see. The older man shuddered and closed his eyes.

Elton stiffened when he opened them once more.

"The sword was what I wanted to show you. Now, I must tell you the thing you need to hear." Karl's voice hardened. "Do *not* let Artemus follow Drake if the dark angel falls to Hell."

∽

THE FIRST CREATURE TO GREET THEM WHEN THEY CAME out of the golden rift was Daisy.

Something squelched beneath Artemus's right foot. He looked from the happy goat to the warm, squishy poop he had just stepped into.

"Great." He rubbed his boot clean and looked around the backyard with a scowl. "Where the hell is everybody?"

"Can we *not* say the word hell?" Serena muttered.

"Yeah," Callie groaned. "I don't want to see demons for a while."

"Same here," Daniel murmured. "I'm all demoned out."

Sebastian and Otis nodded. Smokey huffed.

Haruki was frowning.

Barbara Nolan had insisted that Leah accompany her family to her estate, along with Jeremiah. The cop had woken up shortly after Otis had sealed away Astaroth and destroyed the gate of Hell. He had no recollection of the time he had spent inside the portal.

Naomi had found Patrick among the dead and taken the young man with them.

Artemus studied Haruki with a wry grin. *I'd love to be a fly on the wall the day Jeremiah Chase finds out the Dragon wants to date his daughter.*

Haruki narrowed his eyes. "Why are you smiling at me like that?"

"No reason."

A suspicious squawk rose from the side of the mansion.

Gertrude's crooked head poked around the corner of the building.

"Oh God." Drake paled. "She's still around?"

The chicken's eyes flashed.

"Quick, let's get inside!" Artemus said hastily.

They found some of the LeBlancs in the foyer. Elton stood among his dead relatives, his expression forlorn.

Dread filled Artemus. He fisted his hands. "Is it time?"

Karl returned his stiff stare steadily. "We have a few hours left."

They spent them having a leisurely breakfast and taking a stroll around the estate. It was early afternoon by the time the LeBlancs started returning to their graves. Karl was the last one to leave.

Elton, Artemus, and Smokey accompanied him to the mausoleum. Aunt Bessy and Uncle Winston had already returned to their tombs inside the building.

Karl paused just beyond the threshold to the crypt, his hand on the door. "Well, this is it."

"Do you, er, need a hand?" Artemus said awkwardly.

Karl sighed. "I managed to climb my way out of there. I think I can get back in."

Artemus nodded and swallowed. All the words he wanted to say had vanished from his mind.

Karl's face softened. "Come here."

Artemus blinked back tears and walked into Karl's open arms. He shuddered as the older man hugged him tightly to his chest.

"Do you have to leave?" he mumbled.

Karl straightened and looked at him. "I do."

They stayed with their arms around one another for a while longer. The door creaked as Karl finally pushed it closed. Artemus stood staring at it for a long time.

"Let's go," Elton said quietly.

Smokey stayed close to Artemus as they turned and headed toward the woods.

An alarmed squawk echoed from inside the mausoleum. They stopped and turned. Karl opened the crypt and cast out an indignant Gertrude.

"The chicken stays," he said, disgruntled.

CHAPTER FORTY-THREE

Artemus opened the drawer and paused. The sword he had made for Karl lay within the oilskin they had wrapped it in.

He hesitated, his fingers hovering above the weapon, before glancing toward his bed. Smokey slept atop the covers, paws in the air and a faint snore ruffling his jowls.

Well, he knows about it. I'll just tell the others later.

Artemus removed a T-shirt from the drawer and headed inside the bathroom.

Ten days had passed since Leah had awakened and her gate had been destroyed. Most of the dead had returned to the places they had risen from. Some were being more stubborn and were currently being rounded up by determined Nolans.

Since it was her granddaughter's fault that the dead had risen, Barbara had assigned her family the unsavory task of fixing the problem. From what Artemus had heard through Sebastian, there had even been an epic showdown in one of the city's main cemeteries between Violet, Miles, and a horde of undead.

As for Patrick, he had a fresh grave in the grounds of Daniel's church.

Artemus soon headed out of his room, a sleepy Smokey at his side. He still wasn't sure why he hadn't revealed his new abilities to the others. For one thing, he wasn't even sure *what* his new abilities were.

"I mean, I can't exactly just come out and say, *'Oh, hey guys, I think I created a new metal with just fire and my bare hands,'*" Artemus muttered to Smokey. *"'And the weapon I made with it can cut through steel and probably any object on Earth.'"*

The rabbit stayed silent. Having been a witness to the making of the sword, he had been strangely quiet about the matter.

Artemus frowned. There were many things about their recent encounter with Ba'al that still troubled him. One was the new symbols on Otis's palm. His assistant hadn't uncovered anything in his mother's journals that could clue them in as to their meaning. What he and Sebastian had found in the last few days, however, was a paragraph that stated that a human sacrifice would be required for at least one of the gates of Hell, which likely explained what had happened to Jeremiah Chase.

Another disturbing issue was Drake's now almost constant battle with the demon inside him. Artemus had suspected Drake had been finding it more and more difficult to fight the darkness within his soul. He just hadn't realized how bad it had become until their latest clash with Ba'al.

The third, and by far the most worrying concern, was Jane McMillan's revelation of the name of Ba'al's supreme leader and her transformation when she had called upon him to amplify her powers.

According to Sebastian and Otis, Belial was one of the four principal Princes of Hell. He was a ruling member of the Council of the Underworld, along with Lucifer, Leviathan, and Satanael.

Jane McMillan's words of warning echoed in Artemus's mind once more.

Damn it. Is he really that much stronger than us?

His frown deepened. He knew the answer to his own question.

As for the painting that had turned out to be a gate of Hell, Artemus was pretty certain the one currently on exhibition in the Metropolitan Museum of Art in New York was a fake.

Haruki was taking a delivery when he came down the stairs.

Artemus grimaced when he spied the label on the box the Yakuza heir set down on a console table. "More sake? Really?"

Smokey's ears perked up. He bounced clear of the last steps and scurried over to Haruki, his eyes gleaming with excitement.

"Yeah, well, hopefully it's good sake this time," Haruki muttered. "Hey, watch where you're—*dammit!*"

He stumbled over the rabbit and took Artemus to the ground.

Stars exploded in front of Artemus's eyes as the back of his head struck the marble floor. He cursed.

Haruki rose on his hands and knees above him. "Are you okay?" Alarm clouded his face. "How many fingers am I holding up?"

"Your knee," Artemus groaned. "It's on my—"

Haruki looked down. "Oh. Sorry."

He shifted. Artemus groaned again.

Haruki grimaced. "My bad. That was my hand."

A voice came to them from the stairs.

"I do not wish to interrupt whatever—shenanigans you two have going on, but we have visitors," Sebastian said glacially.

Callie strolled past her brother. "Yeah, get a room."

Artemus scowled and climbed to his feet. "What visitors?"

Haruki berated a sheepish Smokey behind him.

"I believe it is the Nolans."

Artemus made a face. "Great. What the hell do they want now?"

∾

"I would like to live here," Leah declared in a defiant tone.

"*What?!*" Artemus snapped.

"What?!" Jeremiah growled.

Drake masked a grimace. *Here we go again.*

"Oh." Barbara Nolan smiled. "What a splendid idea. It's not too far from your college, either."

Nate put two plates of warm cookies on the table.

"Why, thank you, young man." Carmen Nolan dipped her chin at the super soldier before biting into one of the baked goods. She froze, her eyes rounding. "*Oh my God! You have got to give me the recipe for this!*"

The tips of Nate's ears reddened. "Hmm, sure."

Floyd Nolan munched happily before giving some crumbs to his parrot. "This is good."

"Excuse me," Artemus said in a hard voice. "Can we get back to the subject at hand?" He scowled at Leah. "You are not moving in!"

She gave him a mutinous look. "Why not? All the other Guardians live here."

"Because you are a minor, Leah," Jeremiah said between gritted teeth. "I am not having you stay under the same roof as a group of," he glanced around the kitchen, "—well, single men with what I can only describe as dubious occupations!" He paused. "Except for Father Lenton, obviously. And Otis."

Daniel sighed. Otis became fascinated with his coffee. Drake swallowed a grin.

Artemus, Sebastian, and Haruki glowered at Jeremiah.

"What do you mean, dubious occupations?" the Sphinx asked, incensed. "I will have you know that I am an Earl!"

"The Kuroda Group is engaged in legitimate business activities," Haruki protested.

"And I own an antique business," Artemus snarled.

Esther Nolan passed a cookie to Daniela Nolan, the witches' avid stares swinging from Jeremiah to the other occupants of the room.

"You run a bookstore," Jeremiah told Sebastian.

"Yes." Sebastian narrowed his eyes. "What of it?"

Jeremiah steepled his fingers under his chin. "Which almost never opens."

"Yes. So?"

"And which deals in rare items?"

"Get to the point," Sebastian snapped.

"It's a perfect front for drug dealing," Jeremiah declared confidently.

"I can see why he'd think that," Haruki told Sebastian.

"Anyway, I digress." The detective turned to his daughter, his expression thunderous. "Over my dead body are you moving in here!"

Leah's chair scraped noisily across the floor as she

stood up. She leaned her hands on the table and glared at Jeremiah. "I would like to see you stop me!"

"Oh dear," Barbara murmured.

"How about I make us some more tea?" Nate said soothingly. "Maybe some chamomile?"

"My money's on Leah," Callie murmured to Esther and Daniela.

The witches nodded in agreement.

Jeremiah cut his eyes to them before rising and facing his daughter. "I know very well why you want to live here!" He pointed a finger at Haruki. "You want to—to *cavort* with that man!"

Barbara raised an eyebrow. "'*Cavort*'? Really, Jeremiah?"

"What century does he think this is?" Drake muttered to Artemus.

Sebastian sighed and pinched the bridge of his nose. Haruki opened and closed his mouth soundlessly, too shocked to utter a single sound.

Thunder rumbled in the distance. The grounds of the estate darkened as clouds gathered above the hill.

"Uh-oh," Callie mumbled. "He's done it now."

Leah's pupils flashed gold. "I will not deny that I want to be with Haruki. Nor that he wants to be with me."

"Er," Haruki said, pale-faced. "Wait a second, we've not really talked about—"

"I forbid you to go out with him!" Jeremiah roared.

"Oh yeah?! Well, forbid this!"

Leah stormed across the kitchen, tugged Haruki by the front of his T-shirt, and kissed him forcefully.

Gasps rose all around the room.

"Wow. I did not see that coming." Carmen peered into Esther's tea leaves. "Did you?"

The color returned to Haruki's face in spades. He

closed his arms tightly around Leah. She melted in his embrace with a soft sigh.

"You know, you look mighty relaxed for someone whose wife's lips are being violated," Drake told Artemus.

"Shut up."

Jeremiah swayed before sitting down heavily in his chair.

Barbara patted him lightly on the arm. "Come now. You can't expect her to save the world one day and be grounded the next."

"Where did I go wrong?" Jeremiah mumbled.

"I asked myself the same thing when Joanna started dating you and look how that turned out," Barbara said sharply.

This seemed to snap Jeremiah out of his daze.

"How's Tony, by the way?" Artemus muttered.

"He's alright," the detective said distractedly. "He'll be discharged by the end of the week." He scowled at Leah and Haruki. "Are they ever going to come up for air?!"

The back door opened.

"Hey, did you guys know there's a dead chicken wandering around in your back yard?" Violet froze when she saw Leah liplocked with Haruki. "What did I miss?!"

Miles's alarmed voice came from outside. "No, Millie. You can't eat that bird! It's dead. *Millicent Nolan, spit out that fowl right now!*"

An outraged and slightly wet squawk followed.

"The boa constrictor is called Millicent?" Drake asked Carmen.

The witch shrugged. "He can be an old-fashioned kid that way."

Serena wandered into the kitchen just as Leah and Haruki finally stopped kissing. She stared from their flushed faces to Jeremiah. "I'm surprised you haven't shot him."

"Trust me, I am sorely tempted," the detective said darkly.

Serena handed Drake his watch. "Here, you left this on the nightstand."

"Thanks."

Artemus studied them with a puzzled frown. "Why was your watch in her bedroom?"

This earned him a battery of stares.

"Wait for it," Haruki murmured.

"He can't be that oblivious, right?" Leah said.

"Trust me," Callie stated with a wise nod. "He can."

Violet grimaced. "So, he's the handsome but dumb type, huh?"

Realization dawned on Artemus's face. He sucked in air, his eyes and mouth rounding to perfect Os. "Wait! *You two are going out?!*"

"Thank God," Serena said wryly. "For a second there, I thought we'd have to make out as well for you to get it."

Artemus spluttered. "How?! *Since when?!*"

Drake rubbed the back of his head guiltily. "Since we got back from Rome."

Artemus's jaw sagged open.

The sound of an engine rose from the driveway. Naomi wandered into the kitchen in a pretty summer dress and a head scarf a moment later, Gemini by her side.

Smokey visibly brightened where he sat by the window. The cat wandered over and greeted him with a nose bump.

The witch took her sunglasses off and eyed her extended family with a jaundiced gaze. "I thought you guys would have left by now."

"Nate made cookies," Carmen said, as if that explained everything.

"Hi, Dad." Naomi bent and pressed her lips to Floyd's left cheek. "Why is Artemus catching flies with his mouth?"

Artemus snapped his jaws closed.

"Hey, sweetheart," Floyd murmured. "He just found out his brother is dating the super soldier."

Naomi made a face. "It took him long enough."

"Wait." Sebastian stared from Floyd to Naomi. "He is your father?!"

Naomi shrugged. "Well, yeah. That's why we have the same colored magic. Anyway, are you ready to go?"

Faint lines furrowed Sebastian's brow. "Am I ready to go where?"

"On our date."

Floyd choked on his tea. Artemus handed him a napkin.

Sebastian's eyes widened. "Er, we are, hmm, courting?" He ran a finger around the inside of his collar, as if he were finding it suddenly difficult to breathe. "Wait. There are traditions we must follow." He glanced at Floyd. "I must visit your family home and officially ask your father—"

"Yeah, no." Naomi took his hand and dragged him toward the foyer. "That sounds incredibly boring. Come on, we're taking a drive to this great little restaurant I know up the coast. Who knows, if you're lucky, you might even get to second base."

Sebastian made a strangled sound as they disappeared down the corridor. "*I—I beg your pardon?!*"

"Does he even know what second base is?" Callie said worriedly.

"I'm sure he does," Nate murmured. "He has several original copies of the Kama Sutra in his library."

Callie's expression cleared. "Is that why things have been so—" color flooded her cheeks, "—hmm, well, different lately? Not that it wasn't great before!" she added hastily.

Nate's face turned pink. "Ah-huh."

"Oh dear God," Artemus said leadenly.

Drake grinned. "Maybe I should borrow—"

"Trust me, you don't need a copy of the Kama Sutra," Serena muttered. "You could have written the damn thing."

Smokey dropped his head into his paws. Gemini meowed and licked his blushing ears.

"Kill me," Artemus groaned. "Kill me now."

Barbara sipped her tea and beamed at the room. "Well, isn't this nice?"

THE END

AFTERWORD

Thank you for reading HALLOWED GROUND! The next book in LEGION is HEIR.

If you enjoyed HALLOWED GROUND, please consider leaving a review on your favorite book site. Reviews help readers find books! Join my VIP Facebook Group for exclusive sneak peeks at my upcoming books and sign up to my newsletter for new release alerts, exclusive bonus content, and giveaways.

Turn the page to read an extract from HEIR now!

HEIR EXTRACT

2033, Libyan Desert

Shooting stars streaked across the night sky, silent streams of light with barely anyone to witness them but endless desert sand. Solomon Weiss paused to admire the celestial bodies as they burned through Earth's atmosphere. A cool breeze ruffled his thawb and danced across his exposed skin from the north, bringing with it the salty taste of the sea.

It never ceased to surprise him how much more beautiful the world looked now that he had lost everything but his damned soul.

Solomon's gaze wandered down to the ridge he was climbing. He made a clicking noise with his tongue and tugged on the reins of the camel. The creature obeyed his command with a low huff. It wasn't long before they reached the summit of the elevation. Solomon pulled the animal to a stop and studied the landscape before him.

Stretching out as far as the eye could see was a dark ocean of sand dunes, barren hills, and rock plains. A jagged line some hundred miles long blocked out the low-lying stars to the west. Though he should not have been able to see the lights of the closest town at the base of the mountain range, Solomon's otherworldly eyes detected their presence nonetheless.

He wondered if the child had seen them too.

It took him another hour to reach the cave where the boy had sought shelter for the night. Solomon climbed off the camel and looped the creature's reins loosely around a boulder. He stilled and concentrated.

A steady thumping reached his unearthly ears, too fast and thready for his liking.

Solomon frowned and took the water gourd and a bag of dry raisins from the camel's saddle. He followed the sound of the boy's heartbeat into the dark crevice carved in the rockface before him.

The child had crawled into the farthest corner of the cave, where water had dripped down through cracks and fissures in the cliff to form a shallow pool. The puddle was only four inches wide and an inch deep, not enough to quench the boy's raging thirst. He lay on his front, his thin body shuddering with shallow, labored breaths, as if the very air hurt his lungs. His tousled, black hair obscured his eyes where it had fallen across his face, and his lips were cracked and bleeding.

Solomon knelt on the ground and gently rolled the child onto his back before lifting him onto his lap. He cradled his head with one hand and brought the water gourd to his mouth. A trickle of liquid fell between the boy's dry lips.

It took a moment for him to realize what was happening. The first thing he did was lick his lips and swallow. The second thing he did was grasp Solomon's wrist with a speed and strength that surprised him, even though he had half expected it.

He knew the child was only semi-conscious. The boy tugged the gourd close to him and took giant gulps of the water falling across his parched lips.

He finally blinked, his long lashes gritty with desert sand. Dark pupils contracted and dilated as they focused on Solomon. He froze when he registered Solomon's unworldly identity.

Solomon heard an alien heart start to beat somewhere inside the child.

Thump.

He masked a grimace. *Well, it's not as if I wasn't expecting this either.*

Solomon took a deep breath and suppressed his aura.

Thump-thump.

The boy trembled, as if in pain.

But Solomon knew better. It wasn't discomfort that was making the boy shiver in his hold. It was the furious excitement of the beast who was awakening inside his frail body.

Thump-thump. Thump-thump.

Golden light gleamed in the boy's dark eyes.

The beast's stormy gaze scorched Solomon's face as she beheld him for the first time.

Solomon gazed steadily back at the creature. "I have to say, you haven't exactly done a great job of looking after your host."

Irritation filled the beast's gaze, dampening her bloodlust. A sibilant hiss escaped the boy's throat.

"*Who are you to tell me what to do and not to do with my host?!*"

"Ah," Solomon said wryly. "She speaks."

He took some raisins from the bag and offered them to the boy.

The beast blinked.

The boy took a cautious sniff of the food before taking a careful mouthful between his lips. His teeth grazed Solomon's palm as he swallowed the rest with ravenous gusto.

Solomon rose, the boy's limp form in his arms, and headed for the exit. Though the boy's eyes were open and his beast had spoken to Solomon, he was not truly conscious still.

"Where are you taking my host?" the beast demanded haughtily as Solomon came out of the cave and took long strides toward the camel.

"Somewhere he has a better chance of survival."

The camel grunted in faint alarm as Solomon drew near. It could sense the nature of the creature in Solomon's arms.

I can't say I blame it.

"We are doing just fine," the beast said in a disgruntled tone. *"Now, put us down."*

Solomon stopped in his tracks. "Alright."

He let go of the boy.

The child thudded onto the ground next to one of the camel's saucer-shaped feet and bounced once. The camel startled and backed away.

The beast hissed in rage. *"How dare you hurt my host?!"*

"You said to put you down."

"I did not mean for you to drop him so callously!"

Solomon squatted and stared calmly at the mythical creature glaring at him. "I don't want to hurt your host, beast. I want to help him."

Golden eyes narrowed with suspicion. *"Why would you*

come to our aid? I know what you are. Your kind wants nothing more than to kill us."

Solomon smiled faintly and rocked back on his heels. "So, my glamour isn't working on you, huh?"

The beast sniffed. *"No, monster who walks in the form of man."*

A surprisingly comfortable silence fell between them.

"I can sense your intent is genuine," the beast finally said reluctantly. *"But why would you want to help him? Help us?"*

"To atone for my sins and the sins of my kind," Solomon admitted quietly. "To stop what is coming."

The beast observed him for a moment. *"And how do you intend to do that?"*

"By protecting you. And by guiding your host."

"You mean to serve us?"

"Yes."

"And use your powers to do good?" the beast asked insistently.

"Always."

The beast was quiet for a long time. A shudder ran through the boy's body. His eyes flared with brightness.

"Then, I accept. On behalf of my host and myself. But heed my words. If you betray us, if you so much as look at the boy the wrong way, I will *kill you."*

ABOUT A.D. STARRLING

Want to know about AD Starrling's upcoming releases? Sign up to her newsletter for new release alerts, sneak peeks, giveaways, and get a free boxset and exclusive freebies.

Join AD's reader group on Facebook:
The Seventeen Club

Like AD's Author Page

Check out AD's website for extras and more:
www.adstarrling.com

BOOKS BY A.D. STARRLING

SEVENTEEN NOVELS

Hunted - 1

Warrior - 2

Empire - 3

Legacy - 4

Origins - 5

Destiny - 6

SEVENTEEN NOVEL BOXSETS

The Seventeen Collection 1 - Books 1-3

The Seventeen Collection 2 - Books 4-6

SEVENTEEN SHORT STORIES

First Death - 1

Dancing Blades - 2

The Meeting - 3

The Warrior Monk - 4

The Hunger - 5

The Bank Job - 6

The Seventeen Series Short Story Collection 1 (#1-3)

The Seventeen Series Short Story Collection 2 (#4-6)

The Seventeen Series Ultimate Short Story Collection (#1-6)

LEGION

Blood and Bones - 1

Fire and Earth - 2

Awakening - 3

Forsaken - 4

Hallowed Ground - 5

Heir - 6

Legion - 7

DIVISION EIGHT

Mission:Black - 1

Mission: Armor - 2

Mission:Anaconda - 3

MISCELLANEOUS

Void - A Sci-fi Horror Short Story

The Other Side of the Wall - A Horror Short Story

AUDIOBOOKS

Go to Authors Direct for a range of options where you can get AD's audiobooks.